Joyce Windsor was  school, went to work ___ sequently passing the examinations necessary ɪᴏɪ promotion within the service. Moving to Liverpool, she became part of a fascinating circle, living next door to Fritz Spiegl and just around the corner from Beryl Bainbridge. A shortage of money in no way impeded the determined party-givers of that era and, as a devotee of the Liverpool Philharmonic Orchestra, she was delighted to meet people like Efrem Kurtz and François Poulenc.

She then moved south, first to Putney, then Dorset. In 1982 her husband died and she retreated to the Isle of Wight 'to die', but by chance hit upon a flourishing and companionable community of writers. Thus began one of the happiest periods of her life, which culminated in the publication of her first novel, *A Mislaid Magic*, also published by Black Swan, and to which *After the Unicorn* is the sequel.

Also by Joyce Windsor

A MISLAID MAGIC

and published by Black Swan

After the Unicorn

Joyce Windsor

BLACK SWAN

AFTER THE UNICORN
A BLACK SWAN BOOK : 0 552 99651 3

First publication in Great Britain

PRINTING HISTORY
Black Swan edition published 1996

Set in 11pt Linotype Melior by
County Typesetters, Margate, Kent

Black Swan Books are published by Transworld Publishers Ltd,
61–63 Uxbridge Road, London W5 5SA,
in Australia by Transworld Publishers (Australia) Pty Ltd,
15–25 Helles Avenue, Moorebank, NSW 2170
and in New Zealand by Transworld Publishers (NZ) Ltd,
3 William Pickering Drive, Albany, Auckland.

Reproduced, printed and bound in Great Britain by
Cox & Wyman Ltd, Reading, Berks.

Remembering Nanette Owen,
who had a genius for life

Chapter One

'Boys of David's age are quite mysterious until you remember that they think about practically nothing but sex,' my sister Claudia said.

She dropped the remark into an innocuous discussion on the merits of utility furniture which she admires. I examined it for a clue to her sudden appearance in Underhallow and didn't find one. So far she had shown no interest in my house, though she had not seen it before. Dreams do not often come true in every detail, but Garland House, Georgian, square and white, had been a place of my imagination since I was seven years old. By the touch of a sorcerer's hand I had stumbled upon the reality and bought it at once. At the front lay a green longer than it was wide, with buildings big and small strung higgledy-piggledy around it. That made up most of the village of Underhallow. We just about squeeze into Sussex, but with a tendency to overlap into Hampshire.

My family in general had a deflating indifference to each other's activities, but the pride of ownership was strong in me. Claudia might have said *something*. And Rudi Longmire's presence, which ought to have surprised her, had not so much as raised an eyebrow.

I murmured, 'Oh?' with a coolness that passed her by.

'All sweltering hormones, poor dears. Is there any more gin?'

Rudi, my lover and thus far a deep secret, held the bottle to the light and gauged the contents. Our ages are separated by seventeen years. Claudia and I were children when we first knew him, and he was twenty-five. In spite of our deep interest in the subjects of love and sex we viewed him dispassionately as a kind of magician, fascinating and romantic, yet removed from us by the barrier of his great age. I felt myself becoming defensive. Damn Claudia!

Rudi said, 'You've had two large ones already. I don't recommend a third if you're driving back to Dorset.'

'I'm staying for a few days. Didn't I say?'

'You did not.'

'Amy doesn't mind, do you, Amy?'

I did mind a little. 'I thought you were supposed to be at Grandmother's for two weeks, getting your wedding things.'

It was a sunny Saturday early in June of 1946 and we sat idly on the terrace overlooking the garden. Claudia's wedding date had been fixed (I hoped) for September, and the closer it drew the more edgy and erratic she became.

'I'm a patient person,' she said untruthfully, 'but after being sniggered over by a pack of dirty-minded old women and told in crude terms how to please a husband, I felt that I'd had enough. Be a bolster in bed and learn to cook was the gist of it. I asked how many of them could cook and they changed the subject.'

'Perhaps we could both take lessons. I'm pretty rotten at it so far.'

'If that's all William wants to marry me for he can get himself a housekeeper. Anyway I can cook already.' Claudia muttered this shameful confession into her glass. 'I learnt at – in – abroad.'

'In Switzerland, at school, I suppose?'

She relapsed into glum silence and didn't answer. For some reason that I could not fathom a permanent taboo surrounded the subject of Switzerland and finishing-school. Only once, soon after she came home in 1934, did she speak to me of her schooldays, and then to mention rather nervily a German girl who bullied any pupil who was coloured or Jewish. I knew she had Jewish friends. Once or twice I asked her questions and got my head bitten off with such ferocity that I gave up.

At that moment I felt mildly cross with her on several counts. Sweltering hormones indeed! David, our half-brother, in no way resembled the damply-blushing, fidgety boys who hung around us at dances and parties before the War. There was an eager, healthy shine about him. I had adored him since his babyhood. My father's second marriage had proved a disaster and when it ended Sonia, David's mother, took him from us and then left him alone and stranded in London at the Ritz Hotel. He was ten years old. From that moment he became my child. I spirited him away and looked after him as well as a not particularly bright girl could manage. We lived happily together in our rented cottage near Chichester until the War came. Others decided then that he should be sent to America. I wept for him until I tired of weeping.

He had just returned to me after more than seven years, assured, controlled, and with the overwhelming good looks that I had once come close to worshipping in another man. Like any healthy eighteen-year-old he must have thought of sex. I certainly hoped so. But from the questions he asked, or almost asked, that was not the problem uppermost in his mind.

Claudia lay back in a long garden chair holding her third gin and tonic. Her narrow, nylon-clad ankles were crossed. She fidgeted with an expensive straw hat, tilting it at this angle and that to keep the sun out of her eyes. All her clothes except for the stockings, sent by David's American foster-mother, were pre-war and mostly from Paris. They had been absolutely the last word in fashion in the nineteen-thirties. But Claudia had a fine disregard for what other people wore. Her flowered georgette dress, with long-outmoded butterfly sleeves and huge white bows at waist and shoulder, drooped well below her knees. She looked ravishing and entirely odd.

I hoped that she might notice and admire the heavenly view from the terrace. The scent of a *Cuisse de Nymphe* rose loaded the air. Tiger lilies and penstemons burned red and orange, lighting up the borders with their separate small bonfires. Beyond the garden, the cool green hump of Hallow Hill heaved up from the fields like a whale's back.

Figures moved in the landscape. Polly, my maid, walked slowly up the path towards us, attended on one side by Humphrey, a small boy scout, and on the other by David. They had been picking the embarrassingly prolific crop of broad-beans for bottling. A cloud of thwarted, pestering blackfly pursued them, missing their target, the basket, and getting into hair and eyes and mouths.

Remembering his code (A scout's duty is to be useful and to help others.) Scout Humphrey beat gallantly but ineffectually at the pests with his hat, dislodging folded strips of newspaper from the lining. He took terrific pride in the hat, which had been made for a larger head. Of an elderly pattern, pinched to a peak at the crown, it served in place of the coveted, but because of clothes rationing unattainable, full uniform.

Under the brilliant light Polly's yellow hair faded to the colour of cream. The sun shone through her skimpy pink-and-white checked overall melting the undeniably solid outlines of flesh and bone until she appeared to float, an ethereal, insubstantial being. Instinctively the bean-gatherers took advantage of every patch of indigo shadow thrown by the trees, moving with the languor of dreamers.

Rudi, always touched by romance, smiled at me. 'A page from a book of hours, don't you think? There should be leashed hounds and lutes, a unicorn for virginity, and a promise of courtly love.'

'Those three are much too young to fall in love,' Claudia said from under her hat. 'It's damned painful at that age.' Rudi raised an enquiring eyebrow at this uncharacteristic statement. I was equally surprised. Interpreting the sudden silence she added, 'Or so I imagine. Anyway a schoolfriend of mine worked out that unicorns don't represent virginity at all, but the one who takes virginity away – laps and horns and things. A bit rude, but she said it's only logic.'

'Adolescent girls seem every bit as lustful as boys,' Rudi remarked.

'Pippa's French, half-French really; they take a practical view of sex. Out of school she spent an awful lot of time looking for her unicorn.'

'We're almost out of gin. Are you sure you won't go home after lunch?'

'You've got a nerve, Rudi Longmire, this isn't even your house. Why are you here, if I may ask?'

'Certainly you may.' Rudi jumped in and spared my blushes. 'When you're safely off our hands Amy has agreed to let me marry her for her money. I'm quite madly in love with her – besotted in fact – and she's nice enough to love me as well.'

Claudia gaped. 'Amy? Good God, I thought she'd decided to be an old maid!' I could have borne with rather less incredulity, but then she added, 'You're a lot older than she is, of course, but we're comfortable with you. I suppose it's all right.'

'There, Amy, we have a sister's unreserved blessing.'

'D'you think you could not tell the rest of the family yet?' I pleaded. 'It will be much easier if we announce it to everyone at your wedding reception.'

'I never tell,' said Claudia, who always told on me, or

at least hinted so heavily that an idiot could guess. She pretended it was accidental but it can't have been. About her own life she clammed up completely and never let slip a word unless she chose. 'Throwing them a bone to gnaw might liven things up a bit. Wedding receptions are invariably ghastly, worse than funerals because one has to pretend to laugh at the awful old jokes. Guests don't make jokes at funerals. They're just happily superior not to be the one in the coffin.'

Her mouth drooped and some of the light went out of the day. With the first tremendous joy and relief at winning the War behind us it had become rather easy to fall into melancholy. The fruits withered on the vine. Britain was bankrupt, we were shabby and weary, and uncomfortably aware that peace is relative. If not here, war is always somewhere.

Claudia drained her glass. 'Warm and weak. The ice melted.'

'Perhaps you shouldn't be drinking gin,' I said. 'Not if it depresses you.'

'Who says I'm depressed, idiot?' she asked kindly. 'I miss the War, I think. There was always excitement, and you knew you were doing something about foul Nazis. They don't see anything wrong at all with wholesale murder and torture – quite unrepentant and sullen, I'm told.'

Of all people, Claudia, the lazy and frivolous, seemed unable to lay down her arms and accept peace. The trials at Nuremberg obsessed her. She raged against any blinking from the truth, however evil.

I think I would have shunned the film of the opening of the German concentration camps had she not insisted that we go together. I imagined myself inured to bloodshed of which I had seen too much. But no words existed to describe that heart-wrenching, inconceivable obscenity. Tears had dripped from my eyes as we emerged into dull, sane daylight, but Claudia's face might have been cut from stone. 'That's the truth of it, so make sure you remember. Murder without end.' And the dry bitterness in her voice was painful to the ears.

Now in a mistaken attempt to soothe I said, 'Hitler's dead and the others, the ringleaders, are on trial. I suppose it's a compromise, but everybody can't be punished. Sometimes I wonder if *we* could have resisted a dictator with the power of life and death over us, and no compunction about using it.'

Not a bit soothed, she slanted a malign and scornful look at me. 'Must you always be so bloody reasonable? It isn't over yet. Europe's in chaos and the slick and cunning will get away with it unless we catch them quickly.'

'You don't sound a bit like a soon-to-be bride. Nothing's wrong with William or the grandparents or anyone?'

'Of course not, though fifty thousand servicemen are waiting for a divorce and here am I exhausted with trying to get married.'

I began to have forebodings. This was Claudia at her most negative. Twice already the wedding date had been put back and I had no idea why. When pursued she retreated into a fortified place that could not be invaded. She rarely confided, even in me.

Rudi sighed. 'You were an idle, abominable child but full of fight and courage. Now you have the worst case of cold feet I've ever come across. While you're skulking about in hiding from your own wedding what must Bill feel like? Totally fed up, I imagine.'

'He's busy too, and I'm not skulking, damn you.'

'Then make him take time off. Bring him down for our Lammas on the first of August.'

She gave him a blankly uncomprehending look. 'Half the time I can't make out what in the world you're talking about, Rudi Longmire. What's a Lammas?'

'A loaf-festival, peculiar as far as I can make out to Underhallow, with some kind of ritual dancing. There's money left from the victory parties, and we're to have a revel in aid of a new scout hut.'

'What kind of dancing?'

'I'm none too sure – a costume affair for men on the lines of the Abbot's Bromley Horn Dance, I imagine. David knows more about it than I do, he's been asked to learn one of the parts, the Betty, whatever that may be.'

'How absolutely bloody,' Claudia said, 'the Christmas mummers all over again. Amy and I were dragged down to the kitchen, year in year out, to watch them, and an utter bore they were. I can't at all be doing with quaintness. It tries the nerves.' She shut up as David and Polly climbed the steps, carrying the wicker skep of beans between them.

Scout Humphrey, a child of the cinema, crouched low, holding my small tortoiseshell kitten at bay with an imaginary machine-gun. 'Drop the gat or I'll fill you full of lead,' he snarled. The kitten, unimpressed, leapt at his shoelaces and began to worry them. Bashfully he picked it up and tucked it inside his shirt. 'Hallo, Miss Savernake, everybody.'

'Don't forget to take some broad-beans for your mother, Humphrey dear.'

'Swell – I mean thanks ever so much. She'll be pleased.'

Claudia said, 'David's an amazingly handsome boy. Any woman would envy him that curly hair. I can't imagine where he gets his looks, can you?'

'Sonia, I expect,' I said hastily. 'You must agree that she was lovely when she had him. He went to see her but it was less than a success I gather.'

Claudia opened her eyes and sat up, suddenly alert and interested. She regarded me with a familiar probing look. 'Why are you so fussed over Soapy Sonia?'

'I'm not a bit fussed over her. It's a shame she can't make an effort to get closer to Davy, that's all.'

A burden of secrecy I had carried for years had begun to chafe me badly. Those who ought to have been frank with David had not been, and the secrets weren't mine to tell. I had hoped that Sonia might at last relent towards the son she had adored and then abandoned, confide in him, explain about the past. Instead, I gathered from David's account, she retreated into commonplaces.

I saw him emerge on to the terrace and tried for a change of subject, but Claudia pursued full-tilt her ancient grievances. 'She wasn't much of a mother, and a perfectly rotten stepmother. I haven't asked her to my wedding, so I hope David doesn't expect it. Perhaps I should invite Little Polly Flinders to keep him company.' She spoke with restive malice. 'Oh God, the bloody wedding!'

'And oh God, the wicked sister Claudia,' David said, smiling. He poured himself a drink and sat down beside her. 'Mother wouldn't come, you know. She's still a stunner and not much over fifty I'd guess, yet she acts old. We Savernakes are ghosts to her now, all of us. I'm not sure that she remembers much. She spoke of no-one from her past except for Pandel Metkin.' Here he paused for so long that I became nervous. He took from his pocket a small silver monkey reaching up to steal golden fruit from a tree. 'This is surely worth a great deal of money. Metkin gave it to her. Why, I wonder?'

I could not answer him. The charming, pagan thing symbolized so much: the power of ancient instincts carried in the blood, superstitions that endured in the teeth of reason, the present hungers of love and desire. And once again I was eight years old, watching and listening. Sonia, delectable and indifferent, Pan so warm and handsome, and the time rich with music and magic; my first moments of true awareness.

'Oh that, it was the Arts Festival,' Claudia said. 'We all got lovely things from Pan as souvenirs. He's filthy rich. These were mine.' She swung her earrings and the little gold flowers set with chips of rose quartz and faience danced in the sunlight. 'They once belonged to Cleopatra. Amy got the Pisarro in the drawing-room.'

'You were children. It seems strange to give valuable presents to a married woman.' David watched my face which so often betrayed me. I felt strongly the unease in him, a restiveness beneath his calm. 'I'm surprised Father didn't object.'

Claudia raised her eyebrows. 'Why should he? He likes Pan.'

'So I gather, yet that explains nothing. Why does Metkin now offer me a partnership in his fine arts business? What am I to him? I don't know one darn thing about paintings or antiques, and I felt certain that Father would object. But he thinks it a marvellous opportunity.'

I found my voice. Our father is the Earl of Osmington, once rich but no longer so. 'So it is. You belong to a feudal family, you know. Gunville Place and all the estate is entailed, so it will go to Valentine as the eldest son. What with taxation and shortages there'll be precious little left over for you.'

'I don't want anything, I can make my own way.' He turned the monkey between his hands, considering it from under the lashes of his golden-brown eyes. 'Tell me, Amy, were you there, actually there at Gunville Place, when I was born?'

'Well, no; they packed Claudia and me off to Bournemouth out of the way. Why?'

'This is going to sound absurd, it *is* absurd, but for some time now I've had an alien, disjointed feeling. It seems that I belong to everybody and nobody.' I wanted to say, you're mine, you belong to me and always will, but of course it wasn't true except in my heart, which didn't count. 'If I were adopted it would explain a whole lot. Metkin's orphans, the abandoned babies he picks up off the streets in Egypt and Africa, are talked about a good deal in America. Some of them are growing up there. So it did cross my mind – I thought perhaps—'

'You were one of them, and not Sonia's at all?'

Claudia and I exchanged grins. She said, 'Amy and I had never been close to a pregnant woman before and we could hardly keep our eyes off Sonia's middle, especially when gorgeous smocks began arriving from Chanel, and baby-clothes and cribs and things. How she hated us staring! You must have been a big baby and she got absolutely huge and groused all the time about our appalling manners.' Claudia dug the toe of her shoe into a piece of moss between the paving stones and prised it loose. For a moment I saw in her expression the resentful unhappy child. 'She could have talked to us sensibly about it but of course she didn't think it nice. We were pretty ignorant and imagined that at any minute she was going to burst open like a pea-pod. Amy was on pins with nerves.'

'Of course I was. You told me frightful things about explosions and blood and insides.'

'You were dense enough to swallow any tale. Sorry, Davy, there's no getting out of it, you're Sonia's son and nothing whatsoever to do with orphans.'

He stood up and dropped the silver monkey back into his pocket. 'Does that explain it I wonder, a different mother? Certainly there's no family resemblance between us is there?'

Without waiting for an answer he wandered back into the house. 'Who *is* he like?' Claudia asked. 'Not the rest of us, though you're not like Portia and me either.'

'His mother and himself, that's who. Does William know that you're staying with me?'

I could see David standing just inside the French windows to the drawing-room and held my breath. 'Bill? He's in Liverpool.' She seemed to have forgotten who he was. 'It's merciful that Pan's a queer. The oddest thing, but for a few minutes Davy looked exactly like him.'

His broad shoulders tensed. He had heard. 'What absolute nonsense,' I said casually. 'I expect you need glasses, you're getting as blind as a bat.'

'No I'm not.'

She lost interest, closed her eyes and promptly fell asleep. David shrugged and relaxed, but she had created for me the very situation I had been trying so hard to avoid. What did I do now? I needed advice and help.

Rudi, who had remained silent while we talked, looked interested but unsurprised. He took my hand and gave it a reassuring squeeze. 'Come for a walk in the garden.'

We wandered in companionable silence. The gardener had watered early that morning and the rich, damp soil smelt cool, heightening the scents of sweet peas and lavender. Blue damsel flies whisked to and fro above the pond, dipping their tail-ends into the water to lay eggs.

Within the old stable-yard we could talk freely and not be overheard, except by the cockerel pecking between the cobbles and bullying his many wives. 'How long have you known?' I asked Rudi.

'Not as long as you, I think. When I saw the two of them together in America I wondered.'

'If David questions me what do I tell him?'

'Nothing, dearest Amy. He's unlikely to ask the out-right question and you can't take on a debt that isn't yours. If Sonia won't speak then Pandel must. Ring him, or I'll do it if you prefer.'

18

'He's travelling about so much finding looted pictures for the Art Commission and repatriating lost children. He can't always be reached. I'll try.' I stepped back hastily as a shiny bronze bootlace moved suddenly away from my invading foot. A baby slow-worm. It slid under the compost heap. Stupidly I wondered whether slow-worms had emotions and worries.

'Claudia's asked him to her wedding.'

'He might not come. You know, Rudi, that midsummer seemed like pure magic to me, but I didn't know about consequences. Oughtn't they to have thought?'

'At the time they knew what they wanted and got it,' he said. 'I suppose it seemed like an end achieved.'

'And of course it wasn't, was it? Just another beginning.'

Chapter Two

That evening I offered reluctantly to stay in with Claudia while Rudi and David went to their Victory Committee meeting. In some ways Rudi needed protection. He absolutely loved organizing celebrations, but a long illness left him prey to bouts of tropical fever. He suffered nightmares. For a few seconds on waking he lay shivering in my arms, thinking he was still in a makeshift hospital hut in Burma. Those times terrified me. I hated and resented the years between us for shortening our life together. Love had come to me unexpectedly and magically. I feared to lose it.

He rarely spoke of his experiences in the Far East after he became separated from his little troupe of entertainers. To a man who had struggled from a poverty-stricken childhood into an ephemeral world of gaiety and music, tears, laughter, passionate triumphs and regrets, the jungle must have been a descent into sheer torment.

Rudi fretted to get back to the theatre world that was his life. He worked on plans to open his own theatrical agency as soon as he could find a suitable house in London. 'Agents tend to be universally reviled, and some of them deserve it,' he said. 'I can imagine nothing more satisfying than to coax and persuade budding talents into flower.'

Almost as soon as he set foot in Underhallow Dora Slade, the Committee chairwoman, pounced on him. How she knew about Hollywood and his theatrical past mystified me, but there was something of the benign witch in Dora. She kept the village shop (Dora Aphrodite Slade, sole prop. licensed to sell tobacco) and looked after old Mr Slade, her awful cantankerous father-in-law.

Some people, mostly Hallow-born, snorted over the name Aphrodite. Dora had turned fifty and could only be described as stout. She wasn't very tall either. Yet she carried her firm solid body like an empress. Her greying hair curled vigorously and she had perfect skin, smooth, pale and unblemished. When she smiled I fancied a sardonic gleam lurking behind her black eyes. I liked Dora Aphrodite very much and thought her beautiful.

As it turned out I need not have bothered to consider Claudia. She yawned and expressed satisfaction at being left alone. 'I'm waiting for a trunk call, I told them to transfer it here.'

'Who's it from? Bill?'

A closed, obstinate look came down, hardening her expression. 'If I wanted to be asked stupid questions I'd have stayed on at Grandmother's. I need a bit of peace and privacy.'

'But I thought you'd already moved into Hildegarde's house. It's private enough there.'

'Oh is it? That's all you know. Annie Bowells comes every day and fusses around cleaning and polishing. Everybody telephones, Bill, Valentine, Father, Gwennie, Grandmother. Idiots drop in, offering to keep me company. I can't bear it. I don't want bloody company, I don't want to be married, I just want peace!'

This outburst really alarmed me. Claudia moaned and grumbled as a matter of habit but rarely was she so emphatic or so jumpy. Whatever weighed on her mind had a considerable importance to her. I said, 'Just for once you'd better listen to me. You've already postponed the wedding twice, yet I'm perfectly sure that you love Bill as far as you're capable of loving.'

21

She gave me a ferocious glare. I pressed on. 'He's a marvellously patient man but if you mess about like this you'll lose him, and jolly well serve you right. Is that what you want?'

'Oh God, shut up will you? Just shut up.'

'Can't you give him a bit of a break and tell him what's bothering you?'

She shivered. 'No I can't. He's the last person.'

'It seems to me that you badly need to tell someone. I've always been on your side, Claudia, you know I have. I'm not asking for confidences but if you want an ally I'm still that, and though you used to accuse me of sneaking, I never ever did. Do think about it.'

Her light blue eyes stared at or past me for a moment or two. 'Thanks, Amy,' she said with a long sigh. 'I'll do that, I'll think about it.'

All the evening she was on my mind. Our meetings during the War were brief and infrequent. Up until the moment that she confessed in an off-hand manner to being in love with a commander in the RNVR her relationships with men had struck me as tepid and unemotional, or downright jokes. That day she arrived on my doorstep in tearing spirits. Elegant and beautiful in her WRNS uniform, she fizzed and sparkled with happiness. Then, as suddenly as she had fallen for Bill, she dropped him.

'Do you know how many ships we've lost?' she said miserably. 'When Bill's at sea on convoys I never know whether he'll come back. I can't endure the endless waits for the 'phone to ring, and the worry each time he sails, I simply can't. I'm a jinx. If he's killed it will be my fault.'

At that time, early in 1944, U-boat attacks had dwindled and the talk was of an invasion of occupied Europe. Nothing quite justified her agitation. I got dreadfully angry with her, blaming her for a cowardice that could not endure mental pain. I was disappointed, too, because her commander turned out to be an acquaintance of mine from holiday times at Weymouth before the War. His name was William Deering, but his mother called him Frog. A long, angular boy, he looked just like one in bathers when he jumped into the hotel swimming-pool. Since then he had filled out splendidly.

'Are you going to run away from love and the fear of loss all your life?' I had asked, 'And make excuses about being a jinx? It's mad and wrong.'

'You don't understand,' she said, 'you simply don't understand.'

'Explain then.'

A tremendously sad look came over her face and she closed up like an oyster. 'I can't, not now, perhaps not ever.'

She seemed so unlike her carefree self that I didn't press her. From our difficult childhood we had joined in a natural alliance, but she had reached a path that she preferred to travel alone.

My indignation on William's behalf had proved to be unnecessary. He began in the quietest, pleasantest way to drive Claudia mad. 'Wherever I go he's there,' she complained, 'just looking and smiling and saying nothing. If he really loved me he'd rage or plead instead of watching me like a benevolent uncle. I can't stand much more of it.'

Bill, sublimely confident of getting her in the end, not only loved her but would not let go. One evening he tracked her to an obscure pub near Haslemere and, ignoring the group she was with, sat beside her. Goaded beyond discretion she tried a frontal attack. 'Go away,' she hissed, 'stop spying on me, leave me alone.'

'I don't favour long engagements,' he said. 'The War will soon be over and neither of us is in our first youth.

If we're to have children we should begin to plan our wedding at once. You will marry me, of course? I almost forgot to ask.'

Claudia, goggling at him in rage and frustration, shouted, 'Of course I'll bloody-well marry you, if only to stop you following me around and telling me what an old hag I am.'

A silence descended on the bar. Shamefaced and furious, she rushed to me in Sussex. 'Amy, I could have bitten my tongue out but I'll simply have to keep my word. The whole of Portsmouth and Southampton knows about it, including the Wrens at my depot. And if you dare to laugh I'll mince you into fragments.'

'Does Bill truly know what he's in for?'

She took off one of her shoes, a stout black brogue, and threw it at my head. Fortunately it missed. 'I love him, idiot, and he loves me. He knows enough. The rest isn't his business.'

'What rest?'

I thought that I might surprise her into talking about her lovers or the years when we were separated, but she only shrugged. So that's how matters stood when the War ended. The wedding date was fixed, postponed, and postponed again, and still we waited to be relieved of responsibility for Claudia. Poor Frog! He had angelic patience.

A scout hut did not at first sound to me a tremendously exciting or necessary building to get so fussed up about. What could it supply that the village hall couldn't? It was explained to me that, as well as harbouring scouts and guides and their camping-gear, the old hut had served as the cricket pavilion, a handicraft centre, and a place for doing the teas on sportsdays and at bazaars. When not in use its doors were, naturally, locked. How many keys circulated around the village is not certain, but the figure can't have been less than twenty. They were invaluable to lovers. From scandalous remarks ('She got more in that hut than splinters in her backside.') it became plain that over the years a great deal of sex took place among the nets and bats and tarpaulins.

Then on a moonless night during the War came tragedy. A German aircraft missed its target and jettisoned its bombs over Hallow Hill, leaving an ugly crater in the cricket-pitch and demolishing one side of the old wooden building. A small fire started and two lives were lost, those of an American soldier and the coalman's wife. At the fateful moment they were, according to rumour, engaged in an act of love on a pile of deck-chairs, but I doubt whether anyone could swear to it. They might just have been enjoying a friendly talk and smoke.

Not only Underhallow but Uphallow and Hallow Wickens, our two satellite hamlets, had a deep interest in the replacement of their lost haven. Fund-raising went with enthusiasm.

'Is it all right if I sit in?' I asked Dora Aphrodite, 'or shall I wait in the dance hall?'

'Stay if you can find a chair, Amy. We've a full turn-out this evening.'

Looking around the table I felt, in spite of my anxiety over Claudia, quite glad to have come. For one thing – the main one if I'm to be honest – Josie Knapp was there and at her most potent. It wasn't that I distrusted Rudi, but I definitely did not trust Josie. She combined wild and radiant beauty with intellect and a considerable education. Her abundance quenched us lesser women like a candle-snuffer.

Rudi used to do a wonderful line in sweeping women off their feet. As my experience of sex was slight and usually tended towards farce rather than glamour, I felt rather glad that he had enjoyed a misspent youth as long as it was definitely over. In the terms of Claudia's schoolfriend (an odd mention, that, of a forbidden subject) Rudi was my unicorn. Josie trespassed at her peril.

When we entered the committee-room Charlie Hopkins (gentlemen's barber and chemist's sundries) had his eyes positively glued to the low square neck of Josie's blouse. The curve of her breasts just showed, sun-touched and tempting as tropical fruits. She did not acknowledge his interest. Although she enjoyed a rich and varied sex-life Josie left married men alone. This did not seem to console Gloria, Charlie's wife, (ladies' hair-fashions – permanent waving a speciality). From her grim expression I thought she might be praying that he would be struck blind.

Dora called the committee to order. 'Unless anyone wants to hear them, we'll take the minutes of the last meeting as read. We've a lot to settle so let's get on. First the Guisers' dance.'

Old Mr Slade, sitting on Dora's right and handy for the lavatory, woke from a sound slumber. 'I always used to be Hobby till my feet gave out,' he said, and nodded off again.

'Well Charlie's the Hobby now, but as you know we lost the lad who used to dance the part of the Betty at Dunkirk. David here says he'll have a go but he's a novice. Someone'll have to teach him quickly. What do you say, Charlie?'

Reluctantly he wrenched his gaze away from Josie. 'Eh, what's that?'

'The dance, the Six Swords. David here has agreed to take the Betty's part. Who's to show him the steps and the pattern?'

'He's not a Hallow man,' said Gloria. 'It ought to be a Hallow man.'

'Do be realistic; you couldn't find eleven dancers out of Hallow men. Most of us are incomers. I'm from Southampton myself and half-Greek at that.'

Charlie frowned. 'It's been years since we last did the dance. I just about remember my own part. Your old chap there might know the Betty's, I don't.'

You could have warmed your hands at the look that came into Josie's eyes. 'I'll teach David,' she said softly.

An awful mean jealousy hit me like the twinge of a nerve at the thought of David in the arms of Josie Knapp. I suppressed it at once, but I understood how a mother might feel at the intrusion of another woman into the life of her son. But love him as I did, he was nobody's child. At eighteen he was almost a man, and looking amused but non-committal.

Gloria flounced about a bit in her chair, and I could see that she would have liked to pour scorn and put a spoke in Josie's wheel. But she couldn't. At the time that Josie married Ivan Knapp, our village police-sergeant, she was at Cambridge with a potentially brilliant career as historian and archivist in front of her. She specialized in local history and customs. Why she threw up university to marry Ivan remained a mystery. He was not at all a nice man and quite mad at times. Like Claudia, he missed the War.

'Before we go any further, Dora, can someone explain the Six Swords?' Rudi asked. 'I know it's connected with Borgatten Maze, but not much more.'

'It's just one of those funny things that hang on over the years. The maze used to be famous in the old days. I heard there's a copy of it in the floor of some French cathedral. Josie can tell you the meaning, I expect.'

The highly charged gaze moved to Rudi. 'The idea's simple enough and about as old as time. The Rich Man, who's the Harvest King, is mocked by the Fool and then killed by the Six Swords at the prompting of the Betty. She represents the triumphant Goddess. The dead King is resurrected as corn for the people, and the Billy Boots is the young innocent, the new King.

Hobby was probably once a horse goddess. All danced by men, naturally.'

Gloria Hopkins yawned. 'Oh naturally men. No need to show off, dear. We all know you went to a posh college.'

Josie stepped up the voltage and smiled, not at her but at Charlie. She pushed her hands through her dark curls and set her gold hoop earrings swinging and glinting. Her bosom rose gently. She seemed all sinuous movement, a creature with the ease and amiable cruelty of a well-fed cat. Small beads of sweat gathered on Charlie's brow.

Dora tapped the table impatiently. 'Sorry to interrupt but we must get on. I'm sure Josie'll be pleased to tell you the ins and outs after the meeting, and arrange with David for lessons.' Her father-in-law's head rested peacefully on the table. She pushed it out of the way with her elbow. 'Now, the Lammas loaves, real white bread, one for every soul in the three villages.'

'It's rationed,' Gloria said, 'so's the flour. I'm not buying black market, it's against the law.'

'That's as may be. We worked hard to glean and thresh our own corn and the bread comes free, though we hope even the most pinch-purse will give a voluntary donation. The only other thing we've got to find out is whether the Vicar will agree to hold the service. Old Vicar set his face dead against it because the Dean and the Bishop called it heathen practices.'

'Toadies and lickspittles!' Mr Slade roused himself. 'Boring buggers!'

'That'll be quite enough of that language, Father,' Dora said, earning a spiteful glare in return.

Gloria addressed the chair. 'I hope there's to be no cavortings on the hill after sunset, Dora. We all know about the blaspheming and nakedness that goes on, and there's some not far from here'll take their knickers off for any man that asks.'

'What's the matter, dear, doesn't anyone bother with yours now that the Yanks have gone home?' Josie enquired sweetly.

The changing colours of Gloria's complexion told their own story. She struggled for speech. 'That's a lie, I never did. I don't know any Yanks.'

Now thoroughly awake, Mr Slade shook with silent, senile laughter. 'Creeping round by nights. I've seen 'em. A whited sepulchre, that's what she is.'

Dora intervened hastily. 'What people do in the dark isn't the committee's business. Save your quarrels for outside or we'll be here all night. Gloria, would you mind popping into the dance hall and asking the scouts to send us in a cup of tea?'

The doors opened, letting in a blast of Glenn Miller's band playing 'In The Mood'. Under a notice that read, 'No Jitterbugging', the Vicar jitterbugged vigorously with a girl in a pleated circular skirt. Mr Slade muttered, 'Showing her drawers off to the world. It's all right for some.'

Gloria returned and ostentatiously took a different seat as far from Josie as she could get. Scout Humphrey, accompanied by a very small wolf-cub, followed her bearing a tray. 'No hard liquor, the cops are on to us,' he snarled in a passable American accent. 'Sergeant Knapp's just come in but I brought rock-cakes. Evening everybody.'

'Thank you, Humphrey dear. You're such a good boy,' Dora said.

'He holds my hand when we cross the road,' piped the wolf-cub.

Scout Humphrey blushed to the roots of his sandy hair. 'Just cut the crap, Ernie, and put the rock-cakes on the table. You'd never think he was eight, would you? That's one and fourpence, so give. Please.'

The Victory Committee gave. 'Poor Humphrey,' Dora said thoughtfully as the door closed behind him, 'he's quite lost without the Americans. They made a great fuss of him and took him to all their picture shows. He wants to become a gangster or a cowboy but he's far too nice, and it would upset his mother badly. She's set her heart on making him into a chartered accountant. Now, where were we?'

The secretary showed her notes. 'Almost done, I think, Dora. You asked me to remind you about the children.'

'So I did. The party's mainly for them after all, and they're not interested in the mummers nowadays. They'd much rather have something with shooting and blood.' Dora's wicked unfathomable smile flashed on and off. 'So we'll give them Punch and Judy, a sit-down tea and games on the green after. In the morning the Sunday School children will sing a hymn or two and the brownies and cubs want to do their maypole dances.'

'It's not May Day; we've already had May Day,' Gloria protested.

'Tell her to shut up,' old Mr Slade said, 'her voice gets on my wick. What's wrong with having two May Days, or three if you fancy them?'

Gloria opened her mouth to speak but Dora fore-stalled her. 'Stick to the point, Father, and watch your manners or I'll have you voted off this committee.'

'Bloody women, they've got no respect nowadays. If my boy was here he wouldn't let you talk to me like that.'

'If your boy was here he'd put you in an Eventide Home, so think yourself lucky he isn't.'

Gloria tittered. Mr Slade stared at her out of watery blue eyes. 'You've got the face of a costive camel,' he commented, unabashed. 'I want my tea.'

'You've already had your tea,' said Dora.

'Then I want my supper and a nice milky drink.' At the mention of drink an unease caused him to frown. 'No I don't, I want to go – now.'

'Go on then, Father.'

'Aren't you taking me?'

'Into the gents? I should say not, and don't forget to do your buttons up when you've finished.' Dora watched him shamble away with an expression of acute dislike. 'Sorry about him. The people you get stuck with if you're fool enough to marry! Right, what's next?'

'Don't forget the cricket,' said Charlie Hopkins.

The secretary shuffled through some loose scraps of paper. 'Here it is. Charlie thinks we should challenge Uphallow and Hallow Wickens to a cricket match in the afternoon if it's fine. If wet, skittles in the main hall.'

'Good idea. Any objections?' There were none. 'Then Rudi and I can make up a programme and get the Vicar to run copies off on his duplicator. Did I say we've got a reporter coming to do a piece for the local papers? He's bringing an American lady with him who's writing a book. It sounded all right at first, but now I'm none too sure.'

'What's her name?' Josie asked. 'I correspond with several collectors of folk customs.'

'That's just what I thought she'd be, so I asked at the tuppeny library in Petersfield what she'd already published. Her name's Abigail Golightly and she writes novels. You'd better all take a look at them.'

Dora passed a couple of volumes round the table. On the cover of one a leering masked figure leaned over a girl who had rather lost control of her blouse. The title was *Revenge Of The Warlock*. The second was called *Dance Of Lust* and appeared to concern an orgy in the snow among Christmas mummers.

'Well, well,' Rudi said in a pleased tone, 'sex, religion and witchcraft; a splendid mix.'

'I don't know how she gets away with it,' Dora said, 'all thrusting and throbbing and naked bodies. Suffolk,

31

it's supposed to be. She doesn't leave much to the imagination and I'll swear she never saw goings-on like that in England, not even in Suffolk. I suppose there's no chance of keeping her away?'

Rudi shook his head. 'Short of locking her up, no. If we cold-shoulder her she'll imagine we have something sinister to hide. A big welcome with lots of flattery ought to go down well.'

Recalling the steamy trash that Claudia and I devoured in childhood, I rather regretted that Abigail Golightly had not been around then. Her works sounded highly educational. I felt that Underhallow would be a disappointment to her. Apart from a couple of surviving farms, rural life had all but disappeared.

True we had witches of a sort, nature worshippers who wore folk-weave jibbahs and brewed tea out of dried dandelion leaves. They made a great fuss about getting in tune with the earth. Conscientiously removing their clothes they danced naked, lacking true joy and attracting no male voyeurs. Josie had joined them for a while, expecting heaven knows what exotic goings-on. Earnest, comfortable souls and not in the least bit given to lust, they proved a disappointment to her.

At that point our Vicar put his head round the door. Behind him sounded the slow rhythmic shuffling of feet to a scratchy record of 'Goodnight Sweetheart'. 'Last waltz,' he said. 'Just popping in to say it will be okay about the Lammas service. It's an authentic church feast and our patronal, so we'll not worry about the Bishop and his misgivings.'

'Did you enjoy the dancing, Bertie?' Josie Knapp asked in a sultry voice.

He smiled, turned scarlet and bolted. The members of the committee sat up and took notice. Something about the clergy exercises a powerful attraction on women, and Bertie Gooch was youngish, a bachelor and decidedly fun-loving. It was not in Josie's nature to overlook him.

Every woman in Underhallow ought to have hated her yet, with the exception of one or two like Gloria Hopkins who hated most women, we liked her. She told me once that she admired loyalty. When she married Ivan she intended to be absolutely faithful to him for ever. 'I try, Amy, honestly I do, but I can't manage it. An unattached man has only to look at me and I go weak at the knees. It takes so little to make them happy.'

I didn't think seducing them was so very little and I said so. Suddenly she hugged me, which gave me suspicions that she instantly confirmed. 'Don't worry about Rudi for an instant. He was a mistake. The moment I fluttered an eyelid at him he said, "Don't be an idiot my good woman, I'm entirely Amy's." It isn't often a man makes fun of me so I knew he meant it.'

Money changed hands over Josie's conquests. Bets would now be laid a) on her chance of seducing Bertie at all, b) on how long it would take her, c) would Ivan find out, and d) if he did would he do violence to either or both of them. She provided a continuing source of interest to the sportsmen of Underhallow.

'If there's no other business we might as well call it a day,' Dora Aphrodite said. 'Eleven o'clock. We've been talking an age. Cocoa at home for anyone who fancies a cup.'

Josie stood up and shook out her skirts. She usually wore soft flowing dresses decorated with braid or flowers and tightly belted to show off her small waist. They made her look like a very clean and well-nourished film gipsy. 'First lesson on Monday, David?'

'Thanks, Mrs Knapp. As it's a team dance I guess I'd better ask one or two of the other men to join us.'

'Have you ever seen the maze? It's an interesting place. We could stroll up there now if you like.'

'Another time perhaps.'

I got the impression that Davy had fended off approaches from married women before which was as well since Ivan Knapp stood in the doorway, watching and listening. 'Hallo, Ivan,' I said loudly.

Josie cast a glowing smile at us all and said, 'Just coming, my darling. Good-night everyone, good-night.'

I wished I could resent her, but I couldn't, any more than I could have resented a humming-bird. The room became dull and drab without her.

Chapter Three

Claudia needed a lot of sleep and I expected her to be in bed by the time we got home. She was in the kitchen, slumped on a hard chair with her feet planted on the table, eating raisins and listening to a foreign jazz broadcast on Polly's wireless set. As soon as she saw me she jumped up. No need to ask whether she had received the expected telephone call. Her mood had changed to one of barely suppressed excitement and anticipation. She might have been waiting for a lover.

'Come for a drive, Amy, I adore driving at night.'

'Aren't you tired? I am.'

'You'll soon wake up and we can sleep late tomorrow.'

'What about petrol?'

'Grandmother gave me a tankful and an extra can. Now she's got the motor-bike she always has lots.'

I goggled. 'Not a motor-bike! I don't believe it. She can't even drive a car.'

'She doesn't ride it, idiot. She bought it for the chauffeur and goes shopping in the side-car. The Daimler eats petrol.'

It still strained the imagination. Try as I might I could not see our stately grandparent folded up in a side-car. What of her ribbed silk coats? What of her toques? What of her ankle-length skirts and ample bust? 'What,' I asked weakly, 'has got into her?'

'The Labour Government, that's what; a collection of piddling undertakers according to Grandmother. You should hear her lay into Clement Attlee. She says he's got the personality of a guinea-pig, the looks of Crippen, and not the remotest idea of how to woo the populace.'

'But she used to complain that Churchill was a vulgar opportunist. Who *does* she like?'

'Among politicians, not a soul. She's utterly certain that she could run the country far better single-handed, especially if the Queen Mother pitched in and lent a hand.'

Old Queen Mary served as a source of constant inspiration to Grandmother. They were very alike, though I had learned that underneath her imposing exterior our grandmother was by far the softer, more loving, of the two. She doted on Claudia for her likeness to our dead mother.

'What are you mooning over? Come on, let's go,' Claudia said.

She had a rapport with motors. On the empty roads she drove her pre-war Humber fast, roaring over the South Downs until we reached the coast somewhere near Rustington. The moon wore a gigantic halo, presaging rain; a milky calm lay on the sea. For a while we did not speak. Then she asked, 'Did you truly mean it when you said you're still my ally?'

'Of course. Why?'

'So far I've coped on my own, but I'm miserably upset and tired of endless waiting and wondering and looking over my shoulder. If something doesn't happen soon I'll burst.'

'What is it, Claudia, whatever's wrong? You're not in some kind of danger, are you?'

'Not now,' she said, 'I wouldn't drag you in if I were. Life's beastly unfair, throwing up things that happened years ago and ought to be over and forgotten.'

I jumped to a hasty conclusion that turned out to be partly right. 'School, Switzerland, whatever's bothering you happened there, didn't it? That's why you clammed up. It isn't a man is it?'

She resented me guessing. 'Why do you always assume it's a man? I can't talk about it yet anyway. They told me I mustn't, not until it's all over.'

'But when will whatever it is be all over?'

'Soon, I think, if Pan—'

'If Pan what?'

She sat tapping the steering-wheel and gazing at the sea. A medicinal smell of seaweed rolled in with the tide as it rasped gently over the shingle. 'Listen, Amy, will you swear that if I send for you, you'll come and not say a word to a soul until afterwards? I shan't want to be alone.'

Curiosity gnawed at me. 'Come where?'

'Wherever I am, of course.'

I had begun to feel abominably sleepy and muddled but I said, 'I'll do anything you want except for keeping secrets from Rudi. He'll have to know what's going on.'

'Damn, I'd forgotten him.'

'He's tremendously reliable in a crisis.'

'Aren't you worried about other women? He used to charm them like a wizard. I was awestruck.'

'He never pretended it was for ever and nor did they. There's a huge difference between wanting just for now, at this minute, and needing for life. Rudi always keeps a promise.'

'Yes, I remember. Him then, but nobody else. Do you swear your holiest oath?'

'Yes, I swear. Can we go home now please?'

She smiled at me, backed the old car in a wide half-circle and accelerated just as the first drops of rain began to fall.

Claudia stayed for four days. After our drive she lapsed into a state of trance-like immobility, refusing to answer the telephone and scarcely leaving the house. On the third evening the 'phone rang and it was Portia. She is our elder sister and married to the Duke of Coritanum.

'If she asks, I'm not here,' Claudia mouthed.

I felt fairly confident that she would not ask. When Portia called me I rarely understood why, except that she seemed to need somewhere to direct a series of little homilies or complaints. She viewed us both with chilly disapproval. Somehow the early death of our mother left her on the opposite side of an unbridgeable chasm, and we failed in all respects to do her credit.

With the announcement of Claudia's engagement to William the chill became a severe frost. Portia asked questions. 'Is he a man of family? There are Norfolk Deerings I believe, quite acceptable sort of people.'

'Of course he's got a family, why shouldn't he have? They come from Lancashire, not Norfolk.'

'But simply *nobody* comes from Lancashire. Who is he? What does his father do?'

Claudia took no interest in the ramifications of rank and suitability that meant so much to our sister. 'That's rot, thousands of very nice people come from Lancashire,' she said with irritating accuracy. 'His father's a pawnbroker I think.'

Portia nearly died of fright. It came almost as a relief to her to discover later that Mr Deering was in fact a cornbroker, quite a wealthy one, and the idea of keeping pawnshops had never crossed his mind.

Until I could tell her face to face I hid from her the worse affront to her sensibilities that lay ahead. In a changing world she could just about accept trade. But Rudi grew up on a poor street in Battersea with no money, an eye on the stars, and not a single valuable connection to his name. His passion for the stage was to Portia the equivalent of stewing in some vile Dickensian opium den.

On this occasion she declared that, though we were at a time of National Crisis when we were all urged to Make Do And Mend until Britain Was On Its Feet Again, there was no need for Claudia to economize over her wedding attendants. 'Only one bridesmaid and no pages implies a lack of family support.'

I pointed out as gently as possible that it was none of her business. Not that I got through. Beneath the correctness and the pride she sounded rather unhappy. In an offhand manner she added, 'I almost forgot, an American woman may call on you on the first of August. She's connected with the American Embassy, and one has to be polite to them, though they can be so impossibly pushy and overbearing. Her name is something Slavonic and quite unpronounceable. She writes books under a pseudonym.'

'Abigail Golightly?'

'You've heard of her? I can't say I had, and some of her views are incomprehensible to me. She has an interest in villages and wanted to come to Hindlecote, but that's quite out of the question.'

Portia had to be borne with, but unless I squashed her now I should forever be landed with her unwanted guests. A decision waited to be made. 'Sorry, but I can't entertain her, I'm far too busy.'

A long pause while I listened to clicks on the line and thought of hanging up though I knew she was still there. I whistled a tune under my breath. 'Delegate, can't you?' Portia said at length in a huff. 'I'm utterly annoyed that you and Claudia will never do a thing I ask. I have fourteen old people to care for and no help at all from the Coritanums. It's too bad. I never seem to talk to anyone young, and it's two years since I saw a single member of our family.' At the wistfulness in her tone the unlikeliest notion crossed my mind – that she wanted me to propose myself for a visit. Then she said, 'Not that I – oh well, never mind.'

The pips went then and she said goodbye in a hurry, thus relieving me of the necessity for any further speculation.

'The damned cheek, why should we lead our lives to suit her?' Claudia said when I reported the conversation. 'Who are all the old people I wonder?'

'Lots of her in-laws descended on Hindlecote Castle during the blitz, and she looks after them so well that she can't get rid of them. I'm a bit uneasy about her.'

'Oh rot, she wanted to be a duchess and she is one. Too bad if it's beyond her. D'you know, I saw the dreary Duke a few days ago getting into a taxi with a girl. If he's got himself a mistress it jolly well serves her right. I don't remember her ever being particularly nice to us, even at her grim wedding party. All advances spurned.'

'That was the one and only time I saw her during the War. She didn't even come to Great-aunt Hildegarde's funeral, just sent a beastly enormous wreath of madonna lilies. I do so much *not* like white lilies.'

'We won't have them when you die,' Claudia promised.

I sincerely hoped that Portia's husband had not taken to adultery. She was so respectable and concerned with appearances that the breath of scandal withered her. Her wedding to the Duke had been an occasion of such solemnity and stiffness that one ached with the effort of finding correct conversation and not spilling food on the carpet. She mentioned a dozen times that it (the carpet) was three hundred years old and stitched by hand.

Claudia, bored and not disposed to be tactful, stared pointedly at the faded pattern and threadbare patches. 'Poor you,' she said, 'why ever didn't you get a new one at Maples? They've some really cheerful colours. It must be hell marrying into a stingy family.'

After that we were not asked to stay to dinner. I

doubt whether we missed much. The Duke's side showed fewer inhibitions than we did, and distinct signs of collective senility. They attacked the canapés (mostly cod and sardine mocked up to imitate anchovies or smoked salmon) like wolverines, and trod fishy crumbs into the heirloom carpet.

Portia wore our mother's best tiara and looked heavenly and statuesque in acres of white satin and Brussels lace. But her face lacked the expressiveness of the equally beautiful Claudia, nor was she the kind of person whose company was much sought after. If there were competitions for being correct and boring, poor, good conscientious Portia would win every time.

Claudia and I did not receive invitations to the christening of her son, the baby Marquess of Stevenage. The godparents, in the persons of a viscount (our brother, Valentine), two dukes, a duchess and a couple of baronesses, preferred to have no dubious fairies marring the ceremony.

For the remainder of her stay Claudia idled around, turning over my belongings, reading my letters and being generally tiresome and grumpy. She spent more time in the kitchen chattering to Polly than she did with me. I sighed with relief when she roared off too fast around the green. Ivan Knapp tried to wave her down. She hooted and waved back, causing him to jump hurriedly out of the road and make a note in his official notebook.

He came to the house and complained, which gave him an excuse to prowl around, bobbing up and down behind my hedges and watching David's every move. Rudi began inviting him in, so after a while he gave up. In the red-brick police house beside the green the Knapps had tremendous and audible rows. They loved each other, but unwillingly, and with a wild incompatibility that led them to the brink of violence.

'Hell-bent on destruction,' Rudi said. 'In a saner world they would never have met.'

On the Wednesday of the week following my telephone conversation with Portia a formal invitation came from Hindlecote Castle requesting the pleasure of the company of Lady Amity Savernake on Saturday 22nd June, the occasion of Her Grace's thirty-fourth birthday. (The train will be met and overnight accommodation provided.) I stared at it, amazed and baffled. Portia never acknowledged our birthdays so hers had completely slipped my mind.

An hour later Claudia rang. 'What's that wretched woman up to now? She's never invited us before, so why now? Thirty-four isn't anything special, I mean it isn't an anniversary of anything except managing to be born, and that's not exactly a matter for congratulation in Portia's case. I'm not going.'

'It's an awful nuisance when there's so much else happening, and I don't a bit want to leave Rudi and David, but we ought to go, both of us. She sounded so in the dumps.'

'Do we drag her across country when we're feeling down? No we don't.'

'Perhaps it marks a change of heart, a desire for reconciliation or sisterly love, something beautiful like that.'

'I wish you'd stop wittering on like a romantic idiot. She can't bear us, me especially, and I can't bear her and all those prissy airs she puts on. I particularly don't want to be away at the moment.'

'We really must accept, I think, Claudia, and take nice cards and tasteful gifts and be on our best behaviour.'

The tussle took it out of me but I won in the end.

'Don't blame me if it's a disaster.' She positively

ground her teeth with ill-temper. 'And I'm not staying more than one night.'

'That's all we're invited for,' I said, feeling that Portia, cautious as always, was not exactly handing us the keys of the castle. I had a happy thought. 'She might have asked Val too, and I haven't seen him for ages.'

'So she might. That would be great. All right then, I'll say yes, but I must be back before Monday.'

In my eyes Valentine, our elder brother, qualified as just about the nicest man in the world, unassuming and funny in a quiet way. He had a distinguished War, collecting a wounded shoulder in the D-day landings and afterwards going on some kind of diplomatic mission to the Bahamas where the Duke of Windsor was then Governor.

In Nassau he fell in love. This circumstance bothered Portia when she remembered it, but Val kept his emotions firmly to himself and even she was chary of interfering while the romance remained just that and went no further.

At present he faced responsibilities that would have daunted a lesser man. My father, injured years ago in a dreadful accident, had struggled on at Gunville Place, our vast and dilapidated family home, until the end of the War, coping with evacuees of various kinds and becoming steadily more crippled and weary. He had married for a third time, another blow to Portia. She refused to meet him after his sensational divorce from Sonia, and when he committed the social error of marrying Gwennie Hughes, once my nanny, her cup overflowed with bitterness. Father never sought a reconciliation. All he longed for was to lead a retired life with Gwennie to love him and look after him, choosing whom he would see.

It was Val who made that dream a reality. He found Father a country house near the sea at Lulworth, and took over the running of Gunville. Beset by building regulations and an acute shortage of money, he tackled much of the renovation himself, grew as much food as he could and dealt with the remaining tenant farmers. He wanted to marry, I was sure. I wished that he would and that we could meet more often. But knowing his essential modesty I could quite easily imagine him feeling that he had nothing to offer the girl he loved, which was wrong if she wanted him too.

Dora Aphrodite's stock of cards ran rather to red celluloid roses and effusive verses so I had to make a dash into Chichester to find something plain and suitable. Presuming that a duchess could be expected to possess more or less everything I expended clothing coupons on a pair of leather gloves of which people like Portia cannot have too many.

Only heaven knew what Claudia would think suitable. For the journey to Leicester she livened a chill grey June morning with a scarlet coat (circa 1935). The shoulders were exaggerated with high black fur epaulettes, and she wore a tiny red hat perched over one eye. Such exotic elegance was rare among the austerities of post-war London. The porters couldn't keep their eyes off her. She smiled at them like an eccentric angel, then moaned and complained her way into the heart of England. I enjoyed the journey in spite of her. I like trains.

'We're to be met, but I bet it won't be the ducal Rolls,' Claudia said as we chuffed into the station. 'Far too grand for the likes of us. I don't think she really wanted us to come at all, just a polite refusal to make her feel she'd done her duty.'

'Yes she does want us, but she doesn't know how to be informal. Wouldn't it be nice if we could all be friends, the three of us. Sisters ought to like each other oughtn't they?'

'You live in dreamland, idiot. If she says one word against my heavenly William I shall spit on the heirloom carpet.'

We couldn't believe our conveyance, a hybrid affair that could be called neither a car nor a van, but which had the worst features of both. It smelt of grain sacks. We were bowed into it by the station-master himself. For some reason Claudia resented this courtesy, muttering under her breath and gazing longingly at the smooth, immaculately-shining bonnet of an Armstrong-Siddeley parked a few yards away.

The chauffeur watched us with an air of haughty offence. I expect he felt it a come-down to drive such an ignoble vehicle.

'What's up?' Claudia asked, 'Has Her Grace converted the Rolls into a holy icon or does she save it for royalty?'

'Petrol rationing, Lady Claudia,' he said. 'If you're ready, Her Grace asked particularly for the wagon to be returned in good time.'

'Why? Needed for a funeral is it?'

Aggression sprouted from her like branches from a thorn-tree. Hardly a promising beginning. Considering how little I had wanted to come I wished after all that I had not persuaded Claudia. I hissed, 'Cut it out, you ass.'

'Never mind, drive on. The sooner Her Grace has it back the better I shall be pleased,' she said.

The chauffeur permitted himself a small and bitter smile.

Chapter Four

Hindlecote Castle was not so very much bigger than Gunville Place but, standing solitary in the slightest of dips in a flat landscape, it looked immense and reassuring and quite lovely. The year was a wonderful one for roses and they climbed pink and yellow, red and white, over the dun stone of the walls. Beyond the great gateway formal beds confined yet more within a perfect lawn. I suppressed an unworthy thought that Portia had married a castle rather than a duke.

The butler, of bland, enigmatic countenance, took Claudia's coat. I declined to be parted from the jacket of my cardigan suit as the stone flags and the tremendous formality struck decidedly chill. 'Her Grace is in the small salon. This way, if you please.'

'Thank you, Singlet,' Portia said, unfolding herself from an upright chair and presenting a cheek for our kisses. She actually seemed to wince away as I lightly touched her face. It was not exactly an effusive welcome. 'So here you are. I'm afraid you're too late for coffee. Elderly people seem to need a constant supply of drinks and snacks and I have to be firm for the sake of the staff.'

Inspecting the room with a single swift glance, Claudia noticed decanters and glasses. She beamed at the butler, deciding by some selection process of her own to like him. 'Could that be sherry, Singlet?' she asked.

'Isn't it a little early?' Portia asked.

'Just now it was too late. Let's all have one to wish

you a happy birthday. Will you be mother, Singlet?'

'Certainly, Lady Claudia.' The merest suspicion of a wink flickered across the stately countenance, or perhaps Singlet suffered a lazy eye. 'I can recommend the Amontillado.'

'I bet you can.'

Portia made a strangled noise. 'That will be all, thank you.'

'Thank *you*, Your Grace.' He disappeared slowly like the Cheshire cat in Alice, closing the door very softly behind him.

'Really, Claudia, insinuating that Singlet drinks the sherry,' Portia said. 'Have you come here with the express intention of upsetting my staff? It's simply too bad. They're indispensible to me.'

'Oh come off it. Of course he drinks the sherry. Butlers always do, it's part of their perks, and he's not upset. Laughing his head off in his pantry. Where's Val? You have invited him?'

'No I haven't. He was rather short with me the last time we spoke and I thought it uncalled for. Naturally I am interested in the girl he's getting engaged to. After all, she will be the future Countess of Osmington.'

Claudia glared at me as though it were my fault. 'Do go on, Portia. It's something of a feat to annoy Valentine and I'd like to know how you managed it.'

'I'm sure I don't know why he should take it amiss. The photographs that he has show this Cristabel to be of dark complexion and I merely wondered, since he met her in the Bahamas, whether he had so forgotten his position as to think of marrying a person of colour.'

Of all the breathtakingly tactless, snobbish, damaging women, Portia took the gold cup every time. Even Claudia looked dumbfounded. 'I hope you didn't say that.'

'Naturally I did. Isn't that what a Creole is? Some

kind of half-caste? And the family are Roman Catholic, which really won't do at all.'

I felt an angry, shamed heat rise to my face. 'If Val loves her it doesn't matter a damn what colour or creed she is. And it happens that the true Creoles are people of pure Spanish descent who live in the West Indies. Cristabel is a brilliant, beautiful, educated girl from one of the first families and just as white as you are.'

She inspected me with disagreeable disdain. 'You seem to be well-informed, Amy, if what you say is correct, but I see no need for such a diatribe. Clearly the religious difference is obstacle enough.'

I felt hurt for Val. Telling Portia first of his engagement had been an awful mistake. And to argue with that inflated self-righteousness meant the early ruin of the day that had only just begun. Somehow it must be got through without open warfare. 'It's not up to us to criticize his choice, Portia. You'd better have your cards and presents now.'

'And for God's sake get some of that sherry down,' Claudia instructed. 'You look as though you need it even more than I do – tired out with minding other people's business no doubt.'

Portia in repose did indeed look tired and dispirited. She never voluntarily crosses swords with Claudia, who might be described as a dirty fighter. 'Have you ever tried caring for old people? So demanding, and of course there's nothing whatever for them to do here. Only a few shops in the village, no cinema or theatre or tea-parties or gossip, none of the things they enjoyed before the War. They quarrel and argue and complain about the food.' She sighed. 'I'm sure I can't help it. We lost our chef when he was called up, and Cook does her best, but the rations go nowhere and she isn't at all skilful with left-overs.'

'Where are they?' I asked. 'The old people of course, not the left-overs.'

'I've sent them off into the fresh air with sandwiches and flasks and instructions not to come back until four o'clock. They'll be having a tea-party with us then.'

One could sympathize with Portia's desire for an hour or two of freedom, but I wondered how the old people felt to be regimented and dismissed for hours on end. 'Won't they get rather weary?'

'The Colonel's the most active. He's a second-cousin, and he's taking them into Leicester on the bus. They'll probably go to the cinema or the cathedral.'

Claudia finished her sherry, got up and poured another watched anxiously by Portia. 'Poor old things. Where's the noble Duke? Isn't he joining the celebrations?'

'Sadly not. Botolph is in Germany sitting in at the Nuremberg trials.'

Revenge for Valentine offered itself. I saw Claudia's mouth open to say that he most certainly wasn't. I gave her a warning look. 'You must miss him, Portia. He was away so much during the War.'

'He's forgotten that it's my birthday, I think. There it is, men aren't good at the small things of life, they prefer a grand canvas. Would you care to see your rooms and the rest of the Castle?'

Pride and love infused her cold voice with warmth. Claudia strangled a yawn and probably a desire to strangle Portia as well. I rather wanted to look around, it passed the time. The room we sat in, designed, I imagined, for the use of ladies, was charming. The barrel-vaulted ceiling had been plastered and painted with pastoral scenes and nymphs and cherubs. Blue panels edged with pink ribbons decorated the white walls. Unfortunately it made the beautiful Portia, dressed in a brown tweed skirt and baggy fawn cardigan, look too tall, too thin and too plain.

We inspected the picture gallery, mostly the Duke's ancestors dressed to kill but unlovely, though I saw, hiding in a corner, a Caravaggio. Worth a great deal if genuine, but hateful with an atmosphere of perversity and sick decay.

Portia had given us pretty bedrooms, with little four-poster beds and lots of flowered cretonne. The castle conformed not at all to my dreams of what a home should be, but I could understand why Portia loved it so pridefully.

'If you'll come to my room now,' she murmured as though she feared to be overheard, 'there's something I want you to take with you, Claudia, when you leave.'

She occupied a genuine bridal chamber, a vast room divided by gauzy curtains into bedroom and boudoir. Heaven knows how many Coritanum brides had occupied it, or how many little Coritanums had been conceived in the enormous bed. I took an instant dislike to the atmosphere. For all the stately richness of the fittings the room felt forlorn, as though it had seen more of tears than of love and laughter.

A massive door led, I supposed, to the Duke's apartments. The key was in the lock. Contriving to lean against it I stealthily tried the handle. Locked on the inside, Portia's side. I wondered whether marital sex fell seriously short of her expectations, or whether Botolph 'made demands'. Not that she ever showed much interest in the subject. While I was prying she pulled a chair to the bed and climbed on it, groping around on the solid oak tester and descending in a cloud of dust with a flat leather case.

'A safe place. The maids never think of cleaning up there once the spring renovations are over,' she said, handing the box to Claudia. 'Open it. It's Mother's parure of diamonds. I want you to wear them at your wedding and keep them until I ask for them back.'

Claudia and I stared at her with our mouths open. Portia behaved generally with absolute parsimony, and certainly spent next to nothing on herself or her appearance. When our mother died she gloated like mad to find that she was to get most of her jewels. I was only five and too young to care. But seven-year-old Claudia felt left out and managed to snaffle a few pieces that she particularly coveted, more as keepsakes than for their value. Now she opened the box, and the diamonds glittered up at us, bracelet, necklace, double clip brooches, earrings, and an aigrette with two birds and sprung tail-feathers to tremble and nod and catch the light.

'Why keep them up there? Don't you have a safe?' she asked.

'Only Botolph knows the combination, and he's so often away. I might not be able to get them if I wanted them in a hurry.'

'Then they ought to be in the bank.'

'They were until Christmas, when I wore them at a reception. The bank was closed so I put them in a drawer and forgot about them until quite recently. Since then I haven't had a chance to return them. They'll be just as safe with you as they are here.'

The whole affair seemed awfully odd to me. Her staff were unlikely to steal jewels so valuable and readily identifiable and I did not, I'm afraid, credit Portia with an impulse to act generously to a sister she thoroughly disapproved of. Could too much responsibility in isolation be weighing on her nerves? It would certainly have weighed on mine. I felt, after all, that the stone walls of the castle oppressed me.

'Very nice of you, Portia, but I can't wear them all in Gunne Magna church. I'd look a total clot. You can lend me the aigrette though; I'm not mad on artificial orange blossom.'

'No, no,' she said in an agitated voice. 'Take them all, please. Put them in your suitcase now. Someone might find them and it worries me.' She watched while the jewel-case was stowed away, heaved a sigh of relief and immediately became her unpleasing self. 'I'm not giving you the diamonds, remember, they still belong to me so look after them. It's simply an extended loan.'

'Well, don't force yourself,' Claudia replied, looking savage. 'I didn't ask for the damned things and you can have them back now.'

'There's no need for bad language. I don't want my boy picking up words like that.'

'Boy, what boy? I see no boy.'

'He's with Nanny. She can be relied on to keep him safe.'

Claudia began to get very scratchy indeed. 'Safe? Why on earth do you keep harping on about safety? Do you imagine that Amy and I are about to kidnap him and steal the spoons? For the love of heaven, Portia, try not to be such a wet blanket. No wonder you're left alone so much. What you need is an admirer, but you certainly won't get one in that dreary get-up. Don't you ever have fun?'

The clothes of both my sisters were totally outmoded but, oh, the difference between them. Claudia brilliantly fair in a black frock sprinkled with little flowers and with a stand-up frill at the neck, Portia dulled to extinction by sagging woollies. A small enamel brooch in the form of a Scottie dog hardly improved her ensemble. I wondered why on earth she wore that and made Claudia an unwanted loan of valuable diamonds. For once I, the unbeautiful one, felt serene and well dressed.

'What are you suggesting?' Portia asked haughtily. 'That I should carry on over men in the way that you do? My position calls for the strictest moral standards as an example to the villagers. They look to the Castle for guidance, and I have great responsibilities.'

'I bet the poor old villagers would like you a lot better if you flaunted your looks and let your moral standards slip a bit. Go to London, have a spree, waste money, enjoy yourself. You won't have any time left over for minding other people's business.'

Portia did a thing that's often mentioned in novels. She drew herself up to her full height, which is about five foot ten. Her sharp nose (both my lovely sisters are well honed in the nose department) pointed at Claudia with deep offence. 'The upkeep of a castle is no light matter, I assure you, and I am a good wife and mother. How can you speak of squandering money on foolish pleasure?'

'Well, I've done my best,' Claudia said. 'Who'd be a duchess? Is there to be any lunch or does that come under the heading of foolish pleasure?'

Luncheon, as it was still properly called at Hindlecote Castle, proved an uncomfortable meal, consisting of a mess that purported to be chicken fricassee. I discovered exactly what Portia meant when she said that her cook was not skilled with left-overs. For dessert a white 'shape' appeared. These solid offensive objects had gone out in my grandmother's day, and a good thing too. It ought to be a punishable offence to revive them. Claudia refused it. Portia, stiffly enduring, pushed tiny portions of everything down. No wonder she was thin. Fortunately red Leicester cheese followed, but there wasn't enough of it and the water biscuits were soggy. We weren't offered wine. I pinned my hopes on the birthday tea.

The hours passed slowly. At three o'clock Portia disappeared to oversee the preparations. 'It must be later than three,' Claudia said. 'We've been here for centuries already. Never again, never ever again. I as near as dammit told her that I saw the ghastly Duke in London to see if it wouldn't stir her up a bit.'

'Don't. You are absolutely not to. There may be a perfectly reasonable explanation and if there isn't you'll only make things worse. Just let's concentrate on getting through the day. There's a London train at eight in the morning. We'll catch it.'

The room felt chilly, but then the sun came out. We wandered outside and walked to and fro on the broad paved forecourt that separated castle from lawn and shrubbery. Nothing stirred. All was peace. Then at precisely four o'clock Singlet emerged and hammered vigorously on a gong.

Slowly the garden erupted. From behind every bush figures appeared, hobbling, plodding, stumping in the direction of the house and tea. The old Coritanums, released from temporary exile, had arrived. In the rear two old gentlemen leaned on each other, creeping like tortoises in the sunlight.

At the van sped a grinning, sprightly woman on frail sticks of legs, the tiny muscles of her calves bunching like Jerusalem artichokes. Her scalp shone pinkly through hair of an improbable purple-red. As she grew level with Singlet she kicked one leg backwards and sang out, '*Naughty* boy. Who kissed Lettie?'

And to our considerable shock the dignified Singlet gave an agile answering kick. 'What-ho she bumps!'

'Who in the world is that?' Claudia asked.

Recovering his poise, Singlet said, 'I do beg your pardon. That is Lord Polkinhorn's widow, formerly Little Lettie Truscott, the Darling of the Halls. In my younger days I was a great admirer. I recall all the catch-phrases. A loss to the stage was Lettie, when she married His Lordship.'

'Singlet, I think you're a bit of a dog on the quiet.'

'Was, Lady Claudia, was.'

Thanks in great measure to Lettie Polkinhorn's vivacity the birthday tea went rather well. Plenty of fish-paste sandwiches and salad, two plain cakes obviously bought in from the Women's Institute and all the better for it, squashed fly biscuits, the remains

54

of the shape which left the table again exactly as it had arrived, and an iced birthday cake with candles. The cake was a bit lop-sided. Cook had clearly not entirely got the measure of the kitchen range.

Lettie demanded that Portia blow out the candles. Then we toasted her in weak tea and again under Lettie's guidance sang *Happy Birthday*. The Colonel, a charming old gentleman, called for three cheers. Having looked anxious throughout as though expecting the cake to blow up, Portia then excused herself. 'I always help put Baby to bed after his bath.'

'Baby?' Claudia said. 'By my reckoning that boy must have turned three.'

Lettie grinned. 'An only one, duckie. Not a bad kid, but getting spoilt, and guarded like gold-dust. What are you looking at?'

'Everybody. Are they really happy here? Are you?'

'Bored rotten, most of us. Nothing to do, nowhere to go, not even a decent wireless set. Dear Ivor's on at the Hippodrome and I'd give my soul to be there.'

'Do you have to stay? Is this the only home you've got?'

'I've a great big house in Portman Square stuffed with furniture, and you could say mine's modest compared with some of the others. I couldn't run it without staff, and the Colonel says there's some nonsense about the Duke and money.' She raised her voice in a melodious shriek and called him over. 'Darling boy, can you explain to us again about the money?'

The gist of his explanation was that the unspeakable Botolph had persuaded them at the outbreak of war to deposit much of their savings with him 'for safety'. In addition they paid him regular small amounts for their keep.

The Colonel added, obviously manfully pushing aside doubt, 'My cousin doesn't care to be asked for the money back. He fears that we will spend too much, though he has promised to return our capital sum should we choose to go elsewhere. It leaves us embarrassed for ready cash and unable to renovate our homes, which they undoubtedly need.'

'Trapped,' Claudia muttered to me. 'The dukely toad is skinning them.' She smiled very sweetly and addressed the Colonel. 'Have you any idea at all of the way prices for decent houses in London are shooting up? How many do you own between you?'

He indicated the tortoises, still leaning on each other though sleeping peacefully. 'I can get no sense out of the brothers; they are, poor chaps, in their nineties and on their last legs. I have a large mansion flat in Kensington, each of the others owns a substantial property, but unmanageable in these times.'

'Eleven houses and one flat? Heavens, you're worth a fortune between you. If you sold up and shared out you could all move into jolly service flats – at the Mountroyal for instance. Bang in the middle of the West End, handy for everything, a restaurant on the premises and housework done by maids and porters.'

'Do you really think so? I fear we are something of a burden to dear Portia, though she bears with us.'

'You are the man who can organize it, Colonel. Tea at the Savoy, lunch at the Ritz or a cut off the joint at Simpson's, your club every day, evenings on the town,' said Claudia, the temptress.

The faded eyes of Lettie Polkinhorn gleamed. She looked beseechingly at the Colonel, who had fallen into deep thought. Her seat in the stalls for *Perchance To Dream* was as good as booked.

The Colonel coughed. 'If it can be done we must, I think, keep it very quiet indeed until we have it settled. I'll write to some estate agents at once.'

'Mum's the word,' Claudia said. 'I knew you were

the man. Don't be shy of asking old Botolph for your money back. He'll have to stump up if you make a loud enough fuss.'

Portia returned then, reminded them of their various bedtimes, and began to round them up and shepherd them into groups for bridge, jigsaw puzzles, draughts and various other delights.

Full of conscious virtue at a deed well done, Claudia descended to dinner in benign mood. It did not endure for long. Rather less than half an opened bottle of wine appeared and, anticipating that more would follow, she caused the footman to empty most of it into her glass.

'I expected that to be more than enough for us all,' Portia said.

Claudia surveyed with undisguised rancour the bony fish in white sauce congealing on her plate. 'Is lavish hospitality not a feature of Leicestershire life, or do you feel that a tea-party is enough excitement for one day?'

'The cellar is locked at present and money is not unlimited, Claudia, as I have pointed out before. Charitable work is a continual drain, as are the old people.'

'You must do rather well out of the amount they pay for their keep,' she said thoughtlessly.

'Really! Are you insinuating that I take money from Botolph's kinsfolk? It is my duty to care for them. They pay me nothing. Spreading such calumnies is a poor way to reward my kindness.'

Mindful of the footman standing impassive beside the solitary silver dish (containing, as it transpired, tough strips of liver from some unspecified animal) I said quickly, 'The elderly are not always terribly clear; we must have misunderstood them. How is your sister-in-law, the one who was your school friend?'

The choice of subject diverted her nicely. 'You know, Amy, I did my utmost to make her feel welcome here since it was once her home, but she has proved a great disappointment to me. Her second divorce is pending and her behaviour during the War was quite disgracefully immoral. Yet she used to be such a good influence.'

Claudia, always the worst of influences, gnawed at her liver. 'I expect she got thoroughly bored with virtue. One does somehow. I've got a huge piece of gristle. Do you mind if I spit it out, or is it good manners simply to choke?'

At least we got away from the dangerous subject of the machinations of Botolph. Unfortunately it left us open to a recital from Portia, her self-esteem restored, of those good works and tedious events regularly inflicted upon the village of Hindlecote.

I tackled the matter of Abigail Golightly, but Portia dismissed her out of hand. 'Anyone who pretends to be engaged in the Arts is unwelcome here. Their standards are suspect. Were she not a relative by marriage I certainly would not tolerate the presence of Lettie Polkinhorn who once made her living in the Music Hall. A disgraceful match.' (Poor Rudi!)

'I rather like her. She's a gallant old dear.'

'Then I presume that you will not mind Abigail Golightly. After all, living alone as you do, Amy, is not quite the thing is it?'

Claudia could not resist a hint. 'You needn't bother your head about Amy. She has plenty of company.'

I aimed a kick at her under the table and got Portia instead. 'Sorry, a sudden cramp. I think I told you that David is staying with me. You should meet him again, Portia, he's such a charming boy.'

She ignored that. 'Stewed apple and custard to follow, I believe. Shall we have coffee here?'

Quite soon she tired of us and went to bed. We

followed, finding nothing to stay up for. 'Being a duchess is obviously far worse than I imagined,' Claudia said as we parted for our separate rooms. 'Boring I took for granted, but a duke who's a spiv is rather too much. Shall we sneak down to the kitchen and see whether Singlet can raise a bottle of something?'

'Better not. I feel too depressed for festivity.'

The next day Portia saw us off the premises to catch the early train. The Colonel came down in his dressing-gown to say goodbye. Lettie Polkinhorn craned dangerously out of a window over the dry moat and waved vigorously. I hoped that somehow she would get to the Hippodrome before Ivor's show closed. As we clattered away to the station I realized that we had not been allowed so much as a glimpse of the young Marquess of Stevenage. We were not urged to come again.

Chapter Five

The Sunday train back to London crawled along, stopping often for no apparent reason in the middle of deserted fields. It did not boast a dining-car. 'God, I'm hungry,' Claudia complained. 'What's more, I've aged ten years so I just hope you're satisfied, Amy Savernake.'

'Sorry. Not exactly a roaring success, was it? Thoroughly deflating and enough to make one long to take to sin in a big way. Poor old Portia.'

'My foot! The gall of the woman, upsetting Val and giving the thumbs-down to Cristabel before she's even met her.'

'So mean when he's such a dear. Nice, though, that he's getting engaged at last. It's dreary for him struggling with Gunville Place on his own.'

Claudia took off her shoes, put her feet up on the seat opposite and studied them complacently. Though on the large side they were elegant and shapely. 'At least I returned good for evil, which was pretty nice of me. When she finds I've got her guests to leave she's going to be awfully pleased. I expect she'll see me in a new light.'

'Botty doesn't seem to tell her much about money. Those clothes! How can she bear them?'

'Did you notice the Scotty dog? A birthday present from the child, chosen by Nanny, wouldn't you know?'

I speculated about Portia's capacity to love and whether she expended all her emotion on her son. I hoped not. That surely spelled later misery for them both.

'I noticed what a wretch you are, almost giving me away again, hinting about Rudi, trying to make Portia curious.'

'I didn't say a word about Rudi. To be truthful I was thinking that if that damned shape made a third appearance I should probably use it to stun Portia. Anyway you're not important enough for her to pursue, not like the Osmington heir.'

'Don't you believe it. She needs plenty of grievances. How would you like it if I gave away your secret, whatever it is?'

Claudia's mind had already drifted from Hindlecote. Briefly she looked anxious, then she grinned and said, 'You never would. The difference between us is that you're kind and trustworthy and I'm a snake in the grass. I do rather enjoy prodding people to see what happens.'

'It's still on then, perhaps needing me for this thing?'

'Yes, it is. I'm waiting for slow and creaking wheels to turn.'

'Underhallow's getting rather tied up with the fête or fair, whatever they call it. You've no idea when you'll want me I suppose?'

'Not a clue. I'll ring when I have.'

That was the best I could get out of her. My peace in Garland House had not lasted nearly long enough. Her unannounced visit seemed to have stirred up forces. Claudia took on the aspect of harbinger, announcing the return of the family and its troubles into my life and shattering tranquillity to bits.

Like many a bully Portia had her cowardly streak. She made a habit of taking me to task for Claudia's misdeeds. I suppose she regarded me as tamer and less able to bite back. She did not telephone for several weeks. Then in the second week of July she did and a storm broke over my head. I felt quite pleased at first to be able to launch into chatter about Hindlecote, but she cut me short.

'Stop babbling, please, I haven't rung to exchange pleasantries.' (When did she ever?) 'What do you know about this wild plan of the Colonel's to move everyone to London?'

'Oh, they're going then?'

'Botolph is absolutely furious; he thinks it's my fault, that I haven't made them welcome or looked after them properly. I tried so hard. How can I explain twelve of his family moving out and keeping him in the dark until the last moment? I gather Claudia put them up to it. A most shocking abuse of my hospitality and a thoroughly irresponsible thing to do.'

'You're taking it absolutely the wrong way. She was trying to help you. She thought you'd be pleased.'

'Pleased!' The word exploded from the receiver. 'Botolph is so worried about them, and quite rightly. What's to become of them, adrift in London? Oh it was such a mistake to invite you. Neither of you knows how to behave except with inferiors who don't notice your lack of breeding. You can have no idea of the harm Claudia has done.'

She seemed to be on the brink of angry tears, which I thought excessive since her life was about to become easier. 'Oughtn't you to talk to her about it rather than me?' I asked.

'If I ever manage to reach her I certainly will. She deliberately avoids talking to me. Not that she can put things right now. I don't myself know what to do.'

'Portia, I really am most dreadfully sorry if we caused trouble. It wasn't what I meant to happen at all. I hoped we might – you know – get closer to each other, become more like sisters.'

She sniffed loudly. 'I'm better off forgetting that I ever had sisters. Both of you are a disappointment and embarrassment to me.' So agitated was she and so determined to have the last word that she hung up before she had enjoyed the full cost of the call, leaving me bewildered. For the life of me I could not work out the measure of our sin. An event that Portia undoubtedly wanted should not have steeped her in tragedy and tears. Ought I to ring back? I decided against it. There was no stopping her in full flood, and I felt a little hurt at her humourless rejection of us.

Preparations for the Lammas feast so occupied the village that I managed almost to put her out of my mind. I did wonder a little whether she might not be having a nervous breakdown or going off her head in some way. Castles notoriously produce madness, at least in fiction. Since I knew of no-one to ask, speculation was profitless.

David enjoyed being a guiser and learning the ancient athletic form of dance. I thought at first that a woman's role might embarrass him, but the grotesque costume, a tall, clumsy structure of laths and rags, had nothing feminine about it and took considerable skill to manage. He needed even more skill to avoid being alone with Josie Knapp. She tried awfully hard, and I felt certain that he wanted her every bit as much as she wanted him. He baffled Josie. She rarely met with much resistance.

I felt that in David a romantic streak warred with a kind of enforced austerity. He had need of a secure, exclusive love that Josie certainly could not provide, and he looked for the stability that his upbringing had so singularly lacked. Instead of confiding in me he shut me out. Now and again he dropped a provocative remark about Pandel Metkin and watched me with questioning eyes.

I rang Pan's Paris flat but he wasn't there. Jimmy Raikes, his secretary, answered the 'phone and said that he was in Germany but expected to be home quite soon, certainly in time for Claudia's wedding. Was there anything he could do? I said that I would write and perhaps Pan would ring when he got home. 'You had better read the letter first, Jimmy. You might be able to help.'

'Are we speaking of Midsummer's Eve of 1927?' he asked carefully.

'Yes.'

'It was bound to come sooner or later. A delicate matter and Pan refused to be advised. Too close to the heart you know. Don't worry, Amy, he'll deal with it.'

But I did worry. I had already lost David once, when Sonia took him away from us, almost breaking my father's heart and mine. To desert him so casually after that made forgiveness difficult. She suffered, too, in the end.

My grandmother once told me that throughout the Great War the rich continued to throng the Riviera casinos while in the trenches young men died in their thousands. Perhaps Sonia expected our war to be the same. In 1939 she was still in France with her lover, but instead of returning to England she moved south into Vichy France and was trapped.

Pandel Metkin searched Europe for many dangerous months before he found her and brought her home to me. By then David had gone to America. Though we lived under the same roof she never mentioned his name and said not a word about her experiences in France. And because of her silence I had never quite been able to forgive her.

The thought of losing Davy again, and perhaps for ever, made my heart ache. I was even grateful to Josie for diverting his mind into entertaining paths. The time had come, I decided, to stop shilly-shallying and tackle Sonia. I shirked the interview. At first I told myself that July might be her busy time, though I knew it wasn't. Then I decided to wait for a really fine day. But the weather was awful that month – mildew weather, first cold and rainy, then muggy and rainy, sun out, sun in. Horrid.

Rudi watched me struggle with myself. 'Come along, Amy,' he said eventually, 'let's get this over. I'll drive you and wait. If Sonia bites you can run away.'

On my infrequent visits I gave no warning. If I did, she found a dozen reasons to keep me away. Robbie Woolland, her present husband, worked as a bailiff on a large private estate and they lived in a little tied cottage among woodland. I had the most awful qualms about my errand. Forcing her to face the past was no kindly act, and something about Sonia always made me feel guilty and sorry.

I was only six when she married my father. Perhaps because of my youth she felt easier with me than with her other stepchildren. Valentine treated her courteously but without warmth, Portia despised her and Claudia openly loathed her. I had no great reason for fondness. She rather lacked awareness of her own nature, and since she did not relate her actions to their consequences she read our childhood resentments as pure spite.

Pretty well every red-blooded male who saw Sonia in bloom desired her. Love in its fullness constantly eluded her. Her rich beauty ripened without reassurance or comfort in a blaze of scandal. Then it died. Ironically it was in that death that Robbie found her and offered her at last the devotion she had missed.

'You'd better come in, Amy,' she said uneasily as she opened the door. 'Who's that in the car?'

'Rudi, but he won't disturb us. We're going to be married.'

'Ah. I suppose you know what you're doing. He used to be an absolute wretch.'

She led the way to the kitchen. 'If you wouldn't mind

waiting a few minutes. I'm counting egg coupons. We've dozens of registered customers and Robbie hates the job.'

I waited. The rich opulence of her middle years had gone. Unkempt, a little gaunt, she retained more of her beauty than I expected. Her short white hair, originally a smouldering reddish-black, curled vigorously over a head held with the ingrained assurance of a once desired and lovely woman.

'There,' she said, pushing the niggly little bits of paper into an envelope. 'I'll pour us a drink.'

I was unused to large brandies (a drink I don't much care for) in the early afternoon. I hoped for an oiling of the wheels but an uncomfortable silence fell on us that Sonia made no effort to break. I plunged straight in. 'You won't like me interfering, Sonia, but I've come to talk about David. He's nobody's fool. Something – the insecurity of his childhood perhaps – has made him question who exactly he is, where he belongs. Telling him has been left too late, so the harm's done.'

'What is this? What has he not been told?' she asked carefully.

Of course, I was not supposed to know and I had hidden my secret knowledge well. Hot colour flooded into my face. I said with flat honesty, 'I know about that night, Sonia, I've known right from the beginning. At the time I was too young to make the connections and I didn't understand it all for several years. But you've seen Davy. The likeness is unmistakeable isn't it?'

She twisted and untwisted thin fingers in her lap and did not look at me. 'What right have you to do this – to spy on me and question me? I won't talk about it, I've forgotten long ago.'

Naturally she lied. None of us had forgotten 1927, the magic year, when she and Rudi had joined forces to arrange an arts festival at my father's house: two

66

glamorous, exhilarating weeks of dancing and music and theatre. Then Midsummer's Eve when it all came to an end. Sonia certainly remembered. On that night Davy was conceived high up on a hillside in the lap of the Cerne Abbas Giant.

'I don't want to be cruel but we must talk about it. And I didn't mean to spy on you, truly I didn't. I was worried. That night of the play and the party you were so brilliantly warm and lovely and desired, quite out of the world with excitement, and I didn't expect, I didn't know that—'

The bitterness in her face stopped me for a moment. 'Go on. What didn't you expect and know?'

'That Pandel Metkin wanted you so madly that he would track you down and climb up Giant's Hill to find you. It was all part of the strangeness and the beauty.'

'Ah,' she said and fell silent, locked in some intensely private memory long unvisited. Her light greenish eyes darkened as though a shadow of that old passion touched her. I waited, holding my breath. Out of a dream she spoke softly. 'That was the only truly romantic thing I've ever done in my life, to believe that some god had called me. I didn't plan it. I wanted a child so much yet I hated impurity.'

'Yes, Sonia, I know.'

'Pan's homosexuality I accepted as part of an other-wise exemplary character, and at first he meant nothing to me.' She smiled a little wryly. 'Yet for that one night I loved him absolutely. He *was* a god, a god who worshipped me in the flesh, brought me to life. I believed that he loved me too.'

He did in his fashion, I thought, reluctant to inter-rupt. Her voice took on a dry satirical edge. She sounded old and tired. 'And in the morning it was dead, utterly dead. I had become what I most despised, an immoral woman, and I made myself believe that I had dreamt it all. But it changed me, taught me the meaning of physical passion. And virtue once being lost – well, it seemed pointless to pretend. Everything that followed, all the men, stemmed from that night and ultimately proved my ruin. Do you wonder that I prefer to forget?'

'Of course not, but it's long past.'

'Did Pan laugh about me with Jimmy Raikes, I wonder? It can have been little more than a joke to him.'

Her sadness distressed me. Briefly I touched her restless hands. 'Don't ever think that Pan was indifferent or laughed. He's always remembered. I went to see him in Paris before the War. In the salon was a Renoir of a girl with roses, so like that it might have been you. That's why it hung there: he told me so.'

'What does it matter now? I wish you hadn't reminded me. Guilt's such a lonely thing.'

She got up and turned her back while she refilled her glass. The level in the bottle had dropped alarmingly and I knew I must catch her now. 'Davy matters. Pan wept when he knew he had a son, but he's forced to love him secretly. You're all so unhappy. If you'd talked to David before you needn't have been. I want you or Pan to tell him all about it. At my house if you like, or if you'd rather we could go to Paris.'

She shuddered and took a long slurp of brandy. 'Not France, I'll never go there again, ever.'

'But you'll meet and talk to David? I won't leave you alone unless you agree.'

'The conscience of the family.'

The sneer made me feel disgustingly pious and self-satisfied and that in turn made me cross. 'Stop that, Sonia, please. I know you had an appalling time in France but it was Pan who managed to get you out. Now it's your turn to help. Promise, then I'll go. Once it's done you need not see any of us again unless you want to.'

'What about your father?'

I had thought about him a great deal. He knew all along that David was not his son, yet they were devoted to each other. I doubt whether he ever missed Sonia. Losing Davy was his tragedy, the beginning of an abrupt decline in his health and the ultimate dissolution of our family life. Somehow he had never been able to get close to the rest of us.

Yet when David sailed home from America my father had himself driven to Southampton, rejecting his wheelchair and the chauffeur's arm. For the moment of welcome he stood upright. He did not notice me. I held back, guessing that any intrusion on my part upon their reunion would be resented by both men.

Davy's homecoming drove my father to redouble his efforts to find help for his disablement. He loathed his dependence on the wheelchair. Accelerated by the needs of the war-shattered wounded, new miracles were happening in medicine, and he and Gwennie set out around the spas to find one. I could not see how telling the truth to David would harm that tenacious affection.

I said, 'He'll approve, I think. Leave him to me.'

'Why don't you tell David yourself? You seem to know it all.'

'Just promise, Sonia.'

A prolonged silence followed. Outside in the wood the birds sang their heads off and, as rather often in the past, I wanted to shake her. 'Don't you love Davy at all?' I asked. 'You did once.'

A quiver passed over her face. 'You're as romantic as any shop-girl.'

'Am I? I can't help it.'

'I wish I'd never heard of the word love. How can you understand what it's like to be despised by everyone, even your own son?'

'David doesn't despise you, nor do I. Try to trust us.'

Unconvinced, she thought for a moment or two. 'Very well, I promise on one condition, that you'll be there; but I won't lift a finger to arrange it.'

'You won't have to. I'll do that. Thanks a million, Sonia.'

She had begun to incline rather in her chair. Feeling less than sober myself, I took the glass out of her hand and kissed her. In a peevish tone quite like her old self she said, 'A pity you never did that when it would have pleased me.'

Having got what I had come for, all kinds of doubts assailed me. 'Ought I to have meddled?' I asked Rudi. 'Suppose I've driven Sonia back to the drink? Suppose David hates knowing for certain more than just suspecting?'

'That boy has been handed around like a parcel from one pair of loving hands to another. I have absolute faith in Pan's kindness and discretion. The truth will harm less than lies.'

'What a comfort you are. I'm tremendously in love with you, even though Sonia says you used to be an absolute wretch.'

'How cruel to remind you of it. I'm older and wiser and absolutely yours. May I kiss you in full view of Sonia's windows please?'

'Do make free with me.'

Rudi was so absolutely satisfactory as a lover I very much hoped that getting married would not spoil it.

Watching and admiring the dexterity with which David managed to keep Josie at arm's length, I wondered whether my concern for him was not misplaced. Dancing lessons took place in the garden, rain or shine, on an unkempt weedy patch that once had been a hard-court. On the 18th of July the schools broke up for the long summer holiday. I noticed that whenever Josie appeared alone there, too, was Scout Humphrey underfoot, hung at the neck with enormous binoculars. He carried a magnifying-glass and a notebook.

She tried to get rid of him. 'Better go home now, Humphrey, we're rather busy.'

'No dice, Mrs Knapp, thank you. I'm learning to be a bodyguard, but I won't frisk you as you're a lady.'

'Thanks for noticing, Hump, but I'm sure David can manage without you today.'

Humphrey smiled innocently. (A scout is pure in word, thought and deed.) 'He's helping me with my Observer's badge too, so while you're dancing I'll just sit quietly here in the summer-house and watch for birds and things through my binoculars.'

David looked tenderly at her disappointed expression. 'You don't mind do you? I'm sure he won't be any trouble.'

She shrugged and bided her time. At last her moment came. The lure of a day-camp and the ritual burning of sausages over a fire lit with no more than two matches caused Humphrey to defect. David was alone in the garden. I sat in the first-floor drawing-room with the windows wide open. Their voices came clearly across the still air, and by shifting my chair and leaning well forward I could see them perfectly. Of course, anyone with a spark of honour would have coughed loudly, or closed the windows, or left the room. I, being, as Claudia accurately said, an incorrigible spy and eavesdropper, did none of those things.

Josie wasted not a second. She wound her arms around Davy and waited for him to kiss her. Gently he extricated himself from her embrace and put a yard of space between them.

'No, Josie,' he said.

She looked stricken. 'What is it, David, don't you find me attractive?'

71

He smiled down at her. 'Of course I do, I'm a man, but I like to do my own chasing and I don't think I'm ready for adultery.'

'Damn,' she said, 'oh damn, I'm getting too obvious.'

'Not at all; honest and very seductive. You make it darned tough to hold on to principles. Don't you love your husband?'

She bit her lip thoughtfully. 'Yes, I do, or I wouldn't have given up university, but we ought never to have married. Both of us have a destructive streak. We egg each other on just to see how far it will go. Strange, because I hate rows. The men who attract me most are usually the gentle kind.'

I wondered what an eighteen-year-old would make of such a confession. To my surprise he bent and kissed her on the cheek. 'A game of truth and dare isn't it? Taking risks. I've been doing exactly that with dancing lessons I don't need. No more, Josie. I know my part backwards and forwards.'

'Never? Oh David!' He shook his head. 'You're so beautiful, did you know?'

At that he flushed. 'Don't. That's a womanish word.'

'And you're a man. One day when you're down in the dumps and want cheering up I'll help you to prove it.'

'Josie, you're impossible. Go home.'

Because my mind and energies were engaged with David's problems and Claudia's, and to a certain extent Portia's as well, I did not have a deep interest in the Lammas festival. The last few days of preparation had been abominably noisy. Charlie Hopkins mowed the grass on the cricket pitch and a small steam-roller juddered along in his wake, flattening the worst bumps left when the bomb crater was filled in. On the green the brownies and cubs practised their maypole dancing. The guide-mistress, who also taught in

Sunday School, rehearsed the children in the singing of 'Summer Suns Are Glowing' and 'I Saw The Wheatfields Waving'.

The convention that all little children sing sweetly is a fiction put about by doting spinster aunts. In Underhallow natural voices were few. Asked to sing up the boys bellowed like bull-calves, seriously annoying the rest. 'Shut him up, Miss,' wailed a girl with Shirley Temple curls, pushing the boy standing next to her, 'he's shouting in my ear'ole.'

I felt for the child and made a mild protest. 'Deadly, isn't it? Sorry, Amy, but their mothers love the little brutes and I daren't throw any of them out. Tell you what, I'll move them along the green a bit outside the police house. Give the Knapps a dose of their own medicine.'

Hammering went on into the evenings as stalls were built on the green. The Women's Institute (jams, pickles and eggless sponge cakes) and the Mothers' Union (economical handicrafts from unravelled woollens, assorted bric-a-brac, and poker-work texts – orders taken) selected their sites and guarded them jealously. Pride of place went to the bowling alley. The Pig Club had offered the prize of a piglet on the understanding that the winner would hand it back to be fattened to full pighood in exchange for its weight in meat.

'Unless they're nobbled Hallow Wickens'll get it,' Dora said, 'they've a chap who's mustard with the bowls. I might have them in for a drink of Father's home-made parsnip wine first. It's ten years old, tastes like poison and three glasses would lay low an ox. A pity we can't sell it, but Ivan Knapp says he'll arrest anyone he finds peddling drink without a licence. He's in a foul temper. Josie of course.'

She gave me her swift unsettling smile. I could easily imagine Aphrodite in comfortable middle-age, bored

73

with loving the gods and ready for a nice rest and some disinterested mischief. In my mind's eye I arranged the goddess on a well-upholstered cloud, and she looked exactly like Dora.

By Lammas Eve, the 31st of July, Pan had neither rung nor written, so tackling Sonia had brought about no positive benefit. There had been no word from Claudia either. As I rather wanted to know whether she had spoken to Portia I telephoned to the house in Sturminster Newton left to her by our Great-aunt Hildegarde and got no reply. Like a gipsy, Claudia tended to sleep where she happened to alight at bedtime. I tried Gunville Place and Valentine answered.

'Val, it's Amy. Is Claudia with you?'

'How are you, my dear girl? Lovely to hear your voice. No, she isn't just now, though she stayed a night or two last week.'

'Never mind then. Tell me about yourself and Cristabel. Aren't you tremendously excited?'

'Tremendously. It isn't official yet. I'm off to Nassau the week after Claudia's wedding to propose in person. It's never quite safe to assure sisters that they're going to love a sister-in-law, especially with Portia in the family, but I hope you will. She's an absolute darling.'

'If you love her she must be, and I rely on you to squash Portia at every opportunity. She's maddeningly obtuse and insensitive.'

Val laughed. 'Our cross! Did you know that she wrote a magnificently disagreeable letter to Claudia? We thought of framing it. Not a happy birthday, I gather. After her one unsuccessful stab at it, Claudia swears she'll never try to help anyone again.'

'Quite a relief, I think. One sister dedicated to good works is more than enough.'

'Absolutely. No chance of you coming to see me, I suppose?'

'Not immediately, darling, but certainly for the wedding. Underhallow is seething with festivity. I shall have news of my own then and Portia isn't going to like my choice either, not one bit.'

'Who? Can't you tell?'

I was tempted because Val's a comforting person and I love him quite a lot. 'If you don't mind awfully I'll wait until I see you. Father doesn't know yet.'

'OK, I won't badger you. Just be happy. If Claudia turns up again I'll say you rang. See you in September.'

If not in Dorset she might be anywhere. I could have tried other places, but Claudia became waspish when pursued. Waiting was my only course.

Chapter Six

The 1st of August, Lammas Day, decided to be sunny. Bertie Gooch held a brief loaf-mass service at seven in the morning and we gave thanks to our patron saint, Peter ad Vincula, and asked for his continuing favour. The Dance of the Six Swords was due to begin at nine-thirty up at Borgatten Maze. Josie had argued about the time. She could be quite pedantic over the Celts, and she insisted that their day began at evening and that the name Hallow Hill was a Christian corruption.

'It's one of the hollow hills like Glastonbury Tor, an entrance to the otherworld,' she said, 'and the maze is the key to the door. The dance should be by torchlight.'

Borgatten Maze is a lonely spot, set within a ring of trees on the summit of the hill. The lower slopes are densely wooded. Josie's motives for wanting darkness and torches were liable to be mixed.

Dora Aphrodite gave her a speculative stare. 'I rather think not. Most of the men are full of beer at that time of night. If they find a door they'll fall through it and break their necks.'

With the work of the committee over, Dora expressed her intention of peacefully enjoying the party outside her own shop door. 'I'm not climbing to the top of that damned old hill, and if you're wise you and Rudi won't bother either. Wait until they get down to the green and do the dance proper.'

'As long as we don't miss David.'

'Why not sit here with me then, away from the worst of the noise, and have a bite to eat later? I'm shutting

76

Father in the shop in the hope that he'll sleep through it and manage not to offend anyone.'

By nine o'clock we were pleasantly settled with a flask of coffee and the promise of real ham sandwiches to come, when a hire-car nosed its way out of the narrow lane that connected us to the main road. A gloved hand waved from a window.

'Who on earth?' Dora said.

The car drew up. A very young man jumped out and cautiously handed down a soft, well-corseted lady of indeterminate age. From her dress and hat, composed of many layers of stiffened muslin, to her gloves, her shoes and the triple row of huge pearls that hung to her waist, she wore pink. Her straight, unsmiling mouth was painted to match. She was the pinkest person I had ever seen.

'I guess this must be Underhallow,' she said, 'a tiny corner of old England. Am I in time for the fertility dance?'

Revenge Of The Warlock and *Dance Of Lust* had passed entirely from our minds. We had forgotten Abigail Golightly.

Old Mr Slade, refreshed by slumber, wavered through the shop door. 'Bugger me, it's the Queen,' he said, gradually drawing himself to attention. 'What's she doing here? That's not King George with her. If I'd known she was coming I'd have put a tie on.'

'Shut up, Father, go back to bed.'

Mrs Golightly smiled economically. 'The oldest inhabitant, I guess.'

'You guess wrong then.' Ashamed of his burst of chivalry, Mr Slade dragged a chair from the shop and sat down on it. 'There's dozens older than me, you for one. I'm a marvel for my age, I am. I used to be Hobby till my feet gave out.'

Dora hissed, 'We all know that, you're forever telling us.'

77

'She doesn't know, she's not from round here. Where does she get off calling me old? Dressed up like a dog's dinner.'

'Be quiet or I'll put something in your tea.' Dora stepped forward. 'Sorry about my father-in-law, Mrs Golightly, he gets confused. I'm Dora Slade, the committee chairwoman. Welcome to Underhallow.'

After Portia, to whom Mrs Golightly had taken a fancy ('a fair, pure soul!'), I came as the ultimate disappointment. When Dora introduced us she stared over my shoulder, casting around for the true Lady Amity Savernake. 'Why, you're not a mite like the Duchess.'

Impossible to argue. Portia, gowned and bejewelled, had presence and what Jane Austen called countenance. I didn't. Even when she disguised herself in Cinderella rags, her stern beauty, unilluminated by humour, struggled through. If only she could manage to smile now and then.

Declining to announce myself as the plain one, I simply said, 'No I'm not, am I?'

'An aristocrat of high principle. Too bad her schedule of charitable works did not permit me a visit to the Castle at this moment in time. I shall remind her later. The guide books mention a haunting.'

The Hindlecote ghost had always been a feeble affair, quite undistinguished and remarkable mainly for its shyness. It did not warn, threaten or wail about the battlements. Nobody had seen it for at least a century. Ungenerously I kept quiet. Portia would have to pull up the drawbridge or go mad with boiling oil.

The Guisers' dance interested Mrs Golightly less than Borgatten Maze. 'The labyrinth has a truly sinister place in folklore, and I notice from my map that it lies close to Hag's Gibbet. That name reeks of persecution, priests and the black arts.'

'We have none of that here,' Dora said firmly. 'A few

harmless cranks who believe in the earth-mother; and our vicar is a nice ordinary young man. Why not have a word with him? There's a map of the maze in the church, and a lot of old documents. Mrs Knapp, the police sergeant's wife, will help you to decipher them.'

Mrs Golightly looked extremely sceptical. 'I distrust priests, whatever creed they profess. They prey on the fears of the innocent. It's sufficient to the human soul to hold the good thought.'

Her thoughts did not seem particularly good to me. No wonder such cranky ideas had baffled the conventional Portia, Established Church to the core. Abigail was a gift to the joker, and Underhallow had several. Given half a chance Josie would oblige with lurid tales of corrupted souls and Druid sacrifice and murder done at midnight. Rudi and Dora were bad enough.

'You have no history of disappearances or unexplained hauntings connected with the church, or heard rumours of drugged communicants?'

Dora's black eyes glinted. 'Most certainly not, the very idea. If you're thinking of the lady from the Ministry of Food, I'm sure she only fainted. It was a muggy day.'

'You'll be quite safe with Bertie Gooch,' Rudi said smoothly. 'His fangs have been drawn, isn't that so, Dora?'

'Certainly. He'll be at the church until noon with the scoutmaster, giving out the Lammas bread. It won't be drugged, the baker's a Baptist. And if you need a meal, the Castleton's Oak is next door to the church. They do lunches.'

'At the sign of the coffin,' Rudi added. 'It might be as well to avoid the boiled bacon.'

The visitor recoiled, protectively clasping her downy bust. 'Is that so? Rationing of course can lead to extremes, but I had not imagined – surely there are regulations, authorities?'

'Don't mind those two, Mrs Golightly, they're just trying to be interesting and get into your book,' I said.

But the damage was done. The pages of her next novel (*The Cannibal Cleric*?) would burn with haggard, seamy souls and visions of awful wickedness.

'A joke? I see. Where's that boy, Leonard, got to? I shall take an escort, and of course we shall need photographs. Gravestones can be remarkably revealing.' She collected up the reporter and left us.

Rudi's eyes gleamed at me. ' "I could a tale unfold, whose lightest word Would harrow up thy soul; freeze thy young blood." You're cross with me.'

'Gone has she?' Old Mr Slade emerged from the doorway with an ill-tempered scowl. 'Sodding cheek, wearing a cow-pat on her head and pretending to be the Queen. She's nothing like her. I hate bloody foreigners.'

'Meaning me?' Malice flickered between him and Dora. 'I wonder whether there's room for one more at the Chichester almshouses. I could put your name down.'

'Bitch,' said her father-in-law.

I took a walk among the stalls and bought a jar of marrow jam, some home-made glycerine and cucumber hand cream and a hideous knitted multi-striped waistcoat that I thought might keep the gardener's back warm in winter. I also bought a huge cabbage. Too late I remembered rumours about the source of the fertilizer used to bring it to its unusual size. (Chamberpots, oh dear!) None of us much liked cabbage anyway. Stealthily I dumped it in the bole of an elm tree.

Ivan Knapp prowled after law-breakers. He thoroughly upset the ladies of the Women's Institute by examining their harmless bottles of elderberry cordial and apple vinegar for contraband alcohol. A militant cook sailed into battle. 'Don't you dare open that, Sergeant, or you'll have to buy it.'

'It's the law.'

'Rubbish! What law gives you the right to sniff at my sponge cakes, I'd like to know? People don't want them when they've been mauled. Just you leave them alone.'

He returned, defeated, to his pursuit of Josie. 'Has my wife been here?'

'She went past half an hour ago.'

'Where was she going?'

'Don't ask me – that way.' Morosely, Ivan followed the direction of her pointing finger. She said to her companion, 'He's got a screw loose he has, smelling at the produce. I'm glad he's not mine.'

David, whose dancing had been a tremendous success, had shed his costume and was trying to rub off the garish Betty's make-up with a handkerchief. In this he was helped by a knot of girls armed with a pot of Pond's cold-cream. Josie Knapp passed the laughing group with a flick of her skirts. Ivan had missed her again. I could see the back of his head moving swiftly away from her. Next I noticed her talking to Charlie Hopkins, then she vanished in the crowd.

I took my purchases back to the house. As I opened the front door the telephone was ringing with the particularly urgent and melancholy sound that it makes in an empty room. By the time I got to it the line had gone dead. For a little while I waited, speculating about the missed call. Claudia in distress and needing me? Pandel Metkin from Paris denying any responsibility for our problems? Hindlecote Castle burnt to the ground? Grandmother Mottesfont crushed to death in her side-car under a London bus? My fancies became wilder and wilder. I made my mind keep still, drew a long breath and let the atmosphere of the house work on me. It smelt of the past and of home, old wood cared for and polished, soft soap, breakfast toast, my scent and Rudi's cologne. As always I thought of my Great-aunt Hildegarde. In bequeathing me her furniture she had also left to me some enduring part of her happy spirit.

Selfishly, I wished that I need not concern myself with Claudia's problems or David's just now. My life was waiting to be lived. I loved Rudi so very much, and I had never been properly in love before. All I truly wanted was to be alone with him in this house, to look after him all my life, to be married and safe from loneliness.

Outside on the green the coloured pieces had moved and changed like the patterns in a kaleidoscope. Old Mr Slade doddered along in the far distance among hurrying men making for the Castleton's Oak. I guessed it must be past opening time. David and the attendant maidens walked towards the church. They carried between them the Betty costume, returning it to the crypt where it was usually stored. In the churchyard Abigail Golightly stooped over headstones with Scout Humphrey and the small wolf-cub, Ernie, standing by.

As I approached the shop Dora said, 'I'm off to make the sandwiches. You'd better go up and get your loaves while they're still fresh. After twelve they'll lock what's left in the hall until evening.' Rudi stood up, stretched and reached for my hand. 'And if you wouldn't mind looking into the pub on your way back; make sure Father comes home for his lunch. A few beers and he starts fighting the Great War all over again.'

It occurred to me that in time we who had lived through a second conflict would become like those boys of the old brigade. The War stood as a punctuation mark at the centre of our lives. Events were measured by it – before the War, during the War, since the War, after the War.

I said, 'In twenty years we'll probably insist on boring our children with stories of what happened to us in the blitz.'

'And they won't want to know either,' Dora said. 'We shall be quietly and humanely done away with.'

Ivan Knapp lurked around the church porch still, I imagined, in search of Josie. I said hallo but he only grunted. Rudi and I collected our Lammas loaves from the scoutmaster and wandered into the nave. At the top of the chancel Leonard tried to pose Abigail and Scout Humphrey in front of our memorial tomb. It has nice painted stone effigies of some unknown Elizabethan squire and his lady. They recline on an elbow, one above the other. Their smiles are smug and they look quite pleased to be dead.

'Get the figures in, Leonard, never mind about us,' Abigail cried. She crackled with energy. No doubt her brain seethed with awful images of rape and incest and altars defiled. (*Tomb Of Torture*? *Lecherous Stones*? *Church of Doom*?)

Leonard changed camera plates at the speed of light and they passed on. Rudi and I caught them up. 'What's it like in Alcatraz, Mrs Golightly?' Humphrey asked. 'Don't the really clever gangsters break out?'

'Little boy,' Abigail said, unbending, 'I have never been inside a penitentiary, but there are no clever gangsters, believe me. They are brutes in the grip of the Devil who only feel big when they've got a gun in their hands.'

'They're no good then, just crap?' Humphrey showed his bitter disappointment.

'You said it, sonny, crap. In the movies you see the shooting but not the blood and the dying, and you don't feel the pain. Be a doctor or a car salesman.'

'Cowboys?'

'Forget 'em. Unwashed numbskulls, smelling of cow manure. Sell real estate. Where does the Vicar hide out then?'

'The vestry, Mrs Golightly, over there. What's real estate?'

'We'll have a few pictures of me meeting the Vicar, I think, Leonard. They'll go down well in the States.'

A small commotion interrupted the researches. From somewhere close by I heard Josie's voice speaking low. David and his maidens ran up the steps from the crypt and crowded the aisle. 'Hallo, Amy,' he said, 'I hope I did you credit. Off you go now, girls. The Guisers are having lunch at the pub, men only.'

'Shall we kiss him goodbye? Let's do that.'

They tumbled about him like a litter of puppies and ran off shrieking with laughter. Ivan Knapp pushed roughly past them. He glared at the smears of lipstick on David's face and at the open door to the crypt. 'Caught you,' he said in a low voice. 'I know she's down there. Come out, Josie. It's no use hiding.'

He stumbled down the darkened stairs and disappeared among the stone groins and broken furniture. Abigail shrugged. 'A busy place this. Ready with the camera please, Leonard.

She threw open the vestry door. It swung back silently and there was Bertie Gooch holding Josie locked in his arms, about as close as two people can get. They were lost to the world, kissing and kissing as though they could eat each other up. A flash bulb burst close to my face. Bathed for a second in brilliant light they stood shocked and motionless.

David gave a low whistle. Scout Humphrey's ears went pink. 'Gosh,' he murmured, and with enormous presence of mind ran forward and slammed the door.

It sprang back again so he gave it an extra push, not noticing that Mrs Golightly's plump little arm was in the way. She screamed lightly. 'The skin is broken. You did that on purpose, wretched boy.'

'No I didn't. Sorry. It isn't bleeding much. I can tie it up if you want me to, I've got my First Aid badge – this one.'

'Just you leave it alone. By morning I shall be a mass of bruises.'

Meanwhile Ernie stood with one foot on top of the other, watching closely. His mother was a busy, practical woman and kisses only came his way when he cut himself or badly grazed a knee. 'What're they doing in there please, Humphrey? Has Mrs Knapp hurt herself?'

And suddenly I remembered Ivan. Leonard had captured the evidence for all time on his wretched camera and one look at the lovers would, in any case, tell all. Josie's mouth was pale and bruised (Bertie having eaten off her lipstick) and her blouse had slipped from her shoulders almost to the elbows.

'Shut the door to the crypt, Humphrey,' I said, 'and keep watch on it. We don't want anybody falling down the stairs.'

Mrs Golightly's mouth tightened. 'Forgive the inter-ruption, Vicar. I can see you're busy, but I'm rather anxious to know what you have here about Borgatten Maze. I'll walk round the yard a spell and come back in ten minutes. Okay?' All her expectations exceeded, she nodded and gradually withdrew. 'Leonard, you can't print that picture in your paper, but I'd surely like a coupla copies for myself. It might make my cover with an alteration or two.'

'You can't,' I said, 'you'll do dreadful harm. Give me the plate.'

They did not listen. Rudi put an arm round my shoulders. 'We shall have to try later by devious means – the Editor perhaps. Come along, my dearest girl, I'm hungry. Let's have our ham sandwiches and sample some delights. We could bowl for the pig or even run in the three-legged race for the elderly. I take it you have no deep interest in cricket?'

'Oh this is awful. Humphrey, you'd better get Ernie home for his lunch. They'll be locking the church soon.'

'Just a mo',' he said. His eyes were on Leonard carefully removing the plate from his camera to stow away in a neat leather case. Humphrey screwed up his face, grabbed the plate and smashed it to smithereens on the stone floor.

Mrs Golightly took a swing at his head with her handbag. 'That boy is evil!' she shrilled. 'That is an evil little boy.'

He shied nervously. 'Will I get into trouble, Miss Savernake?'

'You can have all my next month's sweet coupons, Humphrey, and as many strawberries as you can eat. That was a shining deed.'

'Gosh, thanks. Gosh what a morning,' he said. 'I like Mrs Knapp, she's pretty. Don't you think she's pretty, David?' His mind ranged far away from gangsters and cowboys. Humphrey was growing up. 'I don't like Mrs Golightly, even if she *is* an American. She gave me the frozen mitt. Do you like her, David?'

'Yes and no, Humphrey. Yes, I think Mrs Knapp's very pretty and no, I don't admire Mrs Golightly. She isn't typical of American ladies, I swear.'

If the scene we had witnessed caused David pain or jealousy he hid it well. He understood Josie, that was plain. Once, when we lived comfortably together in our Sussex cottage, I thought that I understood him. In his place I should have felt relieved to be uncommitted and uninvolved, but the ideas and emotions of boys change such a lot when they become young men. I had to accept that now I had little idea of how his mind worked. Sadly, he would never tell me.

From the front first-floor window of Dora's shop came the noise of heavy snores as Mr Slade slept off his beer. Over our picnic I told Dora about Josie and Bertie Gooch. 'No-one would have known if it hadn't been for Mrs Golightly. That's my sister's fault. She foisted her on to Underhallow.'

'I didn't realize you were related to a duchess. Is that the one you went to see for her birthday? Not just ham sandwiches that day, I imagine.'

My deepening grudge against Portia warred with family loyalty and won. 'How I wish! More eye of newt and toe of frog than caviar and champagne. A cook who can't cook and a deep belief that stewed apple and custard is the ultimate in luxuries. And now the awful interfering Abigail. Portia's the limit, what's more she despises me and everyone who isn't a damned Coritanum.'

'Not close then?' Dora said sardonically.

'She doesn't go in for closeness except with money. You know, Dora, thinking how much gossip there is about Josie, it truly surprises me that I'm not ostracized over Rudi.'

'But I'm such a nice man,' Rudi said, 'loved and admired by all.'

'Shut up,' Dora and I said simultaneously.

He grinned. I added, 'Why aren't Gloria Hopkins and her spy-ring having a field-day?'

'That's easy. Gloria knows about your title and thinks the whole of the English nobility might tear her apart if she offends you. She's a bit of a simpleton, so's Charlie for that matter. He trusted his Army mates to keep quiet about an Italian girl he was sleeping with, but the news got home to Gloria long before Charlie left Rome. It soured her, though she's far from lily-white herself.'

Courtesy titles had become pointless and silly. I

didn't ask how Gloria knew about it. Our gregarious postman dispensed information with the letters and read postcards as a matter of right.

Dora's sandwiches were heavenly. At that time ham came in oblong tins and cost a lot in 'points' coupons rather than money. A flabby pink-and-red tasteless substance, it bore little resemblance to the York, Bradenham and Parma hams once displayed in full glory at Fortnum & Mason.

'However did you manage to get proper ham?' I asked.

'I have my sources,' said Dora Aphrodite, witch extraordinary, folding her hands complacently in her lap then rapidly unfolding them. 'Oh Lord, here comes Mrs Golightly.'

Rudi and I got up. 'Many thanks, Dora, for a wonderful lunch. Time to inspect the stalls. I feel I shall do rather well bowling for the pig.'

'Cowards,' Dora said. 'Hallow Wickens will win the pig. I forgot to nobble their best man, and serves you right.'

Chapter Seven

In due time several photographs of the Lammas festivities appeared in the local paper despite the shortage of newsprint. Mrs Golightly hogged every single one. She struck exotic poses with tremendous exuberance. ('I used to be a photographic model you know.') An unlikely tale. She had a broad nose that the camera flattened into a shapeless lump. The headline read UNDERHALLOW FETE: A GOOD TIME HAD BY ALL. Not entirely true, I found. Ivan Knapp did not have the best of days.

My indignation against Portia for pushing on to us the intrusive Abigail smouldered away. Bertie's vestry was his private room. I detested the sheer meddlesome discourtesy of barging in without knocking. And in the confusion of conflicting emotions neither Rudi nor I had noticed that as he left the church Humphrey, the conscientious scout and server at communion, had turned the key in the crypt door and switched off the light.

Ivan, imprisoned behind four inches of solid oak, hammered and yelled. His cries went unheard for a long time. The Guisers enjoyed their lunch and slept it off at the cricket match until around four o'clock, when the fine weather gave way to a violent thunderstorm. They then remembered that some of the costumes still lay out in the church porch.

After six hours alone in the pitchy dark Ivan emerged white with frustration, ready to fight the whole world. In the meantime Ernie had run home for his dinner and innocently blabbed to his mother. He gave a version of events hastily improvised by Humphrey from a selection of Hollywood films, to the effect that the Vicar had rescued Mrs Knapp from kidnap by a strange criminal and she kissed him out of gratitude.

The attention Ernie received must have surprised him. The story of Josie and the Vicar, embellished with imaginative detail, spread around the village as fast as tongues could wag. The gamblers began counting up their winnings. Within minutes of his release Ivan knew rather more than all.

The last event of the day was the Lammas supper in the village hall. I imagined that Mrs Golightly would already have departed, satisfied with her garner of sin, but she had not done with us yet. She plodded in, expressing grim endurance in the face of intolerable odds. To preserve the stiffened organdie of her pink hat from the weather she carried it in a brown paper bag and wore a mackintosh pixie hood instead.

'I had to bring her along,' Dora Aphrodite said. 'She's made up her mind to talk about her books and I can't get rid of her. I think she's had a few.'

Certainly Abigail's pernickety way of speaking had softened and gradually she relaxed into jollity. One could see why. She waved away the beer and cider provided and occasionally refreshed herself from a pocket flask. 'Bourbon,' she said, 'hard to get in this damned country so I don't pass it around. I carry it for my nerves.'

Opinion was that the Knapps would not come, but they arrived late and took their seats. Josie fussed over Ivan, pouring his beer and settling a napkin in his lap. He accepted her attentions meekly. Perhaps the oddest thing in that stormy marriage was that Ivan never blamed Josie for her lapses. Men were at fault, jealously seducing her away from him.

Bertie Gooch should have been there to welcome us. He loved a party. According to my maid, the pretty but severely practical Polly, on VE Day he led the entire village around the green at midnight with two girls clinging on each side of him, doing the Palais Glide. What remained of the night he spent sleeping on a table-tomb in the churchyard. 'Nearly caught his death,' Polly said. 'Couldn't preach for a fortnight.'

At best he must have worried about rumours reaching the Bishop, at worst an assault on his person to which he would be compelled by his cloth to turn the other cheek. He sent his excuses. Mrs Golightly said, 'I should have liked to talk to your Vicar some more. Running into that little scene sure helped a lot. I had to push a bit but he came across with real goodies from bygone days: diabolic possession, witch-priests, fraudulent relics. All I need is a title. How does *Snare Of The Sanctuary* grab you?'

'It doesn't grab me at all,' I said with the beginnings of anger. 'Snooping around in private places is ill-mannered to say the least, and you can't begin to know the damage that you're doing. This is an ordinary village of ordinary people. If you pry you're bound to come across indiscretions, but they don't amount to the nasty kind of sin you're looking for. You've no right to pretend they do.'

'Hoity toity,' she said gaily. 'By the time my book comes out it will all be history, believe me. That's the poor fish of a husband over there, I take it.'

Some of the men laughed. If only Ivan had been a nicer man and not a policeman they would have ranged themselves on his side. I noticed with a wrench of pity that he was crying quietly. Rarely do I absolutely lose my temper but just then I wanted to get to my feet and shout at them, Abigail Golightly, the grinning men, and most of all wretched, careless, sex-mad Josie. I began to shake. Rudi reached for my hand

and held it very tightly until my rage subsided.

Dora hummed under her breath. In a delicate act of revenge she had seated Abigail opposite to Mr Slade, and she busied herself with settling him and tying a large napkin around his neck. He smiled a frightful smile. Dora did not notice, as I did, that before sitting down he slid the damp bag containing Mrs Golightly's hat underneath him. Dora helped the old man to a slice of spam, a pig's trotter, a wedge of homemade pork pie and some salad.

'I don't want that muck,' he said. 'I want a nice kipper. It's ages since I had a nice kipper.'

'Eat what you're given and be grateful. I haven't the time to go into Petersfield and queue for an hour just to get you a kipper.'

'Why's that old cow still here? Three poached eggs on toast, a tin of peaches with evap. and four fairy cakes – she's eaten half the shop already.'

Mrs Golightly shook a waggish finger at him. 'If you're a good boy I'll give you a little sip out of my flask later.'

'Christ Almighty, did you hear that? She fancies me! Hard luck, missus, you're twenty years too late. I've given up women. Dora, I can't eat the lettuce. Take it away, it gives me wind.'

'Give it here then,' she said, well pleased with herself and him.

He picked up his trotter and sucked on it noisily. He was not a tidy eater. Congealing grease oozed down his chin. Dora flicked her sardonic witch smile at me. 'Couldn't you just hug him sometimes?'

Perhaps it was the rain sweeping noisily over the roof and lashing the windows that caused the sudden silences and destroyed the festive air. The room smelt sadly of wet clothes drying, pickled onions and hot tea-urn. Rudi wore a mournful frown. He hated to see happy occasions go sour and, as Dora predicted, the man from Hallow Wickens had won the pig.

Mrs Golightly – used to prestigious embassy parties – expected nothing more of us. 'If this isn't straight out of Mary Webb: *Precious Bane* to the life,' she said, and then stood up and told us about her books. 'They are not works of literature, friends, but they fill a gap in the American market. I brought a coupla copies with me to sell to you people and I'll be real happy to sign them as well.'

We disappointed her after all with our indifference to the offer. Mr Slade shovelled ersatz sherry trifle (dried egg and dried milk custard liberally doused with sherry-flavoured essence) into his mouth and mumbled, 'Jaw, jaw, jaw! Isn't she ever going home?' He spluttered a bit. Dora, regal in black, could have been a benign Queen Victoria except for her lively crown of greying hair. She took his spoon away and mopped him up.

'Disgusting rude old creature,' Mrs Golightly said.

Mr Slade bared his teeth at her. 'You look a bleeding freak in pink.'

Ivan was getting steadily drunk on the strong home-brewed beer and tears coursed down his face. He had eaten nothing. Josie looked awful, penitent and plain. She talked to him in a low voice, but he refused to be comforted and quite soon she collected their mackintoshes and took him home.

I decided I hated Mrs Golightly. 'That's your doing,' I said.

'Nonsense, she's a woman of light morals. Did I ask her to sin with the Vicar?'

I hated her the more for being right. Conveniently, Rudi yawned. I said, 'How tired you look. I think David's ready. Shall we go?'

In the short walk home we got absolutely soaked. Because of double summer time grey light still lingered in the sky and my house welcomed like a white beacon. I looked at it with love. The brass knocker shone golden on the dark green front door. Behind the iron railings an old magnolia tree dropped fat leathery petals into the cellar area. I danced joyfully in the puddles. The wind blew strongly down from Hallow Hill, the air smelt clean and cold. Goodbye Abigail Golightly. One life of sin – mine – had escaped her notice. A pity, because she could have upset Portia no end.

On the following day Rudi received an offer from a firm of estate agents of a short renewable lease on a house in Great James Street, Bloomsbury – 'adaptable but in need of renovation'. He exclaimed over the details. His dream of a theatrical agency, languishing for want of a suitable setting, suddenly gave every appearance of becoming reality.

'It sounds perfect, Amy. There's a self-contained flat in the attics that we can use as a town place, and the caretaking couple want to stay on.'

It had become next to impossible to find staff to live in, so that was a terrific bonus. Rudi had told me already that he did not much want to act for the famous or preside over a couple of shabby rooms at the top of a wearying flight of uncarpeted stairs. 'No drab offices or dingy waiting-room, but colour, light and a welcome.'

'Can we afford to renovate in the way you want? It might be awfully expensive and I don't suppose you'll make much money, not at first.'

'Time for confessions,' he said penitently. 'I quite forgot to say because it really seemed unimportant, that in spite of my sound Socialist principles I seem to have become dollar-rich. Hollywood showered me with gold, and I was entertained so much and working so hard that I hadn't a hope of spending it. Pan recommended a manager who bought lots of stocks and bonds and tells me that importing dollars is easy since Britain badly needs them.'

'Then you're not marrying me for my money after all. My power over you is gone. What a swiz!'

He smiled at me with such tenderness that a huge lump came into my throat. 'You're the dearest of dears, Amy Savernake. I want to give you the moon and stars, but you'll have to settle for an indecently expensive present. Anything your heart desires.'

'I already have my heart's desire, but if I must be given a present you can choose. Presents tell a lot: how well the giver knows your nature, and whether they love you enough not to show off with big gaudy jewels or stupid things like platinum grape-scissors.'

'I didn't know of grape-scissors. How merciful that you warned me in time. When can we look at the house?'

'Tomorrow's Saturday and Monday's a Bank Holiday. How about Tuesday, August the sixth?'

Everywhere in London looked shabby and tired except for the empty bomb-sites that flowered pink with rose-bay willow-herb. A bomb had flattened the mews behind Great James Street. Pockmarks scarred the dirty white stucco of the house, but nothing could spoil the well-proportioned rooms with their long windows and narrow ornamental balconies.

The caretaker's wife showed us around. When we got to the studio room on the top floor she hesitated. 'Excuse the walls, Stan hasn't got round to them yet. An artist lived here before, but as soon as they started calling up his age-group he cleared off and didn't come back.'

A crude mural covered the whole of one wall. It showed a tropical Garden of Eden and an extremely undisguised Adam and Eve. 'Good Lord,' Rudi said in an awed voice, 'not so much as a fig-leaf.'

'That's him, and she's his girlfriend. Near the knuckle, i'n't it?' We stood together and examined it thoughtfully. It would have taken an awfully big fig-leaf to make Adam decent. 'Exaggeration, I bet. He should be so lucky! Stan'll paint over it for you though it wants plastering first.'

'That's not possible is it, a w—' I began to say.

Rudi put his hand on my cheek, effectively closing my mouth. 'Murals are a good idea,' he said. 'Don't bother Stan with it, I'll get a plasterer in, and I've a friend who might care to paint something more suitable.'

He hurried me downstairs. 'You shut me up,' I said. 'I was only going to ask whether it's possible to have a winkle that long, but I thought better of it. Do tell.'

'Not a question to fire at strangers.'

'Sorry,' I said, 'it was rather startling and I knew what the caretaker was thinking. Great-aunt Hilde-garde used to be splendid at tellings things like that and I miss her. Who's the friend who'll paint some-thing else for you?'

'Cyril Fox. D'you remember him? He's out of the Army, his agent's just died and he's rather at a loose end. Theatres aren't putting on many expensive pro-ductions at the moment. Perhaps he'll join me, perhaps not, but I'm sure he'll consider a commission.'

Before the War Mr Fox had been regarded as the best stage artist in the business. We called on him and found him sitting morosely among pots of paint and canvas flats, drinking beer out of the bottle. He was dressed up in his pale grey demob. suit over a singlet without a collar. Around his bare neck he wore a striped tie. His white plimsolls had no laces and his big toes protruded through ragged holes in the canvas tops. A trilby hat clung precariously to the back of his head.

'Well I'm a son of a bitch,' he said, almost smiling. 'I

hope you've got some work for me, Rudi, I'm bored out of my skull. No elegance, no charm, it's all bleeding airfields and guns.'

Rudi signed a lease that day and took Cyril Fox to see our mural. 'Christ Jesus,' he said, 'there's a liar for you. Who wants to live with that? It'd frighten an elephant.' I could tell that he felt tremendously pleased and enthusiastic as he wanted to do the plastering himself. 'I'll give it a bit of texture and send you some sketches.'

When we left he dived into the nearest pub. Rudi walked me in and out of secondhand shops looking for fittings and the right pieces of furniture. He bought me an eighteenth-century necklace composed of tiny topaz and diamond flowers and a round gold box to keep it in. Inside the enamelled lid, Cupid leaned amorously on the shoulder of Venus.

'Perfect,' I said. 'You definitely love me.'

All I got in the way of correspondence that day was a postcard by the late delivery showing Gertie Miller in her prime. I had some trouble deciphering the spiky handwriting but I discovered eventually that it had been sent by Lettie Polkinhorn from the Savoy Hotel.

It read, *'Well, duckie, we made it. Ta everso. Such a to-do, Duke yelling blue murder, Portia looking like we were a bad smell under her nose, poor cow. House etc. brought in a packet, hope to move into apt. next month. What-ho she bumps! Come any time. Affectly, Lettie. PS Seen Ivor's show twice. Smashing.'*

There went a happy woman. I felt ridiculously pleased for her.

Two days later, while I still mulled over the novelty of having a Town residence, Claudia telephoned. I looked forward to chatting over Lettie and telling her about the mural and Cyril Fox, but I got no chance.

'Hallo, Amy. I forgot to ask if you've got a passport.'

'I renewed it a few months ago. Why?'

'Good,' she said and rang off.

First Portia slanging me, now Claudia cutting me off. It was too much. Hardly anybody went abroad so soon after the War, what with the dozens of restrictions and small wars breaking out here and there. I wanted to know where I was going. Nettled, I dialled her Dorset number and let it ring for a long time. At last a cautious voice said, 'Is that you, Miss Claudia?'

'That's Annie Bowells, isn't it? This is Amy Savernake. Isn't my sister there?'

'Why hallo, Miss Amy, she's away just now. How you doing then?'

'Fine, Annie. Do you know where she is?'

'Mr Deering, he was asking only she didn't say.'

The horse had bolted. For the umpteenth time I wished for the ability to take a firm line with my family as Portia did. They pushed me into a role for which I felt unsuited, close to those stupefyingly helpful and angelic creatures in Victorian storybooks. Twenty-seven years old and no backbone at all!

The mystery came no nearer to solution when a letter arrived from Pan. He wrote that as we should be meeting very soon we could discuss the problem that concerned us both, by which I supposed that he meant David. And very soon must be Claudia's wedding day on the 28th of September. More than seven weeks to wait. His lack of urgency disappointed me.

In an unsettled summer the children were bored. The haystacks, their natural playground, alternately soaked by rain and scorched by sun, collapsed when climbed on or spontaneously combusted. Either way they were dangerous. Ivan Knapp spent a lot of time following the sound of breaking glass. Twice he lost his cold-frame, Dora's shop window was broken by a badly aimed tennis ball, and Ernie's older brothers had a fight and fell together through a lean-to on the allotments. Ivan indiscriminately clipped the handiest ears and returned to watching Josie.

She must, I think, have known that by wilfully trying to seduce Bertie Gooch she had gone much too far. In an effort to make amends she stayed close to home and within Ivan's sight. In the end her penitence did no good at all. On the day following our visit to London I had an errand at Hartings Farm across the flank of the hill and I overtook her by chance. It was a sweltering, muggy day.

'Strawberries. The last of the season and spoiling with the wet,' she said.

'Me too.'

She cleared her throat awkwardly. 'About Bertie.'

'Please, you don't have to explain to me, in fact I wish you wouldn't. It's far too hot and I've gone off minding other people's business.'

'I only wanted to say that I know I'm hopeless. I get sorry for men – a whore's stupidity without the excuse. Bertie simply hates being a parson – his father you know, family tradition, all that tripe. He loves dancing and girls and cutting loose now and again, and he gets no fun, poor boy.'

'But poor Ivan too.'

She pushed her hair back from her face and frowned. 'It's nothing against him. I love him. He was no angel in the Army and he used not to mind so much. A tame marriage wouldn't suit him at all. He's still fighting off horrors and he's dreadfully claustrophobic since a shell buried him under tons of sand in the Western Desert. He was half-dead when they dug him out. Getting locked in the crypt made it much, much worse.'

Then I began to feel guilty. 'Josie, people do what they do. That awful woman was the worst of bad luck and if I hadn't been so flustered by her I would have remembered about Ivan being down there.'

'No blame to anyone but me,' she said. 'The act of loving makes me feel joyful. I've a trollop's soul and a rusting brain. What a waste. But in case anyone's interested, I've decided to turn over a new leaf. Let's hope it lasts.'

We picked strawberries for an hour, wandering apart along the rows. When we paid the farmer's wife she sold us cream and brought us each a glass of ice-cold buttermilk. A group of children played in a field of stubble, clambering up the useful steps of a partly cut haystack and making a nest.

They did not notice, nor did we, the little filaments of smoke filtering from the bottom of the stack. Ivan, plodding along in Josie's wake, appeared out of nowhere. She raised a hand in greeting but he did not look in our direction. For a second he stood still, then he began to run, pounding up the path shouting as he went. 'Get down from there at once, you stupid brats, get down, hurry.'

Frightened, they clambered out of the loosened hay as it began to sink under them. The two littlest struggled and fell back. Ivan charged. He reached the top in a series of leaps and threw the wailing children down. Then with a terrible suddenness he disappeared.

Josie screamed and tried to run to him. A labourer held her back, pressing her face against his sweat-stained shirt. The farmer's men dared not use a cutter. They attacked the stack with pitchforks and bare hands, hurling the grey smouldering hay away from them. It took nearly an hour to reach Ivan, by which time Josie was a sobbing, inarticulate wreck and he was already dead.

The farmer called the doctor, more for Josie than for Ivan, who was past help. He drove her home. Our strawberries lay forgotten in the field where we had dropped them. Six men carried the blackened, distorted body back to the police-house on a hurdle. I trudged blankly along behind.

Everyone from the three Hallows who could walk or hobble went to the funeral. The atmosphere was uncomfortable with our guilt. Ivan had died a hero's death, but we had not liked him alive and many of us found it hypocritical to try to like him dead. Mercifully, since the scandal still occupied the front of our minds, Bertie Gooch could not conduct the ceremony, being absent from us. The curate came over from Uphallow. Since he barely knew Ivan he was able to praise his noble actions with sincerity.

Adversity had Bertie in its grip. Piqued by Humphrey's destruction of her precious photographic plate, Mrs Golightly lost no time in complaining of him by letter to the Bishop. Not that she was the only sneak. In general Underhallow followed the principle of live and let live but we had our self-righteous minority.

On the 8th of August, only a week after Lammas Day, the Bishop sent for him and kept him. Aggravated by Ivan's death, Bertie's minor lapse ballooned into a huge black sin. He returned to us ten days later, long-faced and miserable, to await his punishment.

Josie moved through the ceremony in a pathetic state of dumb bewilderment. She was treated quite kindly except by Gloria Hopkins and a few of her cronies, but it would scarcely have mattered to her if she had been tarred and feathered and driven out of the village. Like a doll she went where we took her, all the time looking over her shoulder for Ivan.

David, genuinely sorry and concerned, could do little. Two days after Ivan's burial he was to leave on an indefinite visit to spend time with my father and get to know Gwennie, our second step-mother. He had been looking forward to it for weeks. Several times before he left us he 'phoned Josie but got no answer. He had to let it go at that.

Eventually a group of strangers, probably Josie's relations, came down and moved her into a small cottage on the opposite side of the green, shut the door on her and went away. Dora left her rations on the step. They were taken in after dark, but otherwise the door remained firmly closed.

Unenlivened by rackety quarrels in the police house, normal life and peace of a kind returned to us. A new policeman arrived with his wife and two small children. Only I knew of Josie's determination, left too late, to reform for Ivan's sake, and I mourned the pathos of her failure.

No word about David came from Pan but Portia called, having more or less got over her huff. She did not once refer to the old Coritanums and her concern now (far from vague) was for the fate of our mother's diamonds. 'I'm not at all sure that I ought to have entrusted them to Claudia. She is never at home and they ought not to be left in an empty house.'

'Haven't you spoken to her yet?'

'No. I shan't try again. I wrote to her and received an offensive and vulgar missive in return.'

Having no idea where the diamonds were I said, 'She'll have passed them to Val to put in his safe.'

'Are you sure of that? Please oblige me by confirming it and letting me know at once. Which reminds me, I haven't received Claudia's wedding present list yet. I suppose she has made one?'

How sweet the opportunity to take Portia down a peg. 'She would feel a list to be not quite the thing.'

'Oh? I cannot agree.' Did I detect a note of uncertainty in her voice? She recovered quickly. 'A modern idea, but practical in these difficult times. A connection of Botolph's received nine sets of pictorial table-mats in the most vulgar taste. I shall prepare and circulate to relatives a list of suitable objects. When they have made their choice the item can be deleted.'

'Oh dear,' I said. What she regarded as suitable Claudia was liable to find dreary. 'Perhaps I ought to see the list first, Portia, to make sure I don't give what someone else is giving.'

'Very well. Do please remember that gifts will be displayed. Were it not to save face in the family I should not expend time and effort on her behalf, I assure you. When you have made your choice send the list to Grandmother. She is expecting it. Those of the London people who are too old to trudge to the shops can order by telephone.' One of Portia's silences followed. 'By the way, has Claudia reconsidered the matter of bridal attendants?'

'As far as I know I'm still the only bridesmaid. Why?'

She did not answer that. 'Please don't forget about the diamonds. I shall be anxious until I know they are in a secure place.'

Portia had foisted the wretched things on Claudia and I had no intention of chasing after them. Did I dare tear up the present list? Regretfully I decided not.

Thus far August had been a tiresome and busy month. I looked forward to settling down for some peaceful and heavy reading. Inspired by Rudi's knowledge of the theatre and conscious of my ignorance, I gathered to me a life of Shakespeare, his plays, poems and sonnets.

My true taste lay in lighter works. I had just about waded through the preface and Chapter One of the life when, in the third week of August, Claudia rang. This time she meant business. 'You'll need a visa right away.'

'Where for?'

'France. Go to the Embassy in person, and don't let them say it'll be ready in two days or next week. Tell them it's urgent family affairs. Mention that Father's an earl if you have to, and throw in Portia, but stay there until you get it.'

'Then what?'

'We have two days to wait so there's not much point in you going home. You'd better come on here.'

'To Sturminster Newton?'

'For heaven's sake not. I don't want Bill barging in at this stage. Bournemouth.'

The prospect did not attract me. Only a few weeks earlier a girl on holiday in a Bournemouth hotel had been murdered, savagely and sadistically. 'Where are you staying? Not the Tollard Royal I hope?'

'What's wrong with it?'

'Nothing, just the associations – Neville Heath.'

'Idiot woman, he's in jug. We're at the Sandringham Guest House – it's Ivy's place and very central.'

I sighed with relief. Ivy used to be our maid, but I had no idea she ran a guest-house. 'How did you know where to find her?'

'She sent you a Christmas card with a letter to Gunville Place.'

'Claudia! If you really had to read it first you might have sent it on and let me read it too.'

'I forgot. Just get here.'

At that point Rudi took the 'phone from me. 'I don't like the idea of Amy – or you for that matter – disappearing into the blue. I want to know where you're going.'

A muffled voice said, 'Oh bugger! All right but promise absolutely not to go and tell Bill.'

'The Post Office frowns on language like that. I make no promises.'

'If you must know we're going to Paris to see Pan.

It's a legal thing. Come if you like. With luck I shan't have to give evidence to the French court as it happened in Switzerland.'

'Conversations with you are beginning to take on a surreal element. What happened in Switzerland that could interest a French court?'

'Not now, I'll tell you later.'

'How exasperating you are. I shall certainly go with you. It will be good to see Pan again.'

'Put Amy back on please.'

'I was listening in,' I said. 'Are you all right? You sound fussed.'

'Only a bit. You don't mind coming to Paris?'

'No, I want to talk to Pan anyway.'

'He told me. What's it all about?'

'The pips will go at any minute. Do we have to book or anything?'

'I'll do that – the Golden Arrow, ten o'clock on Thursday. We'll have to share a bed, is that okay? It means we can talk.'

'I suppose so.'

It wasn't what I would have chosen. Claudia at such close quarters could be quite tiring and she hogged all the bed, squeezing me into a corner. Goodbye rest, goodbye peace, Shakespeare *au revoir*.

105

Chapter Eight

Once upon a time Ivy had been a fixed and secure point in my life; less than a mother, something more than a maid. She saw me through the awkward years to adolescence and after, while Sonia dallied around Europe with her lovers and Davy and I clung together waiting for the shipwreck. She may have guessed before I did that Pandel Metkin had fathered David. If so, she kept the knowledge to herself.

'Lady Amity,' she said, holding out her hand, 'I'm right pleased to see you again.'

She looked so tremendously smart and businesslike in a navy-blue tailored costume that I felt overawed. But I hurled myself at her and hugged her. 'Don't be stuffy, Ivy dear, I can't bear it. What a lovely place you have.'

'Ten rooms and all full,' she said proudly. 'I like to keep a decent house. It's for Mother really, out of what I made working in munitions. This is her room you've got while she's up the hospital having her feet done, so be careful with her knick-knacks.'

'We will, Ivy.'

There were rather a lot of them. I especially liked an enormous teacup that had 'Father' written on the side enclosed by a wreath of roses and forget-me-nots, and an owl in shawl and spectacles reading a book. Altogether it was a satisfying room. Crocheted antimacassars hung on the backs of the two hard little armchairs, and the cloth on the round tea-table had deep crochet at the edges. I did not envy Rudi, staying all alone in a luxurious hotel.

Claudia flopped full-length on the bed with her hands behind her head. I made her hump up so that I could take the white bedspread off and she glowered at me. 'Clear off now, Ivy,' she commanded. 'You can bring us coffee when it's made.'

Ivy's dignity remained unimpaired. 'Not learnt the meaning of please yet, Lady Claudia? My room's just along the passage. You come in later, Miss Amy, and we'll have a chat.'

When she had gone Claudia said, 'Damn, I was rude and I meant to be good. There's so much going on in my head. I'll be extra nice to her when all this is over.'

'Aren't you going to unpack?' I asked, quickly putting away my clothes in the chest of drawers and finding a place for my book on the night-table (complete with flowery chamber-pot).

'Later on. What have you brought a book for? You won't have time to read.'

'It's Shakespeare's sonnets. Rudi's starting a theatrical agency and I'm trying to educate myself a bit.' I sighed. 'You can't believe how difficult!'

'Not the sonnets surely?'

Claudia once acted in a Shakespeare play and she studied him some more at school, so she regarded herself as an authority. 'But they start out all beautiful and romantic and then get odd, like this one.

  "To me, fair friend, you never can be old,

  For as you were when first your eye I eyed" –

It's ridiculous, aye aye ayed.'

'They were terribly keen on jokes and dreadful puns in those days, the longer the better so that the slower-witted got time to grasp them and know when to laugh.'

'I bet they roared over that one down at the Mermaid,' I said, cross with culture.

'Forget it and settle down. I've an enormous amount

to tell you before we get to France or you won't understand a thing about that either.'

Once assured of my complete attention she began to talk without preamble like someone released from a lifetime's vow of silence. She spoke lightly, allowing herself to drift into self-mockery. Yet underneath murmured the voice of the gullible and cheated schoolgirl, and I began to understand why Switzerland went so hugely wrong.

'As you know, I imagined I wasn't the kind to fall in love,' she said. 'The idea of having to kow-tow to men who, let's face it, Amy, do tend to be boring in concentrated doses, didn't appeal at all.'

'So it *was* a love-affair?'

'Not at first. During terms we were always chaperoned and it didn't matter because our days were pretty full, not just with lessons but all kinds of pleasantness. Though I hate to say it of school it was heavenly fun. The other girls were nice and for the first time in my life I had friends who actually liked me. In the holidays we had as much freedom as our families allowed.'

Claudia's schooldays began in the unthreatened peace of 1931 when she was already fourteen. Usually she came home to Gunville Place for Christmas and part of the long summer vacation. But at lesser holiday times she got herself invited to all kinds of interesting houses abroad where the people did not a bit mind idleness or the intimate discussion of indiscretions. She wasn't so keen on country places. The men generally did not take their mistresses and they suffered from *ennui* with only their wives to talk to. Much of the time they hung around the house playing cards or went out and killed small birds. '*Really* small,' she said, 'linnets and sparrows; disgusting!'

Paris she adored. Lots of invitations came her way. Pandel Metkin, who loved aristocrats and sold them expensive and beautiful things, was delighted to see her again. Her careless attitude to clothes shocked Jimmy Raikes. He took her in hand, introducing her to the Paris fashion-houses and choosing her dresses and costumes, coats and furs, even her underwear down to frilly but practical little corsets. Claudia abandoned the scruffy in favour of stunning. The two of them became thick as thieves.

Her closest school friend, Pippa, was Anglo-French, with a grandmother living in Paris who proved a great convenience. Claudia discovered that even old ladies had lovers. Madame, though positively antique, had lots – dukes and marquesses, all rather creaky but still game. 'Only the good God knows what they do together,' Pippa said. 'One must hope for the sake of their bones that it is nothing too athletic.'

At Easter of 1932 Pan gave a party at his apartment off the Faubourg St Honoré. 'It's really too vast and splendid to be called an apartment,' Claudia said, 'but I felt so exhausted with sightseeing that I couldn't enjoy the evening. Paris social functions used to start so late.'

She wore a new white silk evening gown with concealed scarlet panels in the skirt that peeped out as she moved, and she knew that, thanks to Jimmy, she looked elegant and correct. To be correct was of the first importance abroad. Distinguished and amusing chat came next.

'I've never been the slightest use at polite conversation. Pippa and I hovered on the fringes and watched the poor ancient dukes and counts flirting like boys.'

After a while Pippa had said, 'It's lovely of Pan to invite us, but this is an affair of business politics and no place to encounter unicorns. Not,' she added thoughtfully, 'that there are a great many virgins present either.'

Early ruin, once so thrilling a prospect to Claudia, was far from her mind. She received a great deal of admiration from foreign gentlemen, but she discovered that they unfairly despised single girls who gave in to their importunities. Pippa recommended marriage, preferably to a French aristocrat and *homme du monde*. Tolerance of minor affairs would be useful, and plenty of new money as well as old.

A quartet from Germany was to play in the intervals of dancing, and they had brought with them a singer and his pianist. 'Could you not have invited French artists?' Pippa's grandmother asked Pandel. 'I do not at all care for Prussians. When they besieged Paris I was five years old, yet I remember how they starved us. We were forced to eat rats and dogs, even the poor animals from the Zoo.'

'Ancient history, my dear, and these are not Prussians. Art is international. You will find them pleasing, and the tenor is becoming renowned. His friendliness interests me. I sense an ambivalence there.'

'Is that him, the tiger with the striped hair? He has a singer's chest I grant you, though I prefer to hear a baritone. An opportunist I should say. You don't trust him?'

'Not entirely. For a musician he is over-prosperous and he interests himself too much in my affairs.'

The idea of serious music made Claudia wearier than ever. She did try hard to like it, mainly to please her German friend, Hadassah Abraams, whom she very much admired. The school rather specialized in musicians. Haddie played the piano and the viola well and the violin superbly. She hungered for the concert stage. If she had worries about the obstacles in her way she spared Claudia, a Philistine in politics as well as music, and did not mention them.

Young men and old arrived, bowed to Madame and asked permission to dance with her charges. Claudia danced and fought back yawns. At the interval she flopped down on a window-seat and decided that she simply must go home. In a minute or two she was fast asleep. She awoke to find the tenor leaning over her, studying her face with intent bright blue eyes.

'You are Lady Claudia Savernake. I am Dieter Flynn Huppner. Did you enjoy the singing?'

'Naturally.'

'Little liar, you heard not a note. Come and dance with me.'

Claudia stood up. 'I'm about to leave.'

'Are you ill? You look in excellent health but I'll gladly escort you home.'

'Impossible. My chaperone will arrange it.'

'Surely you no longer need a chaperone? We must talk a little, become friends.'

'But I certainly do. I'm still a pupil at school and I'm on my honour not to cheat in the smallest way.'

'Mother of God, how old are you?'

'Fifteen and a half.'

'An English girl who dresses like a Parisienne! I imagined you to be twenty at least. We are almost compatriots. I understand and must respect your notion of honour.'

Of course Claudia felt immensely flattered, but she did not much take to Dieter Huppner. Knowing, too, that Pan distrusted him made her wary. 'We're not compatriots at all. You're a German aren't you?'

'Only on my father's side. My mother was Irish, that's how I come to speak English so well.'

'But with an awfully odd accent,' she said, taking him down a peg or two. 'Besides, being Irish is completely different from being English. Any fool knows that.'

He roared with laughter. 'Allow me my small effort to ingratiate myself. I did say *almost* compatriots. You shall teach me how to speak like an English lord, and perhaps there are some things I can teach you too.

Lunch with me tomorrow – and of course your chaperone.'

'I have an engagement already.'

'Then I shall telephone you the day after.'

She did not argue. On that day she and Pippa were returning to Switzerland, and he would get no encouragement from Madame.

'Weren't you even a little bit interested in him?' I asked.

'Blissful Paris and so much to do – I forgot him at once. The next day Pan took us all to Montmartre to buy souvenirs at the stalls and admire the pictures. It was a blustery showery day; quite chilly too. Jimmy groused like mad at my abysmal taste because I bought a white plaster Sacré Cœur that played *Ave Maria*.'

'You gave it to me. I've still got it.'

'He despised it and went off in a huff with the only umbrella just as it began to pour with rain. That's how I came to be sheltering in the actual church when Dieter crept up on me.'

'Not in church?' I said, rather stunned by this evidence of foreign wickedness. 'So absolutely the wrong setting.'

'That's by the way, because Dieter pounced out of nowhere. Rudolph Valentino wasn't in it. He pressed burning kisses on my lips and other places and his hands got everywhere. I began to think that the last hours of my virginity were at hand.'

'Heavens, not ravishment?'

'We were in a church, idiot. I'd started to wonder whether I wasn't rather enjoying it when I fell through the door of one of those little hut things. Fortunately empty at the time.' Claudia smiled in a faintly shame-faced way.

How did one confess, I wondered, to sinning actually inside a confessional-box, and would the penance be much steeper? 'Didn't anyone come to your rescue?'

'Not a bit of it. A few people wandered about and looked at us, but in France they smooch anywhere and in broad daylight. I started thinking about scandal and the family. Mother had such high standards. She would have been horribly ashamed of me; and imagine poor Father's frustration at not being able to horsewhip Dieter.'

We both fell silent. I was sitting on a hard, uncomfortable chair by the dressing-table and I noticed in the looking-glass a wincing expression cross Claudia's face as though her thoughts were painful. 'He didn't behave fairly,' I said.

'Men don't. You must have noticed. My understanding of them was absolutely nil of course, certainly those like Dieter. I wish that instead of just slating him then I'd told Grandmother or Pan at the time. It might have stopped the worst things.'

'I suppose he persisted. In the War I found foreigners hard to snub.'

'Only some; Dieter was one. I put him out of my mind and forgot the whole episode until the quartet turned up quite close to Lucerne at a château place that did concerts. The manager sent tickets to the school. Chamber music. You can imagine the tedium! But Haddie Abraams was wild to go and said she wouldn't unless Pippa and I did, so that was that.' She fished in her handbag. 'One of the girls took some snaps on my camera. Here.'

There is something poignant and touching about old black-and-white snapshots. Claudia's young, unsmiling face looked out at me. Her hair was long then, and a thick fair plait fell forward almost to her waist. Pippa and Haddie stood beside her. Behind them a dark, haggard woman stared fiercely out of black, cavernous eyes. I had no trouble in finding Dieter among the three men. Light-haired and tall, he smiled for the camera, resting a hand on Claudia's shoulder.

'Who's the intense lady?'

Claudia's face paled and she gave a violent shudder. I thought she was about to faint but she collected herself as the door opened. Ivy carried in coffee. She showed an inclination to linger and chat but Claudia's blank silence dissuaded her. 'Luncheon from twelve-thirty in the dining-room,' she said grandly.

'Just bring us something on a tray. We don't mind what. And a bottle of wine.'

'Meals aren't served in the bedrooms.' Claudia frowned. 'Oh well, you look a bit washed out, but it'll be cold and I can't do you wine. I don't have a licence.'

She closed the door with a snap and we heard her firm footsteps retreat along the passage. 'I've brought a half-bottle of Scotch,' I said. 'Don't go on if you'd rather not.'

Claudia shrugged. 'Pilar Romero, the dark one, played the piano for Dieter. She was his mistress, though I didn't know then or for a long time afterwards. He rented a villa above Lake Lucerne and they lived there together between tours.'

She still shivered a little. Hurriedly I fished the whisky out of the drawer and poured a couple of inches into a tooth-glass. 'Here,' I said, 'you're going green. Let's talk about something else.'

But she couldn't, not while her whole mind was intent on the past. She said, 'Poor Pilar adored him. He was handsome and he had tremendous charm when he chose. I noticed that when he smiled women kind of swayed towards him like those dolls that have weights in their feet. I began to wobble rather myself.' She took a swig of whisky and coughed, but the colour crept back into her cheeks. She even smiled. 'All Dieter's passions were sudden, and I believe he really did love me. There's definitely something catching about being adored and before I quite knew what had happened I fell in love too. The rest is predictable except that Hitler, of whom I'd never so much as heard, became Chancellor of Germany, and suddenly we were plunged into politics.'

I think that Claudia's love for Dieter Huppner, passionate though it was, must have ended almost at the moment of birth. Wounded by our mother's death and Father's ill-starred marriage to Sonia, she needed a supporting strength. Not that she would ever have admitted it. Being naturally wrong-headed she inter- preted her hunger for affection in terms of sex and trivial pleasures.

In August of 1933 she had only two more school terms in front of her. Her seventeenth birthday was a couple of months away. At the beginning of the summer holiday she, Pippa and Haddie spent a long week-end with a friend of Pandel Metkin's, a countess, at her villa on the lake near Weggis.

Earlier that year a sinister note had disturbed the harmony of the school, an intrusion of discord into Arcady. The German girl Claudia had later mentioned to me brought Nazi ideals with her. Because of the sketchy, intermittent nature of our upbringing much of the English social snobbery had passed us by. The distinctions we made were between them, the uncar- ing adults and spiteful hags, and us, the dear neglected children. Sometimes our manners slipped. In general we followed our grandmother's precept, 'Never be rude by accident.' To hear her friend, Haddie Abraams, referred to as a filthy Jewess threw Claudia into a violent and bruising rage.

'But why do you attack me, Claudia? They are like rats in a corn-store, the Jews, growing fat on the German race. Hitler, our Leader, will not rest until our land is free of them.'

Adept at avoiding what did not please her, Claudia grudged her new insight into wholesale persecution. Her attachments were always to individuals. She had never before had cause to interest herself in differences of race, religion or nationality. 'I often met Germans at holiday times and I liked them. They were ordinary and jolly and nice to me, and so polite. Did they all change in the end? Even now it's hard to believe.'

She knew, of course, that both Haddie Abraams and Pandel Metkin were Jewish. Only when she overheard a conversation between Pan and the Countess did it truly strike home to her that Haddie, a German living in Berlin, might be in peril in her own country, and her father even more so.

The villa was a haven that Claudia loved. On that day, she told me, it looked entirely beautiful. The lake lay still, striped with many blues. The horizon disappeared, dissolved by the heat to a milky pallor. Barefooted, she wandered out on to the terrace and down the marble steps to dabble her feet in the water.

Pippa swam like a dolphin far out. 'I watched the top of Haddie's head moving to and fro in the garden and thought how unreal we all seemed under the blazing sun. There was a bird that called maddeningly on two notes, over and over. Pan spoke very low. I felt dazed and I didn't consciously listen until I heard Haddie's name.'

'I must do something about Professor Abraams,' Pan said. 'Does he know, dear Countess, how great the danger?'

'Oblivious, Haddie says. His work is immensely valuable to Germany, and the country needs scientists. Surely they won't harm him?'

'Einstein is driven out, why not Abraams? He should leave now, legally with an exit visa or illegally any way he can; his family too. The trains already roll daily to

Dachau. I can help if he will only be persuaded before it's too late.'

Claudia began to shiver though the sun still shone strongly. Paddling silently through the shallows she moved further along the shore out of earshot. She could see no sign of Haddie. Suddenly panicking, she clambered over the low wall and pushed through the myrtles, scattering golden pollen on her skin and hair. She said, 'I sneezed violently. From the salon came the sound of the piano, soft and searching. So far all was well with her.'

I took a swig of coffee and pulled a face. 'Cold sludge. Camp, I think. I wonder if we shall ever get the real thing again?'

'In England we've never known how to make it. Have some whisky.'

'No thanks.'

'I will, I rather need it for the next bit. You see, that evening Dieter turned up from the lake in a handsome white yacht, looking madly handsome himself. He brought the tour-manager and two of the musicians with him. Charm oozed out of him, though he must have noticed that it wasn't working terribly well. That girl had made me wary of Germans. Haddie was playing for us and we were singing all kinds of silly songs. We didn't welcome them, we wanted them to go really.'

'Weren't they put off?'

'Not a bit, too thick-skinned.' Claudia sounded savage and bad-tempered still. 'The Countess asked me to show them the garden, which really was amazing. It climbed up the cliff-face in steps, and there were streams and huge jars and troughs of flowers and funny statues. Some of the shrubs and trees had lights hidden behind them. Right at the very top, on a shelf of rock, there was a gilded statue of a ram. I knew they'd

117

never get that far, so I tore up the cliff and left them to puff around in the dark. I hadn't reckoned with Dieter.' She paused vaguely. 'So that was that.'

'Oh no you don't, Claudia Savernake,' I protested, 'you're cheating. Tell properly. What was what?'

She went red as fire. 'You can't believe how hard it is to talk about. That garden was definitely bewitched. There was a heavenly smell of night-scented stocks and the sound of the stream rushing out of the rocks and down to the lake. The night felt warm and gentle, and naturally there was a damned moon. By then I was madly in love with Dieter and perhaps I wanted him to follow me. I can't remember.'

From the dining-room below I heard voices and the clattering of chairs. I held my breath and prayed that Ivy wouldn't burst in on us now. If Claudia's mood changed I would get no more out of her. But she went on.

'The temptation is to pretend that I found it utterly sordid, but I didn't. Dieter undressed me, and the soft air against my skin felt nice. Fascinating to see a naked man in the flesh at last, though no surprises after living next door to Cerne Abbas, except the hot and cold bits of his body. In the moonlight he had an awesome golden splendour. Not that doing sex was madly enjoyable. Definitely uncomfortable on bare rock, and I banged my head on that damned ram's hindquarters. It got very much better afterwards.'

'It ought to have been a unicorn, not a ram,' I said. 'So there was an afterwards?'

She bent her head and began to trace the flowery pattern of the carpet with a foot. In a voice gone dull she said, 'Oh yes, there was an afterwards, until I found out about Dieter's second profession and the true nature of the man. That's why I have to go to France.'

Chapter Nine

Claudia fidgeted about the room when Ivy appeared with our lunch. Her head drooped. She looked bored with her surroundings and herself.

'Can you clear us the table, Miss Amy, while I put the tray down? There's a few eggs spare so I did you an omelette.'

'You needn't make it sound like poison,' Claudia said, irritated as ever by the grieving dove-notes of Ivy's Birmingham accent. 'Eggs are almost festive nowadays.'

'Then eat this while it's hot. Did you say you were having your dinner at the Grand tonight?'

'Why?'

'I hope you're not thinking of wearing those old things you've got on. They went out with fox-furs and halo-hats. You'll not be let in the dining-room in trousers.'

'I can't have worn them more than twice.' Claudia shook out the wide folds of her plaid cotton beach-pyjamas. 'They still fit and anyway I like them.'

'You've no idea, have you? Always a mess unless you was pushed. I read in the paper you're marrying that nice Deering boy we used to meet at Weymouth – Frog was it?'

'William now,' I said, 'he's plumped out a good deal.'

'And how's young Master David these days? Still in America? I'd like to see a photo if you've got one with you.'

I did have one. I had brought it to show to Pandel

119

Metkin, who had not seen his son for several years. To Claudia I had denied the likeness between the two, but once in Paris she was bound to find out the whole story. I fully intended to tell her when the right moment came. When she believed that I had cheated her, Claudia could still deal out a thump or a vicious pinch. Worse, she was quite capable of banishing me and saying no more about her love-affair. I decided to confess while we were eating our omelettes, unless Ivy gave me away first.

But beside knowing everything, trusted servants have a knack of reading minds. After Sonia disappeared Ivy kept house for Davy and me, and I expect she understood my habit of protecting family secrets. 'Just a quick peep,' she said and gave me a reassuring nod. The photograph had a marvellous clarity. David looked as he was meant to be, relaxed, confident, charming. I doubted very much whether the Savernakes were capable of producing so beautiful a son. She took it and smiled with satisfaction. 'There, I knew he'd turn out handsome. We all loved him. Tell him if he's in Bournemouth to look us up; I'd like Mother to see him. Now, Lady Claudia, give me an hour and I'll alter those trouser things into a skirt. You'll have a nice long frock for summer evenings.'

'I don't want a nice long frock.'

They argued and tussled; Ivy won. Claudia couldn't be bothered to get a dress out of her suitcase so she sat down to her meal dressed only in rather ragged satin cami-knickers.

'Let's hope you don't go and get run over in those. They're well fit to go in the bin. Haven't you got anything better?'

'I'm saving my new ones for getting married.'

'Well don't let my guests see you half-naked, that's all.'

Ivy made smashing omelettes, light and moist and

melting. Claudia attacked hers with appetite. I said, 'I owe you a bit of an apology, Claudia – about David.'

'What's wrong with him?'

'Before I say you'd better take a good look at this photograph.'

Her mouth fell open. 'But I said – dear God, it could be Pan.' The vague look vanished and she pinned me like a moth under a microscope. 'Rat, did you or did you not tell me I needed glasses?'

'Sorry, Claudia, but Davy could hear you. He doesn't know exactly what bothers him, though he's close to the truth. Chivalry may inhibit him from laying another sin at his mother's door.'

'It's not just an accidental likeness then? No, it couldn't be, but it's difficult to believe. Pan and Jimmy are such a faithful couple; I've never known them to look sideways at anyone else. And Sonia, a woman! I wonder how Jimmy felt about it? Impossible to know.'

Bald truth leaves out the subtleties. It would have sounded too cynical to say that they had both wanted Sonia and sort of tossed up for her, so that David might equally well have been Jimmy's child.

I said, 'You weren't interested enough in her to notice how desperately she struggled to escape from that awful cocoon of dullness and prudery and always trying to do the conventional thing. I expect she hardly realized it herself. She bored people, poor thing, until she began to enjoy being desired, and all of the men did, even those who'd never liked her before.'

'Miserable beast, you knew and kept it dark.'

Echoes of that night still sounded faintly in my head: words and music, spells and stardust. A time of joy, but sorrows came after. We had called up an ancient sorcery and let loose the sleeping gods. 'I told you that Sonia went to Giant's Hill that night.'

'You never mentioned Pan.'

'If I had you'd have blabbed it. Anyway I was only

eight and I didn't understand what it meant.'

I quite thought that Claudia would say something rotten about Sonia, but she showed a degree of sympathy. 'Poor old Soapy, all her high standards gone to pot. How she must have agonized when she found out she was pregnant by the wrong man. There's the earldom naturally, and David second in line after Val. Father could easily have gone to law and had her baby declared illegitimate.'

'Foisting off a potential heir of alien blood onto the Savernakes might very well amuse him, you know, and he loved Davy too much ever to give him up voluntarily.' I thought with indignation of how destructive those misdirected loves had been to us, the coldly forgotten children, the left out. 'They should have told him, damn them, instead of tussling over him like a piece of property. Davy's close to Father and proud to be his son.'

'Ought we to do something, let him know that we know?'

'No we ought not. How would you like it if Portia came along and said that you were illegitimate?'

'I can't imagine liking anything she says. She wrote me a perfectly foul letter. Not a bit grateful.'

'Valentine told me. On the 'phone she got ever so haughty about a missive you sent her. I'm surprised you answered.'

'I didn't exactly answer. I found a pretty coloured advertisement in a magazine so I cut it out and stuck it on a card. It looked rather nice. Keep your health by taking Bile Beans, the medically approved laxative. Good advice you must admit.'

'Excellent but not appreciated. I bet the naughty Singlet had a good snigger. He must feel dull without Lettie. Anyway, about David, I feel that he deserves to be given back something of worth in place of what he's losing. Told bluntly it's utterly bleak – not even an affair. Too much champagne and one quick kerfuffle in the dark.'

'It might have been two or three kerfuffles.'

'Ho ho, very funny! It doesn't make any difference. Only Sonia and Pan can know and explain what emotions and enchantments drove them. My mind's absolutely made up. They're going to tell him and do it kindly if I have to put a gun to their heads to make them.'

Claudia grinned. 'And I'm supposed to be the one with fangs! Sonia might be difficult, but I've come to believe that Pan's a wizard who can transform us.'

I was glad to have diverted her mind for a few moments but having begun on her story she was set upon total purging. Pushing her plate aside she thrashed around with the newspaper examining every item though she had already looked at it twice earlier. She dropped it on the floor.

'Eight rotten pages, there's no room for *anything* in eight rotten pages.'

'What are you looking for?'

'Confirmation, justice, vengeance for the dead, expiation, unlikely though it sounds. You can't know how suddenly and disastrously things went wrong.'

Reflecting on her undoubted ruin, Claudia had smothered a small sense of disappointment. Sex, which generated so much anticipation and excitement, had turned out at first, she decided, to be rather a fuss about nothing.

'A sad pity that I've always been light-minded and incapable of proper reasoning. I know that I ought to have felt smirched and dishonoured, and rushed off to the nearest nunnery. But I seemed to have lost my virginity for next to nothing. We had regular medical examinations at school and I imagined that there might be outward signs and that I'd be denounced as a fallen woman. I didn't relish trying to explain to Father about moonlight and unicorns; or want to face Sonia's sneer, for that matter.'

'She was tremendously busy frying other fish so you needn't have worried,' I said. 'Tutors, secretaries, budding geniuses, she tried them all.'

'She – you can't mean it? Right there under Father's nose? And I missed it. Damn.'

'You might have guessed that the boy she ran away with wasn't the only one. After Pan I expect she found out that love-affairs were much more fun than virtue. Having begun so late she went right over the top.'

'At least she could sin in comfort. Meeting a lover in secret threw up all kinds of difficulty. It also involved lying to everyone, which I hated, especially to Pippa.'

It occurred to me that if Dieter had not persisted, the episode in the Countess's garden might have been the first and last of Claudia's affair. But in the summing-up, he emerged as an unstable, supremely selfish man of jaded amorality. Amused by her ignorance he told her a great deal about music. 'Educational you'd think, Amy, but it turned out to be mostly about Wagner and sex. Just another way of seducing a stupid schoolgirl. Remind me to tell you about *Tristan and Isolde* some time, you won't believe.'

Claudia knew nothing of Dieter's life or background, and it never occurred to her to ask until it was far too late. His obsession with her coloured all their meetings. Her chatter amused him and if he mentioned politics it was to scoff at Hitler and the Nazis. She did not mind that he asked rather a lot of questions about her friends. They interested her and it seemed natural that they should interest him too.

'Pandel Metkin, he is a good man is he not? He helps many unfortunate people of his own race.'

'Anyone of any race if they're cruelly treated.'

'And Europe is becoming an exceptionally cruel

place. So much persecution of Jews, or Communists, or churchmen,' Dieter sighed. 'My friends suffer from these thugs and no doubt some of yours also, the Abraams family for instance. The Professor is a prominent man, one of our leading scientists.'

'Why should the Nazis harm him then?'

'Can I read their minds? No. Two members of our quartet, accomplished musicians, are Jews deprived of citizenship. Pilar also is a Jew, but with Spanish and French passports. Happily they have a certain freedom to travel abroad and their plans are made.'

'What about you?'

'I'm the lucky one, a German national with a second country if that fails me.'

He may have noticed Claudia's waning enthusiasm. Her days were full enough with friends and there was really no room for a lover. She said wonderingly, 'Perhaps the oddest part of him was the way he loved possessions, things. If he had a craze for a tie or a book or a cigarette-case and I gave it to him, he would be utterly thrilled and content. But that only lasted a day and then he wanted something else. He was quite out of temper until he got whatever it was, as though he mustn't ever be denied.'

This evidence of greed did not really strike home to her until quite suddenly he asked her to marry him. The image of romance carried in Claudia's heart from a tender age crumbled, she told me, into dust, and she saw with appalling clarity that she neither loved nor very much liked Dieter Huppner. 'I got a nasty feeling while he went on about adoring me that I was just another desired object – a natty foulard cravat or a pair of gold cufflinks.'

'You seem to have a fatal weakness for the wrong kind of foreigners,' I said.

'A pity they so lack style, and of course conscience. He looked quite heavenly, fair and Teuton, the slightest bit rumpled and tremendously bedworthy. I had one twinge of regret and turned him down flat. He threw tantrums and threatened to go to Father which alarmed me a little, but I simply said blackmail wouldn't wash if he had any idea of seeing me again. Imagine Grandmother! She would drink his blood for breakfast!'

She had at that time other things on her mind as well. Pippa left school in the middle of their last term and Claudia missed her abominably. 'As if that weren't enough, Haddie simply disappeared. One day she was there, the next we were told that she had gone back to Berlin for good. I wrote, but she didn't answer.' She screwed her face into a defensive scowl yet she could not completely disguise a true anguish. 'I never knew how or when Pan tried to get the Abraams out of Germany. There were little signs. I was on the very brink of leaving school, and to be truthful I put off thinking about much except freedom. I imagined there would be time for Haddie later, but time had already run out.'

In her very last week of school Claudia went to Lucerne to buy small presents for the Mademoiselles. Laden with parcels she drifted into a restaurant, ordered coffee and a plate of cream cakes, and waited for her chaperone to turn up.

It surprised her when Pilar Romero walked in and up to her table. 'We had only ever exchanged a couple of words. I certainly didn't imagine that she had been following me about, waiting for a chance to pounce, but she had. I found out then that she was Dieter's mistress. In a way it came as a huge relief, though I felt angry at being deceived and ashamed of my idiocy.'

But that was only the beginning. Pilar, fuelled by jealousy, spoke with convincing venom. Dieter was, she said, a spy and a paid informer, who had made use of Claudia to betray her friends for money.

126

'In the first shock I thought it monstrous and unbelievable, then I knew that I believed utterly. She told me that Professor Abraams had been arrested and it was my fault, I had sent my friends to die in a labour camp. You can imagine the awful hurt. She hated me, poor woman.'

'But was it really true – about Dieter?'

'Oh yes, he worshipped money, and informing paid well. Switzerland was a well-established escape route for German Jews, and full of spies. Sometimes he managed to collect twice, from the hare and the hounds, but I'm sure I never said anything about Haddie that could have been dangerous. Can I have helped unknowingly? Pan says not, but it's been an agony to me all these years. I've never quite been sure.'

'What about Pilar? Did he go back to her in the end?'

Claudia sank her teeth so fiercely into her bottom lip that she drew spots of blood. In a tight, strained voice that tried to be offhand, she said, 'Instead of simply ditching him as any girl with half a brain would do, I felt that I must have it out with him before I came home. I arranged to meet him in Lucerne. He never turned up. She must have told him about warning me off.'

Her painful jauntiness disappeared. She gave a small moan and rolled up on the bed in a ball of absolute misery. I went over to her and held her, feeling the coldness of her flesh through the inadequate satin underwear.

'It's all right, Claudia, it's all right.'

She sat up against my shoulder. 'Sorry, Amy, you don't know how grim and horrifying the end of it was. Three days later Pilar was dead, murdered. Dieter killed her.'

My heart gave a sickening bump. 'Are you certain it was Dieter, and murder?'

'Absolutely sure.'

She had booked on the evening train to Paris. When Dieter failed to appear she decided to walk up to his villa on the way to the station. 'I can't say I felt keen. Under the mountains it was already dark, and rain dripped from those dismal pine trees and slithered in runnels down the road. And the villa! Gloomy beyond description, a steep, steep garden and not a soul about. Through the door I heard the most peculiar noises; bangs and crashes and a kind of wailing howl. I knocked but nobody came so I crept along under the eaves and peered through the window.'

Her hand gripped my arm tightly and my fingers went white. I eased it off gently and held it between mine, muttering something inarticulate. She didn't notice. 'They were only a foot away from me, shouting at each other in different languages. I couldn't understand Pilar until she suddenly yelled out in French, "Twelve years I've loved and protected you. I protect you no more." The look on Dieter's face, I'll never forget it.' Claudia swallowed hard. 'Oh dear, even now I get a bit sick.'

'Stop for a while then. Have another whisky.'

She shook her head. 'In a hateful, quiet voice he called her the vilest names, a Jew whore and an unclean pig. Her face went ashy and old, but she flew at him like a fury. She had a knife, very long and shiny. Dieter grabbed her by the hair and quite gently took it out of her hand. She stopped struggling. I think she knew what was about to happen and perhaps didn't truly care any more.' Out in the street a boy wolf-whistled and a girl gave a high, self-conscious laugh. Claudia paused. Then she said, 'It was like watching a film. Everything happened so slowly. Pilar just looked up into Dieter's face with those dark, dead eyes and very carefully he pushed the knife into her neck.'

'You were there, you saw,' I whispered, appalled.

'Blood spurted everywhere. They were by the

window and a long splash hit the glass in front of my eyes. I couldn't budge. I felt as though I would never be able to move again. Dieter stood there looking down at her for a moment and frowned as if he were thinking what to do next. Then he turned and saw me. That awful streak of blood crawled slowly down the pane between us. He gave the kind of nod that means wait, I'll be with you in a minute, and smiled tenderly at me.'

A huge hiccupping sob forced its way from Claudia's throat and her teeth began to chatter. 'Then he walked over to the window and slowly pulled the curtains. My legs wobbled like jelly and I was in wild terror of the front door opening. I behaved so badly, Amy, like a stupid, wretched coward.'

A couple of tears ran down her face but she brushed them away. 'Don't worry, I'm not going to cry. I went totally weak and sick in my stomach and lost my head. I knew that I ought to do something, scream for help, go for the police, but I just ran away. In the blinding rain the road down to the station seemed endless. The thought that Dieter might be close behind me with the knife made me faint and terrified.

'My train had long gone. I'd managed to lose my tammy and my purse with the tickets and most of my money. All I had was the little emergency fund we were made to carry pinned into our vests.'

She scraped up enough for the cheapest ticket on a slow train, changing twice, at Basle and Dijon. Police-men, Swiss and French, seemed to be everywhere and she imagined that they could read guilty knowledge in her face. In Paris it was still raining. She felt too hunted and notorious to take a taxi without the money to pay for it. With the stoicism that had often been her salvation she slogged through the drowned streets to Pandel Metkin's apartment.

The concierge tried to stop her. 'If I hadn't kept going I would have fallen down with exhaustion. I squelched across the lovely coloured marble floor and into the lift, looking-glasses all round me. You've never seen such an absolute fright, a chalk-white, elderly hag. My hair had come unplaited and water ran off it in rivulets. My coat stuck to me.

'The concierge must have rung through because Jimmy waited by the lift-door. He held out his arms and I simply fell into them, dripping all over him and Pan's priceless carpets. That was it. Pretty soon I expected to have to brave scandal and talk to the police, but I was safe from Dieter. I felt like fainting but I didn't. It was enough to be free, to be alive.'

'There never was a scandal, was there?'

'Pan took over entirely. He knew all about Dieter's activities and guessed that whoever paid him would protect him. And that was what happened. They fixed everything. Eventually the police and the newspapers wrote it off as murder in the course of a robbery. Dieter, who leased the villa, was proved to have been a hundred miles away in Berlin.'

Pandel Metkin, realizing her danger, advised Claudia not to go back to Switzerland and not to talk to the police. The unsupported evidence of a seventeen-year-old girl would be put down to hysteria, spite or jealousy and not believed. Nevertheless the Nazis might have found it expedient to silence her for ever. While Dieter remained in Germany he could not be touched, and Pan's agents adjusted their plans to neutralize him.

'He and Jimmy looked after me until I got my nerve back,' Claudia said. 'They advised me to put the whole experience out of mind. I did try, and I almost managed to forget. But I made jolly sure that I steered clear of love.'

'And you didn't hear from him again. That was the end of him?'

'Yes it was.' She hesitated. 'For ten years. Pan kept an eye on him, but when we declared war on Germany he sank from sight and couldn't be traced. Then – oh damn the man, they must get him this time, they simply must, whatever it does to me.'

'You should have told someone, not just endured it on your own.'

'Who could I tell? Not Father or Grandmother or Sonia, and you were too young.'

Her eyes were dry, her expression coldly controlled, but at the drop of a hat I could have cried my head off for her, for us and all children like us, fed legends of our importance with every mouthful of Farina stuffed into us by our elderly Victorian nursemaids.

The neat room had become stuffy and I longed to be home with the walls of my house secure around me and sunlight spilling over the garden. I couldn't believe I had been away only a day. I tried to open a window but the sashes were nailed up. Outside gulls screamed and I could hear the sound of the sea.

Rapidly I emptied Claudia's case into the chest-of-drawers, and threw her the plainest skirt and blouse I could find. 'Put those on for now. We're going for a walk, then we'll find Rudi.'

Holidays had not got properly into their stride since the War ended. A few groups sat in deck-chairs or sprawled on the sand, enjoying the capricious August sun. Children staggered around with buckets of sea-water. Murder of a peculiarly chilling nature might have been done there yet compared with abroad Bournemouth seemed homely and parochial, perhaps a little dull, but sane and safe.

Once past the pier Claudia and I were virtually alone. She said, 'One unpleasant thing happened soon after I got back to Gunville Place. A parcel came for me. Inside were my handbag and tam-o-shanter. The money and tickets hadn't been touched. No note. But it had the feeling of a nasty little reminder. I took the lot down to the kitchen-garden and burned them on the bonfire.'

Chapter Ten

After Switzerland Claudia skimmed the surface of life like a swallow over a pond. She spent much of her time in London, where she frittered away the years buying hats and collecting young men. Quite a lot of them proposed. At a night-club she danced with the Prince of Wales, and an absurd rumour circulated that the Savernakes and Mottesfonts were holding out for a royal marriage. For all the true interest of the family Claudia could have married Bluebeard!

Her sharply focused view of the social scene produced some remarkably accurate observations. 'Look at the women he escorts. One step away from hagdom and quite ineligible. He's looking for a mother not a wife, the poor sap. I don't exactly see Queen Mary as brimming over with cuddles, do you?'

When she was formally out she became engaged – with no view to marriage – to the wealthy playboy heir of a Scottish estate. She amused him, but gave him a dog's life. He didn't seem to mind.

Our Grandmother Mottesfont worried about the pointlessness of her favourite grandchild's activities. 'When will she settle down to serious matters?' she asked my grandfather.

'Not too soon I hope,' he said soothingly. He was a great peacemaker. 'Claudia is simply Claudia. To look at her is to smile for pure pleasure and remember one's salad days. She reminds me very much of you when we first met.'

That had to be a lie – I had seen photographs of my

grandmother in her youth – but it was a tactful one. She simpered and went pink. Recollecting my presence (it was my sixteenth birthday visit) she pulled herself together. 'Then she is not to turn the head of my chauffeur. I won't countenance it. He's an efficient, reliable young man and I have become used to his presence behind the wheel. It would be a great waste to have to dismiss him.'

'My dear, he's teaching her to drive, that's all, and he's tremendously pleased with her. I doubt whether he notices how she looks. His veins run pure Castrol and his heart is given to the internal combustion engine.'

'Just the same I shall forbid her the mews. Thank heavens Amy is never likely to turn heads.'

A foul blow, kindly meant. Grandfather sugared the pill, a smile lurking underneath his moustache. 'Be careful, Helena. Amy and I both resemble my late mother. We may not enjoy striking beauty but our charm is second to none.'

'Of course, Robert. Amy's a very good sort of child.'

I detested having such damningly tepid things said about me to my face. Grandpa gave me a brand new five-pound note when I left. I recall wondering whether a box of Poudre Tokalon and a long cigarette holder like Claudia's might make me fascinating. But the note, so white and crackly, unsullied by the signatures of previous owners, possessed too great a mystique to squander.

I had only the smallest idea of Claudia's activities. Occasionally she disappeared from her London haunts and said vaguely that she had been abroad, so I assumed that she had lots of exciting lovers. She never – to me at least – spoke of politics or the ever more frightening situation in Europe. By the autumn of 1938 we did not doubt our coming fate. When I told her that

Pandel Metkin had arranged to take David, then eleven years old, to a foster family in America, she simply said, 'Good idea, in case the rest of us are wiped out,' and went on to chatter about sailing lessons and buying a new car.

We were together on that heart-breakingly lovely September day when Chamberlain told us that we were at war with Germany. She and Ivy and I listened in silence. As I got up to switch off the wireless-set Claudia said, 'I'm so very glad it's here at last.'

A few months later she was in Rochester, learning to drill, scrubbing floors, cleaning lavatories and generally practising to be a Wren. Once commissioned, she was posted to Southampton. Now as we walked the Bournemouth beach she told me what she did not hint at then, that Pandel Metkin's agents had tracked the Abraams family from one labour-camp to another. The Professor was already dead. His widow and children had disappeared into the ever-widening Fascist hell.

'I'm not at all prone to worrying about moral questions,' Claudia said as we took our seats for dinner, 'but I felt it a tremendous shame that I had lost my virginity for next to nothing, and so shabbily. No sense of occasion at all. You can't know how earnestly I tried to imagine myself *intacta*, which meant forgetting Dieter and pretending the night in the villa garden had never happened. It was far from easy because of the murder. For ages I had awful nightmares. Haddie, of course, lingered at the back of my mind – painfully, because not even Pan could tell me for certain whether I had said or done something to help Dieter.'

'So far,' Rudi said, 'I'm baffled. Will I understand better as we go on?'

'Amy knows, she'll explain. I didn't too much want to tell you about my foolish mistakes. It's rather shaming.'

'You'll probably be proud of them in old age. Mine were many.'

'Don't we know it? Amy and I were amazed that the ladies you seduced so absolutely enjoyed themselves. In books it was a totally grim and unsporting business. The men working ruin and chortling into their moustaches; and the poor girls then being shown the door by unfeeling brutes of fathers. And always in such inclement weather!'

Claudia's voice is not loud, but clear and ringing. We had an interested audience. 'Everyone can hear you. Do pipe down or we'll be thrown out.'

'Nonsense, Amy, think how speculation brightens the dullest life.' She smiled demurely at a waiter and beckoned. He dashed over and asked if he could do anything for her (like letting her walk all over him, or hurling himself off the pier, or immolating himself on his little spirit-lamp). She had that enviable effect, especially on older men. 'Will the dance-band be playing this evening? If so, could they play now?'

'At once, Madame.'

'There, we can be quite private.'

'One moment, Claudia, before you continue,' Rudi said with a pained air. 'I wish to put it on record that I have never worked ruin nor chortled in my life. Nor have I ever been able successfully to grow moustaches. There are rules, and you must have noticed by now that women very much appreciate a properly-conducted affair on terms of equal pleasure.'

'How would I know?' she asked, leaving me to wonder whether her experience of lovers was as wide as I had imagined.

'I assure you that we parted with smiles all round. Hurting people is anathema to me.'

'Don't be so stuffy, Rudi, I wasn't casting aspersions. Can I get on, please? I've never talked so much in all my life and I'm finding it rather a strain.'

'Sorry,' he said, smiling at me. 'It's a little unnerving to be reminded that Amy had a ringside seat at the sowing of my wild oats.'

'For heaven's sake do stop going on. This isn't about sex, or you for that matter. You're beginning to confuse me. Is the wine list for ornament or do you intend to order? I'm dying of drought.'

The wine waiter was made of sterner stuff. He cared nothing for frail womanhood, drinkers of sweet sherry and cheap white wine. He drew Rudi's attention to various vintages ('We have a pre-war cellar, sir.') and allowed his ecclesiastical countenance to relax the merest fraction when the order pleased him.

'Why are they always so po-faced?' Claudia asked before he was out of earshot. 'I'll press on if you don't mind. I'm getting the teeniest bit bored with intense conversation, and I'm sure Amy's in a stupor. By 1943, when a faint gleam of hope appeared, Southampton had been horribly bombed and battered, and I had fallen in love with William. I felt happy but unbearably tense, as one did with bombs and U-boats ever in mind. Then just as 1944 began in tremendous optimism I got the fright of my life. At a variety concert. I almost didn't go.'

Memories of the time were recent. From counties north, east and west of Southampton troops and equipment had begun to move in. At night I used to lie in bed listening to the eerie tramp, tramp of booted feet passing my door, or feel the house shake to the rumble of tanks and armoured cars cautiously negotiating the narrow Sussex lanes. One didn't have to be bright to guess that the invasion of France was coming at last.

Claudia knew. Her section of Wrens went out under cover of darkness on secret errands to garages and engineering depots across the country. They carried back with them the small vital parts for equipment carefully immobilized until wanted. She existed in a state peculiar to the times, of weariness and anxiety combined with elation. Sleep became a luxury. Bill had been at sea for weeks, and rumours circulated of U-boats dodging about in the southern approaches to pick off ships as they entered or left the Solent. Going out interfered with her need to concentrate.

'The concert-hall was packed with Army and Navy, Americans, Canadians and the usual all-sorts. If it had been anything but a hen-party of fellow officers I should have refused,' she said. 'They told me it would take my mind off things. Stupid. Nothing ever does.'

Forces concerts followed fairly predictable lines. She sat yawning through the tap-dancing and the jugglers and scarcely heard the blue jokes, none of which were new. 'I began to feel decidedly peculiar, floaty and unreal, and I decided that I would never survive the second half. The tremendous relief when they announced the last act before the interval! Harry Gabriel, the well-known singer, fresh from his triumphs in the North.'

During this narrative Claudia had drunk quite a lot of wine. She barely picked at the delicious food. Now she sat motionless, her knife and fork suspended in mid-air, staring straight in front of her. Her friend the waiter received the full force of her blinded blue eyes. He darted forward. I waved him away.

'What, Claudia?' I asked, 'what was it that happened?'

Stirring, she looked vaguely about her. 'Yes, Harry Gabriel, the well-known Irish singer, only it was Dieter Flynn Huppner.'

'No more until you've eaten some of that lovely duck,' I said firmly.

The nannyish tone worked. 'God, I'm ravenous,' she said, and piled sauté potatoes onto her plate. 'I wonder whether they have chocolate pudding for afters.'

The food worked magic. As a film vampire plumps out after a lovely drink of blood, Claudia glowed with life and colour came into her cheeks. The waiter regarded her tenderly. Though it did not appear on the menu at her word he snapped his fingers and chocolate pudding arrived. She did not speak again until he brought seconds.

'That's better, and a super-duper pud. You should have had some.'

'I wasn't offered any. Waiters never notice me.'

'You should make more fuss. Now, having heard nothing of Dieter for ten years, I had persuaded myself that he must be dead. I felt an instant of total panic. Then my brain unfroze and began to work with extraordinary clarity. Only one lure drew him – the invasion. Southampton and the country around was, as you know, a vast holding-station for troops and equipment. The city seethed with rumour. If I didn't move quickly each scrap of information Dieter collected would soon be on its way to Germany.'

'But how? The security net took in every part of the city and miles around; radio signals monitored, telephone calls intercepted, cars searched, ships under constant watch.'

She ignored my question and went on in her own way. 'I'm not a bit sloppy or liberal-minded, and I really cannot be bothered with causes or groups or races or religions. I like who I like, so that's that. For instance, I loved Haddie because she was herself and my friend, not because of or in spite of her being Jewish. My only pure hate is Fascism.'

'Do hold on a moment, Claudia,' I said. 'What about Dieter? You told me he *wasn't* a Nazi.'

'Damn, I've lost the thread. This wine is heaven but tipsy-making. Did I drink rather a lot of Scotch earlier? Wait. Oh yes, got it. The point I meant to make is that Dieter would be anything it paid him to be. I had good reason to know that he would not stop at murder. If I got in his way or if he thought me a threat he wouldn't hesitate to murder me too. It was the purest bad luck that he happened to be half-German and half-Irish.'

'What difference did that make?'

'Eire ostensibly remained a neutral country, but Eamon de Valera, the President, hated us: not utterly surprising since we messed around so much over Home Rule and kept putting him in prison. Anyhow, he favoured the Germans. Yet when war broke out our government indulged in the usual enlightened madness and continued to allow travel between us and the whole of Ireland.'

'But I thought it was strictly controlled with passes. Part of my duties took me to the ports.'

Claudia glanced at me with derision. 'Getting past you would really have given spies a headache.'

Feeling indignant and a failure I said, 'I knew my job and we had full detachments everywhere. It wasn't just me, you know.'

'All right, all right. Allow me a little joke. Pretty clever of me to absorb all these politics when I'm so dim, *I* think.'

'You're not nearly as stupid as you pretend, no-one could be.'

'Stop bickering please,' Rudi said. 'We're a complacent people and we find it difficult to understand why we should be hated. Also we're far too polite to believe that the nice man in the pub is a spy. A great mistake to take forgiveness of the past for granted.'

I thought of the many Irishmen I had met, in the Navy and the Army, fighting like heroes, and the family of a seaman that Claudia and I had helped to bring out of the rubble of their home near the Southampton Docks. Mother and five children blown to pieces, two more babies injured and orphaned.

'Didn't they care about destroying their own?'

'Did the Nazis? Fanatics don't, I'm afraid, Amy, that's the pity of it,' said Rudi.

Claudia said, 'We knew that information judiciously whispered in the right quarters would be in Dublin the same day and Berlin the next. I presume you know what happened when we started to plan for the invasion of Europe.'

I did, of course. My duties as a Wren changed and I took up a new, most secret attachment. President Roosevelt expressed extreme anxiety about Eire and possible leaks of information endangering American lives. He asked de Valera to expel all German envoys and consular staff. That request was refused. We took the only sensible alternative by imposing a blockade on the whole of Ireland and stopping travel to the country entirely, both north and south.

Claudia said, 'When Pan's agents lost sight of Dieter as the War began, it seems that the Nazis sent him to Eire. An obvious choice, as he spoke quite good English and had no particular moral sense. He lived there in two identities for some time. Useful that he could sing and travel to and fro more or less legitimately while the borders were open.'

'How did he beat the blockade then?'

'He was already in England, doing concerts and entertaining troops. If he'd wanted to, and I bet he didn't with money to be made elsewhere, he couldn't have got back into Ireland without taking risks.'

How many more, I wondered, had there been like him? Cold, grasping intelligences at work behind smiling faces, killers at one remove, smelling out our home-bred Judases.

Frowning, Claudia echoed my thoughts. 'The audience loved him. He sang weepy songs and had the troops in floods. Yet he dealt in betrayal and death and would have watched them all die without a qualm. The thought that for years he had been tripping back and forth to Eire, destroying, not for love of Germany which one could understand, but for money, made my flesh creep. My teeth simply chattered with rage and tension. Someone asked me if I was cold.'

Bitterly conscious that she had panicked once and let him get away with murder, she did not mean him to escape again. At the interval she eased clear of the crowd at the bar, intending to slip away. She was actually through the doors when she walked slap into Huppner/Gabriel, mingling affably with a group of American soldiers. 'Why, Claudia,' he said, startled but not yet alarmed. 'It *is* Lady Claudia Savernake, is it not?' Just as though they had been casual acquaintances and nothing more.

'He'd acquired an Irish accent and that wisha-wisha kind of charm that sounds phony,' she said, 'yet looking at him I could see perfectly well how I came to fall for him as I did. That streaky fair hair carefully falling in a lock over his forehead, broad shoulders and smooth muscles under a white shirt. Absolutely the answer to a maiden's prayer, except that his eyes were too blue and hot and bright. Honestly, I believe he thought I still loved him.'

He held out a hand. 'Delightful to see you. I have to sing again, but do let's meet afterwards.'

A burst of fury half-blinded her then. 'I saw that damned hand as I had last seen it, holding a knife, smeared wet with Pilar Romero's blood. Disgust almost choked me. I forced myself to touch it and smile, and say, Lovely idea, but I'm almost due back on watch.'

He stared into her face. 'The Navy, yes. You look well in uniform, but then you were always beautiful. I truly loved you, Claudia. I still do.' The bell rang for the end of the interval. 'I can't stop now but I must talk to you. Wait for me after the show. Please.'

Claudia did not sound emotional, but I felt that she

had reached the most difficult part of her long narrative. She signalled. The waiter shot over and filled her glass. He approved of us. We were on our third bottle and it was an expensive wine. Instead of drinking, she lit a cigarette and watched the thread of smoke uncurl, lapsing into thought. The malice in her had always been immediate and temporary. An innate laziness made her incapable of deliberate acts of revenge which, in any case, trail behind them a nasty sense of guilt and meanness and are ultimately unnecessary. Infinitely more satisfying is simply to wait. Time itself has a trick of exacting vengeance where it is due. But the reappearance of Dieter Huppner forced her, against her nature, to act.

Stubbing out her cigarette, she immediately lit another, coughed and took a long drink of water. 'God, I'm thirsty,' she said, 'so much chit-chat.'

Claudia did not return for the rest of the concert. Sensibly, she first telephoned our brother, Valentine, at the War Office. He took over, driving down to Southampton to fetch her, arranging interviews with the right people and listening to her confession sympathetically. The Secret Services moved fast but not fast enough. Dieter must have read rejection in Claudia's face. Army and Navy Intelligence picked up two of his contacts – one in Portsmouth, the other on the Isle of Wight – but he had vanished again.

She was held in loose 'protective' custody for a week and then released. Now her mouth drooped in a woebegone fashion at the corners. 'They told me it was in case Dieter thought of trying to kill me, which might have been part of it. The truth was that they thought because I had once had an affair with a German I couldn't be trusted. The questions they asked! Heaven knows what would have happened without Val, who risked his own career to fight for me.'

Rudi said, 'Officials tend to be obtuse, and I imagine

they are chosen for their dry and suspicious natures.'

'And how! They really hurt my feelings. If my father taught us nothing else, he at least taught us to be patriotic and ready to die for King and country. But there it is, men are so vain and big-headed. Their reasoning was that a man can do everything foul to a woman who once loved him and she's bound to be grateful and keep on loving him for ever. Fools!'

'Awfully wrong of us. I apologize on behalf of all men.'

'Thanks, Rudi, apology accepted.'

For a long time Claudia did not know a moment's peace. Every casualty at sea she laid at Dieter's door and her own. In a state of depression and anxiety she decided that she brought bad luck to anyone she loved.

'Dieter had so unnerved me, I felt hunted. At night I lay awake seething with misery because they didn't seem able to catch him, and it looked as though he would get away with it. That's when I tried to throw Bill over. I might have known he wouldn't be thrown. Pig-headed.'

'I wish you'd told me instead of letting me call you a coward,' I said.

'It doesn't matter, I'm telling you now because Dieter's under arrest in France and Pan's told them about Pilar's murder.'

'Now I see,' Rudi said. 'It happened in Switzerland and you may have to give evidence to a French court. That's what our little jaunt is all about.'

'Mostly. There's something else: Pan's managed to trace Haddie.'

Rudi raised his eyebrows at me in enquiry. 'Haddie?'

'A school friend, a German Jewish girl. The whole family disappeared into a concentration camp.'

'And she's alive?'

'In a displaced persons' refuge. She's on her way to

Paris. The good things are coming at once, so that's all, folks.'

Claudia, who in spite of the whisky she had consumed earlier scarcely seemed tipsy, picked up her neglected glass of wine and drained it in a few gulps. The result astonished me. Immediately she became quite definitely and happily drunk. She smiled a starry, crooked smile. 'But you do see how awkward to tell William? And I really love him too much not to. I love him.' Her voice, enunciating carefully, faded and rose. 'I love him. Let's toast that.'

'We understand,' Rudi said, moving the bottle out of her reach, 'you love him, but I think we'll save the toast for tomorrow.'

'Tomorrow is a splendid day. Things to do, people to see, and heavenly Paris.' In the little ballroom next door the band began to play *Blues In The Night*. She wavered uncertainly to her feet. 'Dance with me, Rudi, we haven't for centuries. Okay, Amy?'

'One dance only, Claudia,' Rudi said sternly, 'then I'm taking you both home. I don't fancy escorting a pair of raddled drunks to Paris tomorrow.'

'Absolutely not,' Claudia mumbled. 'Death before dishonour.'

Now I understood why all the trouble with Claudia, and why we were going to France. I thought of the faces in the snapshot, dead Pilar Romero of the jealous, haunted eyes, and Dieter with a possessive hand on Claudia's shoulder; Pippa looking demure in round owl spectacles, and Hadassah Abraams, half turned away from the camera, her face possessing something of the fierce calm of an Assyrian stone relief. Not precisely beautiful but strong and intent, a musical genius. I hated to imagine what years in the vile camps might have done to her.

Feeling like a wallflower I poured myself another glass of delicious red wine, so smooth and soothing.

Claudia had a cheek, dancing with her head on Rudi's shoulder. I longed to dance, and it ought to be me. She was committing blatant theft. Rudi's face was without expression. I thought of cutting in except that they wouldn't keep still. The waiter gave me a pitying look. (Lost him, eh? No wonder.) I gave him my haughtiest stare, pulled a face at him and poured more wine.

After what seemed hours Rudi led Claudia back and would not let her sit down. I had not wasted my time while left neglected. 'Look in the dining-room, three women wearing trousers,' I said, sniggering quietly and pointing vaguely at the ceiling. 'There's a notice.'

'Wha's it say?'

'Can't remember.'

'It says that rules concerning dress are relaxed because of clothes-rationing,' said Rudi, who was staying at the hotel.

'Bloody, bloody Ivy, my lovely beach-thingies buggered up.' She looked down disgustedly at her nice frock for evenings. 'Can I have 'nother drink?'

'Bottle's empty,' I crowed.

Rudi shot me an anxious look. 'You cannot. You're tight as owls, both of you, and if you don't watch the language, Claudia, the manager will wash your mouth out with soap.'

'Can I watch please?' asked a mean voice that seemed to be mine.

'To bed while you can still stand.'

'Carry me,' Claudia begged with a winning leer.

'A great lump of a girl like you, no fear.' He kissed her on the forehead. 'You've done nobly and you're a credit to the Savernakes.'

'I'm not am I?' Claudia mumbled. 'Oh shit!'

Chapter Eleven

I opened my eyes onto a glare of punishing sunlight and Claudia, awake, bathed, dressed and radiant. 'Oh my head,' I whimpered.

'A teeny hangover, that's all.'

'It's the end, a brain tumour, putrid fever, galloping consumption; I'm never going to see my lovely house again. I want to go home, I want to be buried with Rudi.'

'You'll have to wait,' she said unfeelingly, 'he isn't dead yet and we leave Victoria at ten. Get up and have some breakfast. Come along.'

She pulled the blankets off me. I shuddered and put an exploratory foot to the floor. 'What time is it?'

'A quarter to six.'

'In the morning?'

'Of course in the morning. No, don't get back in bed. The car's coming at eight. Here.'

She hit me full in the face with a spongeful of cold water. I daresay it used to work wonders with her Wrens, but I didn't appreciate it one bit. Trickles ran down my neck. My nightdress was soaked and wet patches spread slowly over Ivy's mother's mattress. I knew that I had some other grievance against her though for the moment the nature of it eluded me.

'I hate you, Claudia Savernake, I really hate you.'

'Good, it's high time you hated someone, now stop being so childish.'

How could I be otherwise, neglected as I was and unloved in a cruel, cruel world? Even Fate had it in for me. Claudia drank herself under the table while I, abstemious Amy, got the hangover. Rotten Fate! I had at that stage rather forgotten my sorrows of the night before and the consoling sumptuousness of the red wine.

The door opened and Ivy came in with a rattling of cups. 'Boozing doesn't suit you,' she said, 'you look like hell on castors. Here's a cup of tea and some arsperins.'

'I'll have you know I don't drink, Ivy, but thank you all the same.'

I rather spoiled the dignified effect by hiccupping loudly. She looked infuriatingly tolerant. 'A bath's what you need, except that Madam here has used all the hot water. Better take the pledge if you're going out with her too often. Proper plastered you was last night.'

'Oh dear, oh dear, oh dear, oh dear.'

Claudia made an exasperated noise. 'For heaven's sake, Amy, don't sit there moaning. Get dressed.'

'Are you meaning to drag the poor little mite to Paris in her state?'

'Shut up, Ivy, do. You'll make her feel worse and there were extenuating circumstances. When's breakfast?'

'Cook's not in yet. Go down to the kitchen; hot toast in the silver dish on the stove and I'll do you bacon in a minute. Just let me see to Miss Amy.'

Somehow Ivy washed me and got me into my clothes. I had slept so heavily that my hair was pushed up on one side and refused to lie down. 'That'll have to do,' she said. 'Perhaps the sea trip'll put colour in your cheeks. You'd best eat a bit of something. Could you fancy porridge?'

The sea, porridge, bacon. I clung to the nearest chair as the room heaved up and down. 'Please, nothing!'

My grievances made me a miserable travelling

companion. In the hired car to Victoria Rudi put an arm round me and held me nicely against his chest. 'My dear darling, how unhappy you are.'

Tears came to my eyes. I felt very, very sorry for myself. 'Of course I am. I was in a dancing mood last night. You danced with her and you didn't even bother to ask me.'

'It was late, you were tired, I was tired. Don't be sad. We've all our lives to dance together.'

'I'm ugly. Just look at my hair. The waiter pitied me because I'm so ugly.'

Rudi got mildly cross. 'That family of yours, a bunch of yahoos without a sensitive nerve between them.' He pushed back the partition and tapped Claudia on the shoulder, interrupting a fascinating discussion about sparking-plugs. 'Is Amy ugly?'

'What? Is Amy what?'

'Ugly.'

'Stupid question, of course she's not. A bit of a dwarf, but if she did something with herself she'd be madly attractive. All she needs is a good beauty salon. I might be able to get her done over in Paris.'

'Don't you dare, and don't dare call her a dwarf either. She's perfect as she is.'

'Have you both quite finished?' I asked, bored with the subject and content to be perfect as I was. 'I'm five foot one in my stockinged feet. That's petite not dwarf.'

'Of all the smug, sickening pairs!' Claudia shut the window with a snap.

My headache had gone by the time we boarded the Golden Arrow. A return to Paris was significant for all of us. On my one and only previous visit years before David had sat confidingly beside me, happy to entrust his life to my inexperienced devotion. And Pandel Metkin discovered that he had a son.

Once again it was Davy rather than Claudia's

problems that drew me. I longed for a kindness, some reconciliation between the three of them, Pan and Sonia and the son they had made, the working of an old magic.

Claudia brooded and said little until the boat left Dover Harbour. We sat on the shady side of the upper deck above a well-behaved tinselly sea. She sighed loudly. 'Pippa and her wretched unicorns! White manes and gilded hoofs, so romantic and such utter drivel.'

I agreed. Anything to do with bodies seemed pretty messy to me, though I didn't say so for fear of a lecture on my feeble sex-appeal and how I should have my eyebrows plucked.

'And yet,' she said, 'one's first lover does have a powerful effect. Nothing's really changed for us since the days of the Druids. We're subjected to constant propaganda about purity when boys are anything but, and blamed for leading men astray, as if they needed any leading. Then in the interests of phallus-worship we're offered up, robed in white, on the sacrificial altar of marriage.'

Rudi wore a slightly stunned look. 'Did you think that out all by yourself?'

'Of course not, thinking encourages wrinkles and leads nowhere. One of my Third Officers came from a long line of Socialist blue-stockings and knew a great deal about what she called the persecution of woman-hood through the ages. Also she changed lovers once a week. Her advice was to bear in mind that virginity is a condition and not a virtue. There's loads more of it but I've forgotten.'

'Heaven be thanked.'

As with all Claudia's dashes at philosophy these ideas contained a certain oblique truth, though they were unlikely to appeal to men. The growing exhilar-ation of her mood puzzled me rather. She told us while

149

crunching her way through a bag of salted peanuts that after Southampton Dieter Huppner next surfaced in France, worming his way into the confidence of the Resistance and systematically betraying them. He joined a cell in the Midi. The Germans paid him in looted gold.

Before the Resistance began to suspect him terrible events took place. As a reprisal for the death of an SS officer the Germans killed an entire village, men, women, children, then set fire to the buildings. One night a family of Jews sheltering undetected in a farmhouse were flushed out, robbed of their small possessions and shot, together with the family who had protected them. Members of the Maquis were ambushed then knifed or strangled in the dark.

After the fighting in Europe came to an end some critics became shamefaced over heroism. They declared that many of those who called themselves fighters of the French Resistance were simply bandits and out for themselves. I preferred to think of them not as heroes but as ordinary people, good or bad. Who, among bandits or honest farmers, would not resent soldiers of a hostile foreign power marching in and forcibly taking over their country and their livelihoods? And among the men and women of the Resistance were the outlawed from every walk of life. After curfew they ventured out to blow up parked German trucks and armoured cars or pick off sentries. Living with the Maquis in the vast complex of caves beneath the wild green Department of Lot were Claudia's friend, Pippa, and her husband.

'Dieter belonged to a neighbouring cell and I imagine that he recognized Pippa and feared that she might recognize him too,' Claudia said. 'He told the Germans, who picked them up when they were about to sabotage the railway line near Brive-le-Gaillard. Scores of soldiers searched for the entrance to the cave where the rest of the cell was hiding. They couldn't find it. So they came up with the bright idea of pulling out Pippa's fingernails one by one in front of her husband to persuade him to lead them there.'

Instinctively I clenched my hands with a shudder. Claudia gave me a grim smile. 'We never saw war at its worst. He knew that even if he agreed he couldn't save Pippa, but he fought. They say he killed three men, including the Nazi in charge, with his bare hands before he was overpowered and shot.'

'And Pippa?' I asked, hoping that she had not died.

'Prison, and no treatment for her hand which went septic. She might have stayed there dying a lingering death if the Allies hadn't opened a second front in the South of France. The guards disappeared overnight. Part of her right arm had to be amputated. She got a medal and one for her husband too.'

Dieter left in a hurry with outraged men at his heels intent on killing him. He had no time to rescue his store of looted gold. Children playing on an isolated dolmen found it by accident hidden under a slab of stone. How he lived was a mystery. With the liberation of Paris the Resistance fighters formally laid down their arms, but they did not forget Dieter or others like him. Nor did Pandel Metkin.

Nine months after the ending of the War in Europe the police picked Dieter up for a number of minor thefts. They would have fined him and let him go except that he was carrying a dead man's papers. More months passed before they managed to establish his true identity.

'It turns out,' Claudia said, 'that Pilar Romero was a French citizen, born in France of an Andalusian father and a French mother. A retired police official remembered her murder. The question now is do they try Dieter for that as well as other more recent crimes? If they do I shall have to face him in a courtroom and tell absolutely all. I might even be charged as an accessory after the fact.'

'How did the police get on to you?'

'They didn't exactly. Pan told me Dieter had been arrested and that the police were digging away into his past. I've been so frustrated and so damned angry – I thought if he were punished poor Pilar might rest and leave me in peace. So I asked Pan to tell the French police all about me.' She threw this out with a nonchalance that belied the bright concentration in her eyes. Claudia did not intend us to get away with thinking her brave or noble, though I felt that in this instance she probably was. I opened my mouth to speak but she gave me a suspicious look and a violent thump in the ribs with an elbow. 'Shut up, whatever you were going to say.'

I gasped out, 'Suppose they decide not to try him? It was a long time ago.'

'And murder by a German subject in another country. Pan thinks they have enough without, and that Dieter will be convicted of the other killings. They count as war crimes. If so, I shall just make a statement sworn before a notary who's bound to be the one Frenchman in the world who disapproves of sex and women. It and Pilar's murder will simply stay on file.'

'I'm sorry, Claudia,' I said, knowing that war crimes carried the death-penalty, 'very sorry.'

She gave me a long, cold Savernake stare, reminding me that the history of our ancestors was littered with acts of bloody justice and revenge. 'Are you? Well, your war's finished, mine isn't, and I'm not here out of love or compassion. I protected Dieter once and let other people die. While he lives he's dangerous. I want him punished as he deserves. I want him dead.'

Conversation faltered after that. The boat docked. We trooped across the quay to the Paris train. 'Amy,' Claudia hissed, 'I shall have to tell Bill, shan't I?'

'I don't see why you should unless you truly want to. You were seventeen, for heaven's sake and you're not the only sinner in the world. London was Sodom and Gomorrah in the black-out.'

'Gosh, so it was,' she said, 'I never thought of that. But while I'm in a confessing frame of mind I think I'd better include him. All this plotty stuff gets on my nerves.'

She really was an odd mixture. I hoped that Bill understood her because I certainly did not.

When I first met Pandel Metkin in 1927 I thought him the handsomest man in the world. Now that he was fifty-two I scarcely expected to be so bowled over again, but I was. His crisply curling hair, dark then, had turned a bright silvery grey. In other ways he had not changed at all. His skin had the same smooth olive pallor, his brown eyes an infinite depth of kindness. He and Claudia were to travel to Limoges the next morning. While they talked Rudi and I wandered with Jimmy Raikes through the vast apartment. German generals had appropriated it during the Occupation. The Renoir that looked like Sonia in her fullest bloom no longer hung in the salon. That, with all the other precious objects, had gone off to America before the War began. Not a trace of the former richness remained.

The rooms looked gaunt and sad. Stripped of furniture and curtains, the small ballroom where Claudia first met Dieter Huppner echoed to our tread. In imagination I heard the playing of a ghostly quartet, a tenor singing 'Der Lindenbaum' and a girl's clear voice saying, 'This is no place to encounter unicorns.'

'Dreaming, Amy?' Jimmy asked. 'Pan will never live here again, but it's useful to him as a temporary base. Pretty trinkets are irrelevant just now and the Paris end of the business is dead. It may revive. He hoped that David — Metkin et Fils you know — but I'll leave him to tell you what he hoped.'

He, Pan and Claudia were away for two days. Rudi and I stayed in an almost deserted hotel and had our first holiday together. On that visit I embraced Paris with an abandon that I never quite managed again. Hardly a motor-car cluttered the streets. A few American soldiers ate éclairs (real cream!) and drank Russian tea in the Crillon, but the city belonged for a while entirely to the people. The tranquillity and the liveliness delighted me.

The few open cinemas showed frightfully well-bred and heroic English films like *Brief Encounter* and *The Way To The Stars*. There were shortages, but on the *quais* the flower-sellers' baskets overflowed, and the cafés were open and busy. That intermission, the revival of innocence, could not survive for long. We sat then on a café terrace overlooking the Place de la Concorde, completely empty of traffic and passers-by. 'I'm glad we've seen it as it was meant to be seen,' Rudi said. 'In a year it will have vanished again for ever.'

As soon as I saw Claudia I knew that the last battle in her private war had been won. She shone like a minor sun. 'True freedom, Amy. The joy is unbeliev-able. I was hauled in front of a judge — I think he was a judge — who went on rather, but fast and in French, so I missed bits. The notary came with me — a grandfatherly lamb with a huge crucifix on his watch-chain and a definite twinkle in the eye. He deplored the English habit of sending girls far from home at a tender age, and he and the judge had a chat about it and decided that things were much better managed in France. Then we all had lunch with Pan.'

'You won't have to go back?'

'They aren't going to charge Dieter with Pilar Romero's murder unless all the other counts fail. I don't think they will – too many of them. Nine counts of deliberate murder and unnumbered accusations of causing death by treachery, not to speak of being an enemy of France.' She frowned slightly. 'They took me to a window overlooking the prison-yard to see whether I could identify him. He's grown a heavy beard, streaky like his hair, so I didn't recognize him at once. Then he looked up, straight at the window, and I saw his eyes. That was enough.'

'Did he see you?'

'I'm not sure. I hope he did. Tomorrow he goes on trial. If he's convicted I want him to die knowing that in the end I had the guts to betray him as he betrayed my friends.'

'More retribution than betrayal, I think. And Claudia.'

'What?'

'Can you stop pretending to be casual and flippant now? You don't need defences any more.'

'How you do go on at times, idiot,' she said and burst into tears. Sniffing, she wiped them away and looked ashamed. Then she grinned. 'Now see what you've made me do, rat. You know, Amy, I did get some final qualms about Dieter. I asked the judge whether I had done the right thing by coming forward. He was tremendously surprised. His shoulders went up so high his neck vanished and he said I was taking the only honourable course. Better late than never was the gist.'

'I should jolly well think so.'

She gave me one of her rare hugs. 'Thanks for putting up with me. I'm glad you came. And now I'm not going to think about it ever again. Let's all go to the Folies Bergères tonight.'

*   *   *

The theatre glittered and shone with opulence. Sometimes the chorus girls had no clothes on. They danced so slowly and sedately that it took me a while to notice. I understood scarcely a word of the jokes, and Jimmy refused to translate. An entire sketch – what could it have been about? – centred upon a cushion that made rude noises when sat upon. The audience roared.

'The French have a mild obsession with bottoms and all that goes with them,' Claudia observed. 'I noticed it at school when we got chicken-pox. Having our temperatures taken quite startled us. I spared pity for the Mademoiselle who had piles!'

After midnight we walked back to the Madeleine. In a little square we chanced on a children's carousel, brightly lit and slowly turning. Claudia stopped and gave it a wistful smile. 'I don't suppose it's going, do you?'

Suddenly it began to move faster, tinkling out a song. The black-moustached owner sat on a kitchen chair rolling an untidy cigarette with one hand and pressing a lever with the other. He grinned and beckoned to us.

'We'd love a ride,' Claudia said to him in French, grinning back.

He bowed an invitation. Claudia stepped over the low gate, he grabbed her by the hand and launched them both at a pair of chickens. We followed. To the tune of 'J'ai perdu le doh de ma clarinette' we revolved sedately on horses, donkeys, dragons and ostriches in the untroubled night.

Pan filled the proprietor's hand with francs as we left. 'Come again!' he called. 'Come again my friends.'

By daylight Claudia and I searched for the square, but we never found it, or the carousel, or the man with the black moustaches. Perhaps we dreamed him.

*　　*　　*

'Hadassah Abraams is with nuns at a house near Chantilly,' Pan said. 'She leaves in a few days for America where she has aunts and cousins. I can arrange a visit if you wish it, dear Claudia, but expect absolute change. Everything has been taken from her, including her health, her music and her sense of identity. She may not react to you at all.'

'Will seeing me – if she remembers anything of school – upset her? I wouldn't want that.'

'It might. Looking back on happy times can be extremely painful. On the other hand, to see a familiar face could provide another thread for her to cling to.'

Claudia said, 'Can we try? Please? I'm her friend, even if she can't be mine any longer.'

She begged me to go with her and I did, though I refused to be present at their reunion. It promised to be an intensely private moment that outsiders could only spoil. The nun who received us said, 'Hadassah is sitting in the conservatory. I will ask if she feels well enough for a visitor.'

I left Claudia then and found a seat in the garden. Another nun bent over a flower-bed, puffing slightly as she dug out weeds. From where I sat I could see a long glassed-in room and a thin grey-haired woman sitting alone with her hands folded in her lap. She moved her head slightly. I saw the Assyrian profile and realized that it was Haddie Abraams. A door behind her opened. Claudia walked in, stopped for a moment, then knelt and took her friend's hands in her own.

The two heads moved close together until Haddie's rested on Claudia's shoulder. After fifteen minutes the nun carried in *tisanes.* I gathered that all must be well since she left the two friends together.

When Claudia emerged her cheeks were wet. 'She's so ill, but they say she'll get better. You should see her hands, old-looking, and the knuckles swollen. And at school she looked after them so carefully. Oh God. Sorry, I can't help crying.'

I passed her a handkerchief and let her mop up. She put her arm through mine as we wandered down to the gates. 'Nuns seem to have quite a nice life,' I said. 'Not all prayer, but lots of work.'

'Dull though, perpetual virginity, even if one does soar straight to heaven. When she gets to America Haddie will go to a hospital run by a Jewish charity. I hope they can do something for her, and I hope we can meet again. She spoke about the time her father was arrested and told me incidentally what I wanted to know. It's so odd. I didn't betray them nor did Dieter, though it's a thing he might easily have done or intended to do.'

A small thing gave the game away, an act of kindness on the part of Frau Abraams. In one of the coldest winters of the century she made up a parcel of clothes, including her second-best fur coat, to help an impoverished friend, saying that she would not need them again. The friend exclaimed to other friends about this generosity. They mentioned it to their friends in shops and at meetings until it reached the ears of hostile listeners. From then on the way to freedom was barred.

'Is that the last of the ghosts?' I asked.

'The very last, but I won't forget all those whose lives were destroyed for nothing. Grandmother used to say I was a ghoulish, bloodthirsty girl and that one day I would meet real violence and be cured. As usual, she was right.'

On our last day in Paris Pan and I talked privately of David. 'If it seems best to you, Amy, I will certainly undertake to see him, though truly I think it unwise unless he seeks me out. I long for my son, an heir to join me in my business. But to claim the privileges of fatherhood now would be an outrage against love. David is mine only by an accident of passion. In all else, all that matters, he is your father's son. Tell me, is Sonia willing to see me?'

'Yes. I had to push her rather but she agreed eventually.'

'Then the better course will be to see her first.'

'Don't offer Davy anything, Pan, money or help or a career. He needs to be independent until he's ready to choose.'

'I know, I know,' he said. 'Tiresome to be able to give to anyone but my son. I won't try to buy affection. Yet Jews and queers make good fathers, though not ones to boast about.'

That upset me. 'Please, you know we're your friends and you'll be David's if you give him time.'

'How short that falls of what the heart desires,' he said with an air of longing, 'but it will have to serve. My fault, my punishment.'

Understanding so little his emotions and heartaches, I had no words to comfort him. 'Pan, may I ask you something?'

'Of course.'

'Why is it, d'you think, that the Jews are so persecuted? How can the camps have happened, how could so many be slaughtered in such appalling ways? We're supposed to be civilized. Even animals are better used.'

'I won't lie to you; I simply don't know. Do we Jews carry a strain of fatalistic guilt in our make-up that leads us to assent to persecution and death? At times I believe it. We rarely fight the evil or shout out our wrongs and make the world listen.' He took my hand and held it gently between his own. 'Christ may or may not have been the Messiah. He was most certainly a Jew.'

159

*   *   *

'Your family provides constant interest, though it is a great distraction,' Rudi said. 'Let me see – I've rather lost track of time – we've been in France three days so this must be the 30th of August.'

'Good heavens, is it still only August? The month seems to have lasted a year. I can't keep up this pace much longer. Whatever happened to our nice quiet, uneventful life?'

'Claudia happened, and various other Savernakes, not to speak of Josie Knapp. Never mind, with luck Claudia will be married in a month or so and become Bill's problem. Promise me that there are no more fates to be settled in which we are expected to play an active part.'

I still had niggling doubts about David, but I didn't mention them. 'Will she settle down to marriage after all this drama, d'you think?'

'For some reason – perhaps I'm becoming psychic – I have a strong feeling that nothing other than the small excitements of living will ever interrupt her days again.'

'Oh dear, you mean she'll become dull?'

'Not at all. Claudia is to dullness as Queen Boadicea was to meek surrender. It should be fun to see how she assaults family life – at a distance of course. Please, Amy, if you love me, apply your mind to wedding dates.'

'Spring would be lovely, especially May.'

'Nine months. Can't it be sooner?'

'But winter's coming. I see myself drifting down the aisle in something white and filmy, amid millions of roses and with sunbeams dancing in my hair. Soon it will be time for woollies and rather cold for honeymoons.'

'All the better,' Rudi said. 'We can stay at home and never get out of bed. Nobody will call and we can keep each other warm.'

'Everyone will call; they always do, but March might not be too bad. As it's you and I love you rather, I'll give it my earnest consideration.'

'There,' Rudi said complacently, 'I knew I could bend you to my will.'

Chapter Twelve

After only one night at home I set off again with the utmost unwillingness to drive Claudia to Dorset. My white house slept peacefully in the early morning sun. The last of the flowers had fallen off the magnolia tree and the dark, denuded leaves drooped like a spaniel's ears. Unaccountably, a rambling rose had appeared from nowhere, showing off like mad and draping the railings with a lavish curtain of pink blossom. I felt homesick. Underhallow might not be a thrilling place, but I hated to think that its small dramas were taking place without me.

Dora's shop had not yet opened its doors. A pile of newspapers wrapped in a poster lay on the step. A strange uniformed policeman emerged from the police-house pushing a bicycle and talking to someone over his shoulder. Across the windows of Josie Knapp's cottage ragged curtains left from the blackout were tightly drawn. The place appeared to be deserted.

Having promised Sonia, I had telephoned my father to ask whether we might talk about David. He said at once in a livelier tone than I had heard from him in ages, 'I think it imperative that we should.'

Naturally I very much cared about Davy's happiness, and hoped that the truth would give him security and freedom. Yet I doubted the purity of my motives. The first light of morning had brought a fearful, inescapable honesty. When I married Rudi I did not immediately want Claudia dropping in, nor did

162

I want reproachful 'phone-calls from Portia. And I did not want to have to worry about David.

I heaved a long sigh. Busybodying, especially when it was done with the best of motives, was a dangerous activity. If it rebounded on me I could not complain. Meddlers will be persecuted!

Claudia trailed a languid hand out of the open window and hummed tunelessly. She looked tremendously pleased with the world. After a while she said, 'Why so glum?'

'David: he must have a life. Staying with me for ever is not it, yet I couldn't bear to throw him out.'

'We're bloodsuckers aren't we? You're going to have to be firm with us or you'll end up like Portia, with a houseful of seedy relatives. Make David go back and finish college when his year's up.'

'Must I? He isn't keen and I'm not very good at firmness.'

'The thing for you and Rudi is to have lots of children. That'll fill up the house and make you fierce with mother-love.'

'It would certainly give me something else to worry about,' I said unenthusiastically. 'What about you?'

'It may never arise. I'd more or less decided to say nothing to Bill about Dieter after all. Then I thought how wearying to have to go through to the grave remembering not to spill the beans accidentally. If he calls it off I'll have to grit my teeth and bear it. After all, Great-aunt Hildegarde lived without men as merry as you please. Why shouldn't I?'

'She had Jesus. It was her deep interest. You're not deeply interested in anything much, are you?'

'Not to say engrossed exactly. I could take up a hobby. Jesus won't do though, I haven't the stamina for sermons and hymns. Bird-watching, perhaps, or dog-breeding, or I could open a hat-shop.'

I groaned in despair. Nervousness I could understand, but in Bill she had found her perfect match and I wished that she would stop these idiotic changes of mind. 'Birds would bore you, dogs in quantity are worse than children and even smellier, and nobody wears hats any more. As for celibacy – what's happened to your girlish enthusiasm for sex? I bet Bill's lovely at it.'

'I wasn't thinking of marriage in those days, and before my deflowering sex was an abstract,' Claudia said austerely. 'What's Rudi like? He ought to be marvellous after all the practice he got in Hollywood.'

'I have no complaints,' I said, 'none at all. More than that I decline to tell.'

'That's a mingy attitude I must say, and you brought the subject up, not me. How does he compare with your other lovers?'

'What other lovers?'

'Not a single one?'

Claudia gave me a look of pitying disbelief. I glared back and nearly ran the car into a hedge. 'God knows I tried,' I said. 'Without love it didn't quite work out, and I'm glad now. To have any man but Rudi as my—'

'Unicorn?'

'Don't sneer, damn you. My wartime postings made jumping into bed with strangers a security risk, and I was bashful enough to hate the idea. I've never felt awkward with Rudi, never.'

'Soulmates! I've always been the teeniest bit jealous because he liked you best.' She patted my bare knee soothingly. 'Seriously, Amy, I know I'm about the worst offender, but you must chuck us all, get rid of us. Don't let us eat you alive.'

It was sound advice, but Claudia would forget that she had given it and be terribly resentful if I applied it to her. She never had the gumption to know when she was heading for misery. And I couldn't withstand her; Bill could. I prayed silently that his resolution and tolerance would hold out long enough to get her to the altar and save her (and us) from a life of aimless spinsterhood.

Great-aunt Hildegarde's house had rather changed its appearance. Claudia perched on the table in the kitchen, kicking her feet to and fro and drinking cooking sherry. She was waiting for the carter to arrive, accompanied by a load of spare furniture from Gunville Place and Bill, who wanted to oversee its disposal. I alternately prowled and chatted.

A brand new refrigerator whirred in a corner and the old oak cupboards had been painted blue and white. Cheap new cotton curtains hung at the windows. She studied them dubiously. 'I wish they wouldn't leer at me in that bold fashion. They didn't look nearly as aggressive in the shop – quite jolly in fact. What do you think?'

'Grim,' I said, hating them too much to lie. 'Why purple and orange zig-zags?'

'Some people aren't cut out for home-making. Can I help it if I have no taste in soft furnishings?'

Upstairs Annie Bowells swept vigorously. She had left the wireless on and a cinema-organ played light classics and selections from the shows. We scarcely noticed until the music stopped and a voice of mellifluous smoothness began to speak.

'A young gerrl wrote to me the other day with a problem that exercised her mind and kept her from sweet sleep. She is to be married to a boy she loves with all her heart. But, alas, she does not go a virgin to the marriage-bed. "Should I speak and risk losing my man?" she asks me. "Or say nothing and hope that he never finds out?"

'How great my responsibility! Over many hours I

pondered her problem and found no perfect answer, only my deep, true feeling that between husband and wife there should be no secrets. Honesty is always best. Where there is perfect love there is perfect understanding. To know all is to forgive all.'

Claudia's expression was an interesting mixture of doubt and disgust. 'Filthy, pernicious rubbish,' she said. 'It's enough to make one lie in one's teeth on principle.' She slid off the table, but before she could switch off the treacly voice said, 'A verse that I would like to share with you popped into my head as I sat in the quiet of my room:

So little truth our old world hears,
So twisted the ways that wind.
Honour and love cast out all fears,
Blest are the ties that bind.

When you are tempted to deceive, imagine that you are the one who has been kept in the dark only to hear whisperings . . .'

Claudia found the switch. 'Bugger, oh bugger,' she said violently, uttering the word she usually kept for her best and biggest rages. 'I'll never be able to get that out of my head. Blest are the bloody ties that bind. That kind of thing gives virtue a bad name. Perhaps after all – oh, I don't know. Have some sherry.'

'No thanks.' A motor-bike shot up the drive, followed by a van. The door crashed open. 'They're here. Hallo, Frog dear. I hoped Val might be with you.'

'Good to see you, Amy. He's coping at the other end. Sends love and drop in if you have a moment.' Bill briefly folded Claudia in his arms. 'Can't stop. I've found a few pieces not too monstrous. Gunville Place in its heyday must have rivalled Castle Dracula.'

'I told you so,' Claudia said. 'Utility's much nicer. I want to talk about something important.'

'Between us we should manage to create the ugliest dwelling place in Dorset. We could do guided tours.

Did you girls have a good time? I'll take you out to lunch when we've finished.'

Relics from the lumber-rooms of our old home crowded in on the shoulders of the carter's men and Bill didn't wait for an answer. Claudia glared at his unconscious back. 'Of all the exasperating wretches! He's at it again, ignoring what I say. Wait till he comes down here.'

'If you're thinking of doing something idiotic, I'm going.'

'Don't you dare.'

'You told me to be firm and chuck you.'

'Not me. Naturally I didn't mean me or today, did I?'

'No,' I said hopelessly, 'I don't suppose you did.'

Bill's calm temperament must have been taxed to its limit by Claudia, yet he listened kindly to her none-too-clear explanation of her change of heart. 'The female on the wireless baffles me rather. Perhaps hunger is making me stupid. Is she a friend at all, and can you go over her again please?'

'Of course she's not a friend, just someone filling in an odd five minutes on the BBC with beastly beautiful thoughts. She thinks there shouldn't be any secrets between husband and wife. I don't at all want to have to drag up the past which will be tremendously wearying, and a lot of it I've forgotten anyway. On the other hand, some things I simply have to tell if I'm to marry you. So I think we'd better not.'

'What a great deal of writing and telephoning you'll have to do. And packing up and returning presents will occupy you for weeks, I should think. I feel that even truth and honour might be easier. Where would you like to eat? Anywhere on the river is bound to have trout and duckling.'

'God,' she said desperately, 'do I have to scream to

make you take notice of me? Let me tell the worst and get it over with.'

'Oh no you don't,' he said. 'It's not my day for hearing confessions. We're both in our thirties—'

'I'm not, I'm only twenty-nine.'

'Be quiet, woman, can't you see that I'm thoroughly exasperated! Kindly keep whatever's bothering you to yourself. I absolutely refuse to listen. Why on earth should I care what you did before we met? My past wouldn't stand minute inspection, and I'm certainly not going to tell you about it. It's none of your business.'

'Oh,' Claudia said, deflated, 'that's a relief. I'd far rather not; I thought it was the done thing.'

Bill took her arm in a tight grip. 'Now you're talking like a Victorian novel. Put on a warm coat, stop embarrassing your sister, and come along before I starve to death. If we don't hurry there'll be nothing left but steamed cod.'

'I can't stay, Frog,' I said. 'Father and Gwennie are expecting me and I think I'll call in at Gunville on my way. It's an age since I last saw Val. But thanks all the same.'

'Another time then.'

Claudia climbed onto the pillion of the motor-bike and clasped Bill around the waist. 'You've bruised my arm.'

'A mere foretaste of what's to come. Regular beatings each Saturday night, social engagements permitting.'

'I can't bear steamed cod. The wedding's on then?'

'If I have to drag you by the hair.'

'Well, I suppose it always was,' she said in a cross voice. 'Blest are the ties that bind, heigh ho.'

Bill turned his head and stared into her face, a few inches from his. The sudden intensity in the look they exchanged made me blink and feel like an interloper. Claudia smiled. She really did have a heavenly smile when she meant it. Strong men melted and old ladies mentioned untruthfully how like her they were at the same age.

'Hold tight, Claude,' Frog said. 'Bye, Amy, we'll see you in church.'

Gunville Place lay in unlovely slumber. My arrival excited no interest except among the crows nesting in the monkey-puzzle tree. Eventually I tracked down Valentine at the far end of the orchard. When he saw me he abandoned his inspection of the cider apples, swung me off my feet and kissed me.

'You don't mind me dropping in?'

'My dear girl! I couldn't be more pleased to see anyone.'

'It's only a flying visit I'm afraid, en route for Lulworth. I have to talk over one or two things with Father.'

'Are you going to tell him about your young man? Is it anyone I know?'

'I am, and I might as well tell you, too. He's not so young. His name's Rudi Longmire, and he organized the big festival in 1927. You and Portia were away at school and couldn't come – exams or something of the sort – so I don't think you can ever have met him. It sounds stupid, since I was just a kid, but we became terrific friends.'

'The name means nothing, or does it? Mr Longmire, yes, I believe I did meet him once, at Grandmother's of all places. He had called to say goodbye to her as he was off to Hollywood with a film star, Marie Dearlove. Is that the chap?'

'It is. Grandmother dotes on him and I'm pretty sure he has a sneaking fondness for her too. I waited eighteeen years for Rudi without ever knowing that I had fallen in love with him *in absentia*.'

Val smiled. He didn't have David's extraordinary

handsomeness, but he was a good-looking man. All my siblings had fair hair without a trace of yellow. Val's was thick and biddable. Outdoor work had given his skin a light, even tan, making his blue Savernake eyes appear startlingly keen.

'You know he was rather decent to me. He drove me back to school and told me lots about the stars he knew. Then he fished out a signed photograph of Miss Dearlove and gave it to me. For all I know it's still there on the wall of what was my study. He certainly pushed up my status with the other chaps.'

'I'm a bit anxious about Father's reaction. He liked Rudi *but* – if you see what I mean.'

I sat down on the grass among the fallen apples and began pulling a daisy to pieces.

Val dropped beside me. 'Watch the nettles, there's a clump just behind you. He used to be devilish difficult to talk to, but he couldn't have been better over Cristabel. None of Portia's insulting inferences. There are problems, of course.'

'Not posterity and religion, I hope. Claudia and I had more than enough of no-Popery and the Thirty-nine Articles during that weird week-end at Hindlecote. Rather a pity that Portia was born too late for martyrdom.'

'If we have children, and I hope we shall, they'll be brought up in Cristabel's faith and kept well away from Portia. I don't trust her ethics. She's not above wrestling for their souls on the quiet. But my chief concern is that I'm proposing to take my bride away from a beautiful home in the sun and bring her to miserable England and Gunville Place. Hardly a fair exchange.'

Pagan that I was, religious niceties passed me by and saved me a great deal of struggle. Occasionally the sentiment of the story or the rituals to which I gave lip-service got to me and made me regret my lack of simple faith. But I could not manage to reconcile the image of a loving Father-God with the flawed and poisoned world around me. Where, for instance, was he when millions of his chosen people were dying horrific deaths in Europe? So many questions and no proper answers, only vague, bland reassurance.

I said, 'I wish I believed in God, but I don't seem able to. Gunville ought to be knocked down.'

'And most of it may be when I can raise the money to pay a decent firm of architects. The central block has twenty rooms, quite enough. The wings could go for all the use they'll be in future. Eventually the land is likely to be valuable and could be let or sold.'

'I shan't miss it a bit. What a wonderful crop of apples you have.'

Portia would have pointed them out as evidence of God's bounty, ignoring the hard work of nurturing them, and the disastrous aphid damage only too apparent on the yellow plum trees.

'We shall be cider-making soon. I've found a second-hand press and some well-seasoned barrels, and made an arrangement with the village that helpers will be paid in cider. Would you like to try last year's? Share my lunch too. It isn't much, I'm afraid, bread and cheese, and the bread's as much chalk as flour. Local cheese, though.'

'I'd love to stay, Val, but I can't. Gwennie's expecting me and I'm going to be rather late. It's been lovely. Only four weeks and I'll be back for Claudia's wedding. I suppose yours will be in Nassau and we won't be able to come?'

'Wait and see,' he said. 'It won't be for a while and we've time to make cunning plans.'

Odd sensations assailed me as I drove on to Lulworth. I felt resentment against the Army for the devastation they had brought to the countryside, and the arrogance of governments who chose to offer up the lovely beaches of Dorset to pointless war-games. And out of nowhere came my one happy memory of Portia. She must have been about ten. I still lived in the nurseries with Gwennie to look after me, and Mother was alive then. Lulworth fascinated me. I would spend as long as Gwennie allowed, lying spreadeagled on the rocks while she held tightly to my chubby legs, gazing down into the calm blue-green water of the cove. I had a deep conviction that if I looked long enough my brown eyes would turn blue like those of my favourite doll. This fantasy I kept to myself.

More often than not Gwennie and I were there alone, building sandcastles and paddling when the sea felt warm enough. Portia must have been on holiday from school on the day I had just remembered. When she had bathed she took me into the shallows and jumped me up and down over the waves, laughing and splashing. She wore a dark-blue bathing-suit with short sleeves. Her unflattering cap of blue rubber had a frilly black and red cockade and made her look bald. Staring into her face, I noticed how soft and pretty her mouth was and the way the long straight lashes veiled her eyes.

One of my longings had been to walk through Durdle Door, for doors in fairy tales always had magic things on the other side. But the coast has only half-tides, so that the sea never goes out very far. Until that day I had managed to be there at the wrong time when the water was too deep for paddling.

Portia tucked my frock into my knickers. 'Come along, baby, we'll go slowly so that we don't splash ourselves.'

Holding my hand she walked me carefully through the limestone arch then back again. It thrilled me, though we found no enchantments on the other side, only more beach and sea and cliffs.

At what point had the smiling schoolgirl begun to turn into the censorious, overbearing duchess of nowadays? True she showed caution, forbidding me to buy a fruit-ice from the handcart pushed by a melancholy Italian, for fear of typhoid. She said they were made in filthy conditions and a swindle too. Once the orange-coloured bit was licked off nothing was left but frozen water. I did get an ice. Portia made Gwennie walk down to the little dairy and bring me a cornet. So I think perhaps her sense of responsibility and love of command already lurked in the background, waiting to develop.

Where had Claudia been all that day? Awake she could not be missed, unerringly finding mischief. But even then she slept a lot. My clearest view of her is as a small rosy bundle abandoned to sleep, so I suppose that was what she was doing. And now Portia despised us, and Claudia teetered on the brink of marriage, and Gwennie had married my father.

I did not delay my arrival more by going down to the cliffs. The blue waters in which we had bathed covered the ribs of sunken ships and the white bones of dead men. Reminders of death and passing things were everywhere. Long barrows and grassed-over towns shaped the down-tops, yet the shades of vanished races seemed wholly alive, reinforcing the life of the present.

My father, of whom I am very slightly nervous, neither barked nor bit. He said of David, 'This astonishes me. I quite imagined that Sonia would have told him the circumstances of his birth long ago, when she took him away from me.'

'She explained nothing to him or to us, about David or about ourselves.'

'But you knew, or so I assumed.'

'Oh I guessed eventually. David guesses too, but

we're all tiptoeing around the truth, not speaking out in case the others aren't already aware. Such a muddle. You're not against him knowing are you?'

'I'm reluctant to tell him myself in case he construes that as rejection, but no. Please do bear in mind, whatever you or Sonia say to him, that I don't give a damn who begot him, he's my son now and always.'

Loving Gwennie and being adored and cosseted in return had changed him. He spoke Sonia's name with none of the bitterness he had harboured for so long, though the accident that crippled him and that she had caused must have been uppermost in his mind. His health had improved and he walked with less pain.

'A new treatment,' he told me, 'a Swiss chap that Gwennie found. He's rather avant-garde, an advocate of bone surgery, replacing damaged joints, that kind of thing. I'm going to let him have a go at me. I've asked David to stay with us and help.'

'And will he?'

'Eagerly, bless the boy. This is a last throw of the dice, a measure of independence or the wheel-chair for life.'

I was tremendously affected. If only I could have surmounted the barriers between us and shown my affection for him. But I felt bogged down in commonplaces. 'I shall worry until it's over,' I said.

'As I've weighed the risks carefully, I don't see why you should.'

'No, of course you don't see,' I said, suddenly irritable, 'none of you ever see *me* at all. That's the same old attitude that made childhood such a misery! Do you think I can't understand about pain and loss, that I have no right to love you?'

'I didn't mean—'

'After Mother died I went in terror that everyone around me would die until I had no-one left at all. Gwennie drew me a picture in coloured chalks of a little girl holding on to a man's coat-tails. She said that I had a father to look after me, there's lucky. What a joke that was! You didn't come near me; there wasn't any safety or affection for us.'

'Amity, please.'

'Everybody pretending to care about us and simply forgetting. Good heavens!'

'Amity—'

'I won't ever do that to my children.'

'Please, my dear.'

'We were shipwrecked and stranded, that's what we were.'

'Will you kindly be quiet a moment,' Father said.

Carried away by my sense of injustice, it took me a moment or two to realize that he was laughing. 'It isn't a bit funny.'

'No,' he agreed, 'but sometimes you are, my dear girl. And sad too. Grief is pretty selfish. I adored your mother and it shattered me when she died. You children seemed almost indifferent. Not a tear from Claudia, or a proper goodbye. The moment the funeral was over she had that gramophone blaring out again.'

'And that was when she did her crying. Sonia butted in so much. If we were sad we must go to her and not bother poor Daddy or let Grandmother see us cry. We hated her. Mother knew she meant to step into her shoes. She told me so while she was ill.'

'Ah,' he said, 'I didn't know that. I was very lonely. Forgive me.'

And then of course I felt sorry, remembering an impression from my nursery days of my father as a man in love and awkwardly tender. But still an unbending earl. Instead of insisting on marrying Gwennie right then as he truly wanted, he let himself be deflected by 'suitability' and married Sonia instead.

After its burst of assertiveness my spirit wilted and turned brown at the edges. 'That was rude of me,' I said humbly, 'and I didn't mean to be self-pitying and sentimental because I'm tremendously happy really. It isn't announced yet, but I'm going to marry Rudi Longmire.'

'Well I'm damned.' He laughed aloud. 'Sonia took a poor view of his morals, I recall, but she outdid him in the end. What do I say to you, that I disapprove on various grounds? I do a little, though I can't help liking the fellow.'

'Just congratulate me please, and if you're well enough, give me away.'

'Are you inviting Sonia? She might be awkward.'

I thought of her counting egg-coupons and making preserves, hitting the brandy bottle at the first reminder of old passions. 'You need not fight her. She's a voluntary prisoner without malice or desire.'

'Yes then, I shall be honoured.' He added suddenly, 'Your sister has been keeping very dubious company, I hear. What do you know about it?'

He would recognize lies instantly. 'You know more than I do, I'm sure. Don't you have sources?'

'An old associate in our Paris Embassy and others here, but I have no idea of how she became involved.'

'Does it matter? Her part's over. Under her nonchalance Claudia's intensely English and patriotic, though it might not be obvious.'

'The fellow will die, you know.'

'Oh yes, she knows that and finds it just.'

David decided to return with me to Underhallow to arrange for the removal of his belongings to Lulworth. I was glad of his company. At Salisbury we stopped for dinner. By the time we left Petersfield behind us a light drizzle was falling from an overcast sky and it was very dark. I dared not hurry. An abominable tiredness had settled on me and the road was unlit.

At the last bend before our lane a dark shape

appeared with appalling suddenness in the headlights. As I braked and swerved I felt a soft thud. We leapt out of the car. Lying slumped against the bank was Josie Knapp. No wonder I had not seen her sooner. She wore black from head to foot and, thank God, she seemed to be uninjured, though I had knocked a sack-like bag out of her hand. She groped for it and clutched it to her.

David picked her up and helped her into the car. 'Are you hurt?' he asked very tenderly.

She lay back against his arm, not speaking but simply staring into his face. In the dim light her eyes seemed huge. 'Should we take her to hospital?' I asked as my pounding heart gradually quieted.

'No, she's all right.' He wrapped her in his arms and she turned her face against his shoulder with a long, sighing breath. Neither of them moved until we reached the gate of her cottage. 'Stay there. I'll get her inside.'

He lifted her and carried her through the front door, shutting it behind him. I waited for half an hour, wondering how often Josie walked by night on the wrong side of unlit roads and how long it would be before she got killed. Love and sex are weird. Strange that she should be inconsolable for an unlikeable man she had loved but persistently deceived. Perhaps, like Sonia, she found guilt unbearably lonely.

David emerged, frowning. For a moment or two he stood looking up at the bedroom window. He tried to close the gate but it was off its hinges. 'She's utterly lost,' he said, 'starving herself and living in squalor. Carrying Ivan's Army uniform about in that sack. I've put her to bed and told her I'll look in tomorrow, though she'll probably lock me out. What else can I do?'

'Only watch her and try to keep her safe.'

He was incredibly calm and patient, visiting each

day, talking of ordinary things while she sat silently looking at the wall. Dora and I took invalid food that could be eaten from a spoon, and David fed her. She still wandered at night, but somehow he managed to steer her towards the village and the relative safety of Hallow Hill. It seemed to me that he had inherited his father's compassion for the lost.

Chapter Thirteen

With an over-exciting August behind me and Claudia on course for the altar I felt a mild pleasure in returning to quieter concerns. Rudi, on the other hand, enjoyed all the fuss and activity of business. He abounded with new energy and, I'm sure, dreamed each night of solicitors and accountants and friendly bank managers wreathed in smiles. Dollars did make such a difference. Lease-lend, so helpful to the war-effort, took on the aspect of an ogre with the presentation of the bill, and we seemed to owe America most of the kingdom.

A cast-iron reason for visiting Sonia cropped up when I had begun to despair of ever getting her and David together. I acted as trustee of a small fund set up for her by my father when she returned penniless from France. Her husband had written asking for it to be wound up. I didn't quite see why Sonia should not have the money for her private use (especially with brandy the price it was) but Robbie possessed the countryman's independence. He chose to support his wife without help.

On September 5th, a Friday, Rudi had a day of appointments in London. Although I quite wanted to see how Cyril Fox's murals were coming along, I decided instead to pounce on Sonia before she completely forgot her promise. I asked David to go with me. 'You haven't visited her for ages. It would be a nice gesture before you settle at Lulworth, and I'll be glad of company.'

'I guess I ought, though she isn't exactly a wow at

conversation. She may open up a bit with you there and put me straight on some facts that are bothering me.'

Getting facts straight usually meant a lot of shouting and unpleasantness. My heart dropped to my boots. 'Do give her a break, Davy. Wouldn't you be defensive in her situation? Like a million other women she ran away with her lover and left her child, and she certainly got punished for it. Men do the same thing every day of the week. And what happens? Their friends nudge them in the ribs and say, young blood, eh, you old rogue.'

'Hold on, Amy, don't lose your hair!'

'Well it makes me cross.'

'I've noticed.' He raised an amiable eyebrow at me, looking so staggeringly like Pan that I almost choked with adoration. 'I promise to be good. Father put me right about a thing or two.'

'He did?'

'Sending me to America may have been kindly meant, but it humiliated me just the same. I felt sick as any boy would to miss the bombing and the dangers. As I reasoned it out, if it were only a question of my physical safety I could have gone to Gunville Place. But Father didn't ask. Nobody seemed to want me around. It wasn't such a big step from there to wondering about myself.'

Even in 1939 Britain was pitifully unprepared for warfare. We faced rapid invasion and defeat, though we never spoke of it aloud but pretended it could never happen to us because of the Navy and our indomitable spirit, etc. David had a Jewish father, Jewish blood. That factor, of which he was still ignorant, decided us to remove him as far from harm as possible.

'None of us wanted to lose you, especially Father – and me of course. He was trapped over custody.'

'Yes, so he tells me. Awkward. Rather significantly I

180

thought, he quoted the family motto, *"Quod petis hic est"*, What you seek is here.' Davy smiled slightly. 'He's another who suggested talking to my mother, but to bear in mind that the Savernakes never let go of what is theirs.'

'We do take it for granted. Even Sonia hasn't entirely managed to escape us. We're pretty selfish and awful.'

'So we are.' I noticed that he included himself. 'But able to sink differences in a crisis.'

It was an accurate observation. By tacit consent we had allowed the War to draw the sting from old grievances. I smiled. 'We kept your place you know.'

'Yes. I hope I haven't outgrown it.'

He seemed so much more relaxed that I began to believe that the meeting would be easy and Sonia's disclosures merely a confirmation. But on the journey his expression gradually hardened and became grim. Poor Sonia faced the sternest judgment of her life.

She was unsmiling but tremendously prim and impassive, as in her palmy days before the lure of sex and adultery so greatly changed her. Her beauty had undergone a renaissance. Down but not out, I thought, admiring her and noticing that the brandy bottle was not in evidence. After the greetings silence descended on us. Every ounce of social grace deserted me. I shuffled my feet and glanced out of the window, thinking what a rotten idea it had been to arrange this meeting. Absolute sentimental rot. I gave Sonia a pleading look.

She nodded coolly. 'I believe you've some papers for me to sign, Amy. Can we do that at once, please? Then you'd better go out. You seem fidgety and I want to talk to David.'

So I collected up the documents and went out as instructed. Robbie was just leaving by the back door with a gun over his arm. 'You come along with me,

Lady Amity, and let those two get on with it,' he said. 'They'll do better together when they've talked.'

'Sonia's okay? She's not upset?'

'Mr Metkin came here to see us and we thrashed things out in a quiet way. A nice enough chap. A bit emotional, but sorry about the boy and taking the blame for what happened between him and Sonia.'

'I'm glad he did. You know, Robbie, it wasn't a bit in her nature as she was then, so pernickety and over-fastidious.'

'You don't need to tell me,' he said peaceably. 'Since we married I've got to know her well. One mistake after another and not a soul to give her a hand up or show her real affection. I'll see to it she's never in the cold again.'

I was immensely glad of his presence. In my heart I knew that the oneness between Davy and me had gone forever, and rightly so. A last wave of sadness swept over me. Then it vanished into the green dankness of the woods leaving me light, unburdened and free. The mischievous gods had intervened with their unnatural passions in the lives of the stuffy, so terribly English Savernakes. It hadn't suited us at all. We were meant to be ordinary.

'Where are we going, Robbie?'

'There's a persistent old beggar of a dog-fox break-ing into my pheasant run in broad daylight. If I don't get him soon I'll not have a bird left by the First.'

'Must you shoot him?'

'Not squeamish, are you?'

'A bit, but I know they over-kill – like people, I suppose.'

'Don't fret, the gun's in case I have the luck to catch him in the run. Not likely. He hears me coming a mile off and has a good old laugh. You sit here while I go on and check the fencing, then we'll share my tea.'

I sat on the mossy trunk of a fallen beech and

wondered how Sonia and David were getting on. Then I thought about myself. When Portia found out about Rudi she would want me, the blot on the family escutcheon, to have a very quiet Registry Office wedding. But I wasn't going to. Virgin or not, I meant to wear white and be married in a church packed out with squabbling relatives.

I picked up a twig and laboriously scratched in the moss, Mrs Longmire, Mrs Rudi Longmire, Amity Longmire. Hearing Robbie's light tread returning, I hurriedly scribbled out the words, scattering my shoes with little bits of green. As Sonia remarked, I'm as romantic as any shopgirl. Bitchy of her, but she made good cakes. Robbie and I shared strong tea with the special taste it gets from a thermos flask, chicken sandwiches an inch thick with meat, and two kinds of cake, Dundee and lemon. It was a jolly good meal. I felt ready for anger, tears, anything at all.

Two accusing faces met me at the cottage. David's likeness to Pan was so marked that I had not noticed until that moment how much he also resembled Sonia. Their expressions of wounded obstinacy were identical. Neither of them cared for me much just then.

Sonia said, 'Why did you make me do this when you know I'm hopeless at telling things? Excuse me, I have to feed the hens.'

Davy sat down and whirled the piano-stool around. He began to play a slow, syncopated blues. Bent over the keys, his back to me, he watched the lazy movements of his hands. 'Since you engineered it, you know what I've just heard. It wasn't exactly a shock. But I imagined a grand passion, a love-affair, not a quick loveless scuffle in the grass. No wonder I was dumped on anyone who'd have me. My God!'

All my so-clever plans had foundered on the belief that I knew Sonia better than she knew herself. What idiocy. I ought to have told him long ago and risked rejection. Wanting to be the best-loved was just another kind of greed.

'Damn,' I said, 'oh damnation. You were the most wanted child there's ever been, and so coveted and adored.'

'Can we go home now, please?'

A feeling of total exasperation hardened my heart a little. We seemed, all of us, to be terminally infected with self-pity, as though we deserved to be protected from unpleasant truths and general nastiness. 'No we can't, not until you stop feeling sorry for yourself. You're not the only one who's been hurt, for heaven's sake; it's a long chronicle of unhappiness.'

Startled by the sharpness of my tone he swung round and gave me a reproachful look. 'Amy?'

'Don't Amy me!' I snapped, resisting the appeal in his golden-brown eyes. 'I've loved you all your life. I was almost there at the moment you were conceived, and it wasn't sordid at all, it was pure magic.'

'Oh? A virgin birth, I suppose.'

And suddenly the thought struck me that in an extraordinary way it very nearly had been. Not that Sonia was precisely a virgin. She had been married to my father for six months or so when the accident happened that crippled him. Yet her emotions remained frozen and untouched. Then I, a gawping eight-year-old, watched entranced as Pandel Metkin flew down from the sky in an aeroplane, and immediately equated him with the Annunciation and the Angel Gabriel. They were both so beautiful, Sonia and Pan. Their looks somehow chimed in perfect harmony and I had seen, but did not recognize, the immediate attraction sparking between them.

'You have to know what kind of woman Sonia was then, tremendously pursued but straitlaced and puritanical. Above all things she longed for a child.

Father's accident left her virtually a widow. We weren't kind to her.'

'Why didn't she tell me this?'

'Because she doesn't understand herself all that well, and I must say that she doesn't whine like we do.'

'Ouch,' David said. 'How come she got me then?'

'A conspiracy of magics; words and music, grotesques and giants, sun, moon and stars, and a heavenly midsummer night.'

'All that? Gee!'

'If you'll listen without sneering I'll explain.'

'Sorry, go ahead.'

Mine was a child's eye view and perhaps for that reason clearer than Sonia's. I told him about everything, not just Rudi's Arts Festival and Sonia singing and acting, but my first encounter with fear and raw sex and learning the facts of life.

I said, sentimental all over again, 'The night was so strange. It frightened me, yet I felt compelled to follow Sonia. When she went up to the Cerne Abbas Giant it was to ask for a child, not to meet a lover. She was alone, looking for supernatural help. That night every man loved and wanted her, Pandel Metkin most of all.'

Lost in remembering, I scarcely noticed Sonia come back into the room and sit down. David made a vague movement with his hand. 'Yes, go on.'

'That's more or less all. Pan followed her and then I thought I'd better go home. David, you've never in your life seen two such overwhelmingly glorious people – god and goddess. They gave the Savernakes a wonderful gift, they gave us you. I've never stopped being grateful.'

He smiled, looking young and confused, then turned back to the piano and played a loud satirical chord, dadah. 'How on earth can you remember after so long?'

'I wrote all about it in my journal. You can read it if you like, though you'll find it childish.'

'Really,' Sonia said in a shocked tone, 'putting down things like that about us. I'd have burned those journals if I'd known. Where are they now?'

'Safe. I keep them locked up because Claudia's so nosy.'

She sighed. 'Secrets are tedious. Whether I forget or remember it doesn't matter any more, does it?'

'No, Sonia, it doesn't matter now.'

Somehow, perhaps because of generous glasses of Robbie's mulberry wine, we moved from antagonism to conviviality. I was cautious with the wine after my Bournemouth binge. David fished a pile of sheet-music out of the rack and leafed through it. 'Who's the singer?' he asked.

'Sonia,' Robbie said. 'Go on, my girl.'

She crossed the room and stood beside David with a hand on his shoulder. 'Choose me something.'

'How about "Oft In The Stilly Night"?'

The whole world had changed since I last heard Sonia's warm, unmistakable mezzo. She sang some ballads, ending with 'My Old Kentucky Home'. Even Claudia, who hated both Sonia and any music except jazz, had liked the song because of its melancholy. It appealed to her feelings of martyrdom when asked to exert herself. Her dismal hooting of 'Just a few more days for to tote the weary load!' dirged through the corridors of Gunville Place and gave singing a bad name.

Robbie said in a pleased and gentle tone, 'Sonia hasn't sung like that for months.'

I overcame an impulse to cry. The trouble with emotions is that the words to express them don't seem to exist, not in English at least. Show them and you're guilty of snivelling sentiment, hide them and you're hard as nails.

'Something modern? I can improvise.'

'No more,' Sonia said. 'Go home now, David. I'm quite worn out.'

'Can I come again before I go down to Dorset?'

'That depends.'

'On what?'

'On not making a parade of your birth. I never deceived Gervase. You're registered as his legitimate son and that's who you are. I don't want more upsets.'

'What about Metkin? Meeting him's going to be pretty strange. I can't possibly accept a post in his business. I don't want to see him again.'

'In eighteen years he's made no claim on you and you can't avoid a family friend for ever. He left a letter for you – here.'

'If only he weren't – well – homosexual.'

Sonia gave him a very dry look indeed. 'It might have been someone far worse, believe me. Read his letter and think again about your attitudes. Now go.'

He bent his head. 'I'm sorry, Mother.'

She ruffled his crop of dark curls. 'Don't be sorry. I've learned never to be and God knows I've plenty to apologize for.'

All that I ever heard of Davy's feelings afterwards was a single remark he made in the car as we drove home. 'Odd, I'm half-Jewish, partly foreign and I feel English. It needs some thought.'

Dinner was a silent meal. Soon afterwards he went out and as Rudi had not yet arrived home I climbed to my attic room at the top of the house and lay propped on a window-seat, looking out on to the green and the road. The window was wide open. Not wanting to attract moths, I did not switch on the light. Houses, trees, figures stood out in dark sharp relief against a lurid yellow twilight. Rain again tomorrow!

I loved the room, the largest of the two attics. It housed my desk, all my private and valueless treasures and some of Great-aunt Hildegarde's books, including her big Bible. Here and there she had marked the pages with comments. At the end of the book of Job: 'Shall not bother to read this nonsense again. Wanton persecution of a perfect and upright man smacks more of Satan than the Lord. Can't admire it.' She did not mince words, even over God.

Once, I imagine, the nurseries were here under the roof. Embedded in cement outside the windows, upright iron bars ensured no accidental falls. Cupboards beneath the high padded seats were perfect storage for toys and games. They now held my diaries of twenty years, programmes from the 1927 Arts Festival with my name printed on them, and the letters Rudi sent to me regularly from America while I was growing up. The room stretched across the house. The window where I lounged commanded a view of Underhallow, the other looked out over the garden and the slope of Hallow Hill.

Dora pulled down the blinds in her shop and Charlie Hopkins walked swiftly towards either the church or the pub, more probably the latter. David had not, I noticed, gone far. He paced to and fro, hands in pockets, along the edge of the green in front of the house.

Then the black figure of Josie Knapp emerged from her gate. She walked slowly, her eyes fixed on the ground. David stopped and waited. As she reached him he put out a hand. 'I'm glad I met you,' he said. 'I wanted to see you very much.'

Caught by the intensity in his voice, I sat up and watched them.

'Why?' Josie asked dully.

'Come and sit down for a moment.'

'I'm taking flowers to Ivan.'

'Dear, you aren't carrying any flowers.'

'They were in the porch. I've forgotten them, I'll have to go back.'

'No. This has got to stop. I won't always be here to

look after you. Winter's coming and if you wander on the roads at night you're going to be killed sooner or later.'

'Why does that matter?'

'Because it's a stupid waste. When my year in England is up I'm going back to America to university. You could do the same, go back to Cambridge.'

'I'm finished, I'm too old.' Suddenly Josie choked and cried out, weeping and keening with wild extravagance, her head bowed onto Davy's shoulder. He folded her in his arms, holding her until she became quiet. She lifted her face. They began to kiss each other over and over again, fiercely, as though they were starving.

He half-led, half-carried her through the side gate. I thought I knew where they were going, but I crossed the room to the other window and stared down into the garden. There has been a dwelling on the site of Garland House more or less for ever and behind the present house stands the ruin of old Garland Cottage. We used it mostly for storage. But the two main rooms I kept furnished as emergency guest-rooms.

I saw their shadows moving along the path and heard the squealing of the hinges as the door swung open. It closed with a slam. Then came silence and I thought I had better stop listening and watching. What happened next was not my business.

How long David stayed with Josie I don't know. He had not come in when Rudi arrived home, but I woke in the night and thought that I heard the front door softly closing.

At breakfast Rudi bubbled over with enthusiasm for the London house. 'Getting Cyril was the most stupendous piece of luck. He can pick up almost anything that's hard to get, and cheaply. My office will be ready in a month and our flat's going to be so nice. You

189

must see it. So must David. Where is he?'

'Out I think. I expect he had breakfast early.'

He wasn't a bit deceived by my casual tone. 'Not upset by Sonia's revelations I hope? I'm rather counting on having you to myself once Claudia's married.'

'Davy's all right,' I said, 'and he's going back to Harvard eventually. Don't mention it, though. I overheard it.'

'Who did he tell, if not you?'

'Josie Knapp.'

Rudi whistled. 'Don't tell me those two—'

'Yes, I think so. I'm jolly glad. He rather tended to condemn Sonia. Lots of illicit passion is the best cure for hardness of heart. Besides, it's not being in love, only mutual comfort.'

'Good. It'll be all over the village by noon.'

He was proved right almost immediately. The doorbell rang and Polly showed in Dora Aphrodite. 'That wretched Golightly woman, can you credit it, she wants compensation for Father squashing her hat; fifteen guineas if you please or she'll sue. I'm not paying it. I don't spend that much on clothes in a year. D'you think she would go to court just for that, Rudi?'

'The Golightlys of the world rather enjoy litigation, but I've been threatened with court action times without number, in my hungry days naturally, and wriggled out of it.' He put on his spectacles and began making notes on a handbill. 'Give me a few minutes.'

'Amy, is it true about David and Josie Knapp?'

'Is what true, Dora?'

'I heard that they're, you know, having a love-affair, and that he's persuading her to go back to Cambridge on a grant as a mature student.'

'You know a lot more than I do.'

'Josie told the milkman and he actually saw David there in the kitchen. She looked as though she'd been up all night and she was in her negligée. Red lace.'

Dora allowed herself a small smile. 'I do hope it's true. Ivan saved those children, I know, but a difficult man and we can't go on mourning him for ever.'

Rudi lifted his head. 'Fifteen guineas you say, Dora?'

'That's right.'

'Fine. You can agree to pay her—'

'What?'

'Less expenses of course. Shall we say five guineas church photography fee; coffee, tea, and poached eggs on toast was it? etc. one guinea; rest and toilet facilities one guinea; admission to stand for entertainment two guineas; supper five guineas.'

'The supper tickets only cost five bob.'

'To residents, not to intrusive ladies in pink. That comes to fourteen guineas. A guinea contribution to scouts' funds then, for porterage and mental cruelty, i.e. Scout Humphrey who, poor lad, has lost his vocation as a gangster and become uncomfortably aware of the opposite sex. Total, fifteen guineas. The Golightly could argue, but I bet she won't. Too expensive.'

'Rudi, you genius.'

'Not at all,' he said modestly. 'It's a waste of time applying to geniuses in matters of this kind. Look for the rogue.'

Chapter Fourteen

The solid spectre of Abigail Golightly continued to brood over Underhallow. Humphrey's scouting enthusiasm waned. He laid aside the precious hat in favour of a dark green beret and took no interest in a rather jolly camp-fire organized to mark the demolishing of the remains of the old scout hut. David and he no longer needed each other. For a while Humphrey was lonely.

Even Ernie deserted him, though unwillingly and only because his mother, suspecting bad influences, kept him in. His place did not stay vacant for long. A small skinny girl of determined character began to dog Humphrey's footsteps. I admired her efforts to attract and keep his attention by swinging over railings and doing cartwheels one after another across the green.

When Gloria Hopkins called to deliver a leaflet she brought me down from the attic where I had been having another stab at the life of Shakespeare. Tutting over the maiden's exposure of her chaste navy-blue school knickers, she said, 'Surely she's old enough at ten to learn a bit of modesty. I told her mother so but it's no use trying to help some people. She called me a name and said I've got a dirty mind. Me! I ask you.'

'Never mind, Gloria. At that age they're still children and they're used to doing gym at school together in shorts.'

'Will you be coming to the lecture? We need to know because of the teas.'

I read the leaflet. A talk by Dr Lynette Smythe on 'The Vexed Question Of Bowels'. Somehow the conjunction of bowels and Gloria was particularly unappealing. 'I don't think so thanks. We're busy with my sister's wedding.'

'And I suppose David's got other fish to fry, in and out of Josie Knapp's cottage? A nice thing, I must say, with Ivan not cold in his grave.'

I studied the mean waves of her tightly permed hair, the pallid bolting blue of her eyes. Whatever had once been loving and warm in her could not be discovered in the spiteful discontent of her expression. Charlie's infidelities and defections had so chilled the marrow in her bones that the attention of American admirers failed to thaw it.

'Ivan's as cold as he's ever going to get,' I said irritably, infected with the merest touch of Portia. 'It's more profitable to help the living and not speculate and gossip too much.'

She snatched the leaflet out of my hand. 'If you're not coming I might as well have that back for someone else. Sorry I'm sure if I spoke out of turn. I thought you ought to know what's going on. No offence meant.'

But plenty taken. Gloria inspired rancour. I felt ill-wished and inclined to point out that poor old mad creatures were once hanged on Hags' Gibbet for lesser malice than hers. I closed the door, just managing not to slam it, and went back upstairs.

The Bard had lost the little attraction he had for me and I seemed to be stuck halfway through Chapter Two. Closing the book, I tidied away my pens and straightened the blotting-pad, detaching an envelope from one corner. Thick, white and crested – heaven preserve me, Portia's wedding-present list! When had it arrived? Certainly in August, not long after Ivan's funeral. I had forgotten to send it to Grandmother and today was the 10th of September, nineteen days until the wedding. Hardly time for anything.

Come to think of it, I had made no enquiries of Claudia or Valentine concerning the whereabouts of the wretched parure of diamonds. Briefly I considered Portia's annoyance. Should I perhaps make a real effort to please her by some useful act? I couldn't immediately think of one. The prospect of explaining to my grandmother the absence of the list more nearly occupied my mind. She would not appreciate one bit a lame letter of explanation. I should have to take the list to her and apologize enough to satisfy her of my true penitence.

So when the next day Rudi asked me if I would go to London with him, I accepted like a shot. He wanted me to see the work that Mr Fox had done at the house and also to collect his altered morning-suit from the tailor. My bridesmaid's dress hung in a spare bedroom wardrobe, waiting for a final trying-on. Once I had disposed of Portia's accursed list I was ready.

I called on Grandmother first. In my childhood she frightened me and although I had come to understand and appreciate her real kindness and quality I still regarded her with wary respect. I began my apology, she cut me short. 'Never mind, child, I guessed you had forgotten and hoped you would go on forgetting. Whatever the opinion in Portia's circles, I feel it an unpardonable rudeness to solicit for presents and I refuse to do so.' She glanced at the neat list. 'Are you really giving that?'

'Of course not. Claudia would kill me.'

She warmed to me at once. 'You're a good child, Amy. I should very much like to see you married as well, instead of dancing attendance on Portia. Are there any suitors in the offing?'

'Wouldn't you be awfully startled if there were?'

'Why should I be?'

'Compared with Claudia and Portia I'm not much to look at. Old maid material, I thought.'

'If I've given the impression that you're not valued you must forgive me. Claudia has caused me so much anxiety over the years. You have no plans then?'

'Wait and see, Grandmother.'

She assumed her Queen Mary expression. 'Ah, I'm to be punished.'

'Of course not. Claudia has turned my life upside down, too, and I shall have to face Portia's rage when the expected useful objects fail to materialize at the wedding. Romance must take a back seat until I can get my breath.'

An elderly maid pushed in an elderly high-wheeled trolley bearing coffee and rugged-looking biscuits that turned out to be rather good, virtually fatless but made with golden syrup instead of sugar. My grandmother had the air of a sibyl, pregnant with news. She remained silent until the coffee had been poured and the maid had departed then said, 'We may both safely ignore the list. Portia has suffered a blow.'

Grandmother understood the drives that created Portia, the Duchess; the sense of betrayal when Father remarried, her fear as family life crumbled, the need for security that could only be assuaged by position and reinforced by the strength of stone castle walls. Consequently she tried always to be patient.

'Nothing serious surely?'

'That depends upon your point of view.' I believe that she was tempted to laugh. 'Her butler has unexpectedly given notice. Worse, he announced simultaneously his engagement to that old variety turn, Lady Polkinhorn. They propose to marry by special licence almost immediately.'

'Singlet and Lettie? That's wonderful. They've known each other an age and they'll have a great life together.'

'While it lasts,' said Grandmother. 'Singlet's constitution will be tested to the full. The woman's incapable of repose. And Portia doesn't consider it wonderful at all.'

I could imagine that after serving for many years at Hindlecote Castle, Singlet, with his secret passions, had taken his fill of repose and looked forward to some action. 'Tiresome for her to lose an excellent butler, of course.'

'Also what your sister describes as a shocking dilemma. Lettie Polkinhorn is still a connection, and a wealthy one, capable alive or dead of heaping riches on the boy. A husband is liable to scotch those hopes. And Portia is suffering agonies at the prospect of perhaps being required to sit at table with her own ex-butler. An interesting problem. She seems in some way to blame Claudia.'

'You *are* laughing,' I said, 'I thought you were.'

'Yet I feel genuinely sorry for Portia. A happy woman would not concern herself so deeply over trifles.'

At Great James Street I found Mr Fox in expansive mood talking to Rudi while mixing paint in a row of buckets. At first acquaintance the keenest observer would have struggled to detect the artist beneath the bulging, unkempt exterior. Unbeautiful himself, he was passionate for beauty. The crude Garden of Eden had gone from the wall. Pale matt colour of a miraculous delicacy replaced it, providing landscapes and pearly translucent distances.

'D'you know what it is?' he asked.

Being barely educated, I sometimes perpetrated dreadful howlers in an attempt to appear highbrow, but in the figures, the birds and the flowers before me I found a piece of Shakespeare that I did know thoroughly. In my schoolroom days Sonia had made

me learn by heart the song from *Love's Labour's Lost*.
Mr Fox had chosen to illustrate it.

'It's amazing,' I said.

'That great dick – er doodah, pardon me, miss, took
some covering. I had to knock half the rendering off.
His mum ought to have taught him not to draw rude
pictures on walls. It's all right for you then?'

'All right? It's absolutely gorgeous!'

Spring with its piping youths and flowers, its
cuckoos and maidens, merged imperceptibly into
winter. Dick (Doo-dah?) the shepherd, blew on his
cold hands, Marian worked her way through a pile of
crab-apples and Joan scoured greasily away at her pots
and pans.

Mr Fox tried out a muted green paint on a piece of
plaster-board, then wiped his hands with rag. Tufts
of hair poked through the holes in his vest and he wore
a cigar-butt like a trophy behind his right ear. The
under-brim of his pearl-grey trilby sported a burnt
patch. But I threw my arms round him and hugged
him. 'Mr Fox, you're a perfectly lovely man and
brilliant.'

He went red and sweated heavily. 'That's nice, miss.
Call me Cyril.'

Walking later down Brewer Street on the way to collect
Rudi's suit, we saw in the middle distance the portly
form of Portia's husband. He looked both ways, shot
into a doorway and disappeared.

'That's Coritanum,' I said. 'What can he be doing
here? Claudia swore she saw him in London, but
Portia told us that he's at the Nuremberg trials.'

We took a close look at the house. Not precisely a
desirable residence. In front lay a small cobbled
courtyard littered with rubbish. A smell of savoury
cooking, dead cabbage leaves and urine hung about it.
Over the basement door a notice read, 'Cracker Club.

Members Only.' There were no names beside the doorbells, only the number of rings for each floor.

Rudi, who wore an irritating, all-boys-together smile, said, 'Better not mention this to your sister.'

'I certainly won't. I'm not an absolute fool, and please take that leer off your face. Men are the absolute limit.'

'Sorry, Amy. How I hate it when you group me with "men". I couldn't help admiring the sheer magnitude of the ducal lie, but I swear never to do so again. Let's have tea at the Ritz.'

'I'd rather go to Fortnum's.'

'You're cross with me.'

'No I'm not.'

'The Ritz, then.'

'Fortnum's.'

'Are we having our first quarrel?'

'I'm quarrelling with the messy way men behave and their horrid unctuousness if women stray an inch. We'll go to Fortnum's.'

'Righto, Amy,' Rudi said meekly, 'Fortnum's it is.'

The serene self-possession with which David organized his next actions excluded any need to advise him. His uncertainties gone, he turned the full force of his considerable power of concentration upon Josie Knapp. Without explanation and only the scantest of apologies, he more or less moved into her cottage. Neither Rudi nor I commented on his absence. I had absolutely and finally done with interfering for the rest of my life.

For practical reasons I wished I dared ask David how long he was to remain immured. At other times it wouldn't have made a pinch of difference, but Claudia's wedding day loomed ever closer and she had grabbed him to be an usher. As the only bridesmaid, responsibility weighed heavily upon me. Claudia, who seemed to know less about the event than anyone, said vaguely that there might be a couple of matrons-of-honour, but she wasn't sure.

Portia telephoned again. She kept the humiliation of Singlet and Lettie Polkinhorn to herself, and made no enquiry about the wretched list or the diamonds. Bafflingly indirect as she was, I grasped far too late that she had expected Claudia to ask her son to be a page. 'I had four pages. How quaint and modern for her to have none, not even her only nephew.'

When I passed the intelligence on to Claudia I got the expected reaction. 'The bloody cheek of that woman! She scorned us with a dreadful scorning. All her attendants were Coritanum's lot, and one of the pages sicked up over the ducal shoes right in front of the altar.'

'You oughtn't to have laughed so loudly,' I said. 'Portia was utterly mortified.'

'Good. Generally children are a complete mistake, but I quite took to that boy. Later he scoffed three-quarters of a sherry trifle without drawing breath. True it was small and abysmally low on sherry, but it showed a proper spirit. It's encouraging when the young know precisely how to behave.'

After the years of self-imposed silences she had become extraordinarily talkative. She rang up and chatted for ages being, as she put it, bored to fragments by arrangements. Dress fittings and rehearsals struck her as quite futile. ('Doesn't one always end up with a shambles and everyone at daggers drawn?')

Mr Moot, once the Vicar of Gunne Magna, had come out of retirement to perform the ceremony. He muddled her with little Christian homilies. 'Can you believe, Amy, he told me a proverb that says a virtuous woman is a crown to her husband: but she that maketh ashamed is as a rottenness in his bones. Have you ever heard it? He got rather huffy when I said I'd never come across it and that I thought it too bad that it was always women who got nagged about virtue. Men need it much more. As far as I'm concerned a virtuous woman is the ultimate pain in the neck. Think of Sonia – disastrous and a definite rottenness in Father's bones, I should say.'

Pan had offered the use of the Paris apartment and his staff for the honeymoon, but Bill would have none of it. He pointed out that Claudia had used up a good slice of her thirty-five pounds currency allowance. 'We can't possibly do Paris on forty pounds between us. I'll book the honeymoon suite at that hotel in Weymouth where we first met.'

'Imagine, he thinks that's romantic, Amy,' she said, 'and I distinctly remember that he once called me a twit because I didn't know that George somebody invented something, railway engines – or was it electric light bulbs?'

'You put a crab down his shorts. Either he's forgotten how you almost ruined his love-life or he took it as a sign of friendship.'

'But Weymouth! What does one *do* in Weymouth for a whole month? Perhaps it'll rain all the time and we can go on to London. At least it won't matter much about clothes, which is a good thing as I haven't a clothing coupon to my name. Unless there's an immediate miracle I shall have to go in an Army blanket.'

'Pooh, we do a good line in miracles. By the next post I'll send you part of our wedding-present.'

'What have you got me?'

'I'm not telling.'

'Not more useful objects I hope, I've simply mountains of those. Give me a hint.'

'No. Wait and see.'

'Mingy beast.'

'Yes. Goodbye.'

'Don't ring off, I've got loads more to say.'

'Goodbye, Claudia.'

After four days (and nights) David asked Rudi to drive him and Josie to Cambridge. 'She wants to find out whether she can get one of these post-war grants and go back to get her degree.'

Friendship accompanied by sex had worked a miracle. Josie was comforted for Ivan, David had broken free of his shyness and restraint. They were fitting lovers. I rather hoped that they were not romantically in love.

'A splendid idea,' Rudi said, 'but I can't take you the whole way because of the petrol. We shall need enough to get us to Dorset and back. Suppose I drive you to Liverpool Street. There's a good train service.'

'Fine. Then you needn't wait. I don't know quite how long I'll be.' The three of them went off the next morning. Josie took a quantity of luggage, and I guessed that she meant to stay away from Underhallow for a while, perhaps permanently. She had abandoned her widow's weeds, not quite reverting to the seductive gipsy look. Her mass of curls was held back by a black velvet Alice band. In a dark grey tailored suit and high-necked blouse, she could happily pass as a student, and very mature.

'Will you be late?' I whispered to Rudi.

'I doubt it. Come with us if you're not too busy.'

I declined. The last impression I wanted to give to David was that of a guard or chaperone. Instead, Polly and I picked the immense crop of William pears. They always ripen suddenly and together, and provide a lovely feast for the wasps. After lunch I took a full basket across the green to Dora.

'Gripy things, pears,' Mr Slade grumbled. 'Don't you have any greengages? I could just fancy a greengage tart. She gives me nothing but slops and sodding Woolton pie.'

'That's a lie,' Dora said. 'You've just eaten your way through a pound of lamb's liver. And Miss Savernake doesn't want to hear that language, so behave yourself.'

He blew his nose and examined the result with interest. 'Catarrh. You should have done more onions, they're a marvel for catarrh. I heard up at the pub that the Bishop's going to kick the Vicar out. Serves him right, shagging that Josie girl in the vestry, though I shouldn't be surprised if he thought it was worth it.'

'He did no such thing, you nasty, vulgar old toad!' Dora yelled in his ear. Her creamy skin turned pink. 'Sorry, Amy. He's common as dirt, like all the Slades.'

'Didn't stop you from marrying my boy, did it?'

'If I'd known you were going to outlive him I'd have thought twice.'

'Is the Bishop really going to move Bertie? It hardly seems fair. Josie made a dead set at him, and he's already been reprimanded.'

'I don't know for sure, but I think Mrs Golightly's been stirring things up for him, and I'm sure Gloria Hopkins complained.'

'Wishes it was herself, does Gloria Hopkins. Sex-starved bitch,' said Mr Slade, cackling.

'Shut up, Father. Bertie isn't taking it too well. He's hung placards on the church railings, and there's a petition going around.'

An idea for wishing Abigail Golightly back on to Portia came into my head. I rejected it with a good deal of regret. No interference. Collecting another smaller basket of pears, I took them round to the vicarage. At the church, notices announced BISHOP UNFAIR TO UNDERHALLOW; CHRIST FORGIVES SINS, BISHOPS DON'T; GUILTY UNTIL PROVED INNOCENT; SAY NO TO INJUSTICE; PLEASE SIGN PETITION IN CHURCH PORCH.

Bertie received my proffered gift with enthusiasm. 'Lord knows what happens to the rations. Nothing but spam! Hebrews thirteen, eight, to borrow a text from a theatre review.'

'Do you honestly think the notices are a good idea, Bertie? They're rather pointed.'

He draped his long frame limply across two armchairs. 'Meant to be, Amy. The Bishop and I are at loggerheads, and for nothing worse than a couple of kisses more or less forced on me. Not that I didn't respond enthusiastically, but I had no idea of letting things go further.'

'I rather think Josie had. She fancied you tremendously.'

'She did, didn't she?' he said happily. 'The dog-collar helps of course. I was glad of poor Ivan. He could always be relied on to stand between me and paradise with an invisible flaming sword.'

'Supposing the petition doesn't work?'

'Hmm, I could try sitting naked in a barrel outside the Bishop's Palace, though I don't actually have one. It's been done before, not with success. Perhaps a cardboard box. Your father doesn't happen to be in with the Lords Spiritual, does he?'

I explained that he now attended the House only for matters of the gravest importance because of his health. 'He usually manages to argue with bishops, but I'll ask him.'

Bertie bit savagely into a pear, and mopped the juice from his chin with a grubby handkerchief. 'Delicious! Do that, my dear girl, please do. I'm threatened with going to the Midlands as assistant priest, locum and perennial dogsbody. Can't be trusted, it seems.'

The parish liked Bertie, but it was a matter for wonder that he had ever managed to become a priest at all. Sitting naked in a cardboard box was unlikely to help his cause in the slightest, rather the reverse. I hoped he wouldn't bother. 'You haven't thought of marriage I suppose?'

'Many times, many many times, but good women do expect rather a lot in the way of piety and renouncing the sins of the flesh. Anything in the slightest degree pleasant comes under that heading you know.'

'Even dancing?'

'Especially dancing, yet there's quite a lot of it in the Old Testament. Miss Right must exist, but she tarries. Pity you're so besotted with Rudi, you're a splendid dancer and uncensorious. Very suitable. I suppose you *are* besotted? I couldn't persuade you to change your mind?'

I grinned nervously. Bertie had a predatory look in his eye and we were alone. The sprawling parsonage had been built a couple of centuries earlier for eighteenth-century vicars in their procreative prime. It was eerily silent. 'Is that an offer?'

'Testing the temperature of the water. I'm terribly ready, how about you?'

'Stone cold, sorry, Bertie. Have another pear. I'd better go.'

'Unsettling woman, go if you must.'

No man had called me unsettling before or made impulsive proposals. I felt tremendously bucked up. It was something to tell Claudia if she made fun of my feeble and unambitious love-life. When I got home I remembered the spam and the theatre critic and looked up Hebrews thirteen, eight. It read, 'Jesus Christ the same yesterday, and to day, and for ever.' Oh Bertie!

Rudi arrived home quite early. 'London's a bore without you. David told me to tell you that he'll be back tomorrow and could he ask you to make sure he has a new shirt for the wedding.'

'If Claudia wants us at Gunville Place two days before I suppose I'd better begin getting us packed.'

We wandered upstairs and I tried on my brides-maid's dress so that Rudi could tell me whether the hem drooped or not. I wasn't entirely sure about it. Gwennie had found the material when she was clearing out the sewing-room at Gunville Place, silk brocade in ivory and gold. I imagine it had been intended originally for curtains.

'Bertie Gooch almost proposed to me today,' I said indistinctly as I pulled it off over my head, 'imagine!'

Rudi looked reproachful. 'I don't care a bit to imagine things like that. Have you been leading him on?'

'I don't fancy him in the least. I only took him some pears to find out whether he's being sacked. Are you jealous?'

'Blind with it. Tempting a man with fruit was what got Eve into the serpent's toils.'

'That was apples. I'm sure pears don't count. He said I'm an unsettling woman, which made me feel quite anxious for my virtue.'

'If you continue to stand there in those revealing cami-knickers you'll find your virtue tested to its utmost.'

'Will resistance be useless?'

'Completely.'

'Then I shan't bother. No sacrifice is too great for you, my darling love.'

'I like your bridesmaid's dress very much,' Rudi said later.

'Do you? I *am* pleased. You don't mind that I'm not a golden princess like Claudia and Portia? More of a Rumpelstiltskin in skirts.'

'An absolute slander. I recognize that your sisters are classic beauties, but there's something chilling in their perfection that's positively the death of lust.' Rudi smiled gently. 'You're a pocket Venus, neat, warm and adorable. That exhausts my range of compliments for today. I hope you love me.'

'Oceans,' I said, feeling that in spite of the miseries of

rationing and shortages, life was quite rich and wonderful.

He took my hand. 'What we need is a child or two of our own to worry about.'

'Must we? Why does everyone want me to have children when I've scarcely had time to be alone with you yet? You might wait until we're officially engaged.'

'Sorry, I'm impatient to marry you. Can it be quick?'

'Not too quick and not a miserable Registry Office. Father will want it to be at Gunne Magna as befits a youngest daughter, though I'd rather like Under-hallow. What do you think?'

'Anywhere in heaven or hell as long as I get you,' Rudi said.

I can understand how he used to mow women down like ninepins. Unlike most Englishmen, he concentrates on being a lover and doesn't get shy or uncomfortable about saying romantic things. A small voice in my head told me that I must keep him concentrated. I decided the thought was unworthy but worth bearing in mind.

Chapter Fifteen

There had not been a wedding from Gunville Place
since Father married Sonia, almost twenty years ago.
On that day we children, clinging to our grudges and
the memory of our dead mother, refused to be
bridesmaids and did our best to make the occasion
miserable. Forlorn and bewildered then, now for
Claudia I twitched with nervous anticipation.

Every tragedy that had ever befallen a bride rattled
through my brain. The imprudent game of hide-and-
seek in *The Mistletoe Bough*; Jane Eyre snatched
rudely from the arms of Rochester at the eleventh hour;
Smilin' Through, and Norma Shearer (did she or did
she not have a squint?) getting shot stone dead at the
altar.

And poor Lucy of Lammermoor hadn't managed to
last out the wedding night before becoming insanely
dangerous with the knives. At that point in my
musings I pulled myself firmly together. A French
prison held Dieter Huppner, the one stumbling-block,
if he were still alive. The main danger to living happily
ever after was Claudia herself. And if she dared to
louse things up now, I should feel tempted to take a
knife to her myself!

It took us ages to load up the car for Dorset. Rudi
patiently stacked away dress and hat boxes, cases and
wedding presents. 'Righto, everything's in,' he said.
'Amy, I feel unsure about our present to Claudia. Can
her heart's desire really be a large fish-kettle with
detachable perforated serving-dish?'

'Of course not; what on earth would she do with it? She isn't a bit keen on fish. We're not giving her that at all.'

'But my dearest girl, I saw you initial it and cross it off a list.'

'The list was Portia's, I told you that. Her world is divided into duchesses and dependants. I don't think she's noticed yet that we're in danger of sliding downhill towards shabby-genteel. Why show off? I simply chose the most hideously useless object and got rid of it in case someone else thought it would make the perfect gift.'

'No wonder I adore you. What, then, are we giving?'

Immediately I became racked with guilt because I had deliberately not confessed my extravagance, feeling that no man could be expected to understand. I said, 'First of all, what every girl in her right mind would want, half a dozen stunning silk nighties that David smuggled from America. And I did mean to give them both some Royal Worcester. But the perfect stuff is export only and it seemed miserable to buy seconds.'

'So what did we do?'

'It's rather odd, but the only value-for-money things worth having are jewels. So many in stock since before the War.' Rudi raised his eyebrows and I floundered apologetically. 'A simply gorgeous necklace, I do hope you don't mind. Claudia's going to love it. It was such a bargain and you gave me lots of money. The pendant's a square emerald set in diamonds. You don't think green's unlucky, do you?'

'Not when it's an emerald,' Rudi said with a thoughtful air. 'Anything else?'

'Only onyx cufflinks for William and some silver spoons that belonged to Great-aunt Hildegarde, the ones we never use with faces on the bowls. Claudia's always coveted them. Oh, and we sent her a hundred clothing coupons in advance for her trousseau. Clever?'

'How generous and criminal we are! I dare not ask what you sacrificed for the coupons.'

'Only the pride of the Savernakes. The landlady at that beer-house outside Rogate, the one with the thrusting bosom and raucous laugh, can get anything at all on the Black Market for a price. One runs the gauntlet of leering men.'

'Amy, you really mustn't. Those places are dangerous. Some of the customers do more than leer. You might well be attacked. Promise me not to go there again, at least not alone.'

I hated him to be worried, but at least his mind was diverted from the frivolity of emeralds which, come to think of it, were a wonderful investment. Having no further need of illicit goods, I promised gladly. 'Not to worry, please, my darling. Great-aunt Hildegarde taught me how to defend myself, and I'm not precisely sizzling with allure for passing sex-maniacs.'

David laughed. He said to Rudi, 'She doesn't know a thing about men, does she?'

'Is one of you proposing to drive, or are you leaving it to me?' I enquired with all the hauteur at my command. 'One thing I do know about men is that they're impossibly overbearing.'

September had made up its mind to go out in a burst of glory. On that fine fair morning we crossed from Hampshire into Dorset over Bokerley Dyke. A solitary kestrel trod on air in the vast singing blue distances above the downs. Tucked under green tumps the ancient unknown dead slept and dreamed for ever in the prehistoric cemetery field.

We drove first to Lulworth, where David was to stay for several months. Before we left Rudi asked to speak to Father privately. I knew what that meant. In a thoroughly polite, old-fashioned theatrical way he was asking for my hand in marriage and a father's blessing.

'I feel rather silly,' I said to Gwennie. 'I'm twenty-seven for goodness sake, and Father does know about us.'

'Not shy, is it?' She glanced at me with some diffidence. 'Gervase is old-fashioned enough to like formality. I've always worried about the way you were left to make what you could of life, and I'm pleased it's come out like this. Old fool aren't I? Rudi's not young, though. Have children quickly or you'll miss the boat like I did.'

'Just because I love who I love, people think I'm loaded down with frustrated maternal instinct,' I said in a slight huff. 'It isn't so. I don't think I'll care too much if I don't have children.'

'And what about him then?' She stretched out a hand to David. 'A man needs sons. You can't think how happy Gervase is to have his boy home with us.'

I nodded, fearing that Davy would reject this sentimental claim upon him. He smiled with great sweetness, took Gwennie's hand and kissed it. The smile and the gesture were Pan Metkin's.

At Gunne Magna I confided Rudi to the care of the landlady at the Running Stag and drove on alone to Gunville Place. I did not want us to be nagged and harried into revealing our secret too soon.

For elegance and comfort my ancestral home scored no points at all. From the outside it looked like a slum with mattresses, bolsters and blankets draped over window-sills to air. Below the terrace, a marquee completed the ruin of what had once been a lawned garden. Most of the smaller trees in the park had been hacked down and used for firewood by the poor freezing evacuees. But the hall, at least, looked festive. Between them, Gwennie and a small army conscripted mainly from the Bowells family, who were Father's best tenants, had worked wonders.

Claudia was in a foul mood. She rarely accepted invitations herself and she had expected most of those invited to refuse. 'Dismal fiends, why must they come? One forgets how they adore to get together and swill and swig and hate each other.'

'But it's a wedding, they're bound to come for a wedding,' I said. 'Poor things, for years it's been nothing but funerals and tears and broken-hearted mothers. So terribly, terribly sad, but they turned out in force just the same and showed sympathy.'

'Stop babbling, ass.'

I felt myself begin to fade as I always seemed to in that vast, unloveable house, but then Valentine came and swept me up in a bear-hug and kissed me. 'I couldn't be more pleased to see you,' he said. 'The invasion starts at dawn tomorrow, so we'll all get our strength up tonight.'

'Errgh,' Claudia said. We turned and inspected her. She lay collapsed on a window-seat, looking boneless. 'What are you two staring at? They're all about a hundred years old and full of boundless energy, and they'll want the band to go on playing all night. If I don't get my sleep you'll have to push me to the altar in a wheelchair.'

'Lazy dog, you're to be charming and make sure that you speak nicely to every single one of them.'

Claudia rolled her eyes to the ceiling. 'No escape. Poor, poor me.'

'She's such a misery,' Val said. 'I'm surprised that any man has the courage to marry her.'

The next morning I awoke late in the turret bedroom that had once been mine. The swathes of pink-and-white muslin chosen by Sonia to hide the Victorian-mediaeval rough-cast walls had been removed when the evacuees arrived and not replaced. Something to be very, very thankful for. It used to have the air of an outstandingly ugly woman inadequately veiled. Now it was just plain ugly. Someone had scratched an unnoticed obscenity low down on the wall beside the bed. Two of the dismal slits of windows were cracked. Someone else, Gwennie I supposed, had redeemed it a little with a huge bowl of roses in the dimmest recess and a few inoffensive water-colours, hung where they could be seen from the bed.

From the noise I guessed that the early birds had begun to arrive. Feet stamped and shuffled, voices loudly squabbled for the best rooms. Best meant nearest to the bathrooms, only one to each floor. In the morning an impatient, grumbling queue would form. The cousins, aunts, uncles, were not a bit inhibited about telling each other to get a move on in there, they didn't have all day, and the corridors rang to the noisy flushing of water and a cry of, 'Lavatory's free.'

My door suddenly shot open. Claudia came in, slammed it behind her and leaned against it panting like a hunted hare. 'Heaven help us, how they've bred,' she said. 'All those snotty cousins from Bury St Edmunds and Norwich and King's Lynn, they've grown up and brought forth young. Dozens of them, and only two nannies between the lot. Why wasn't I warned? Why are you still in bed? Get dressed.'

'A bath and breakfast first.'

'Not up here, madwoman, you'll be trampled to death by mothers with baby-baths and nappy buckets.' She threw me my dressing-gown. 'Grab your clothes. You can use the servants' bathroom and have breakfast with Val and me in the kitchen. The Bowellses are in charge and there's home-cured bacon and brown eggs. Don't hang about, we've got the final rehearsal at eleven.'

Sammy Bowells boomed a welcome, ('You all right

then, my dear?') and Gladys, his wife, gave me a kiss and said, 'Water's hot, Miss Amy. My, don't you look well?'

Around each of the upstairs baths, even the pretty blue-and-white flowered ones, a thick black line had been painted to mark the wartime ration of five inches of hot water. No such squalid disfigurements for the servants. They must have wallowed unpatriotically to their chins until, one by one, they had been called up to share the common discomforts.

I hadn't time to wallow. Claudia didn't trust me to hurry. She sat on the wide mahogany lavatory seat and groused steadily about her guests. When I mentioned mildly that she had an obligation to them, she said that Grandmother and Gwennie had appointed themselves hostesses so it was nothing to do with her. She had more nerves than a cat in a gale.

'It's going to be lovely, you'll see,' I said firmly. Then, with something not far removed from horror, I thought that the sooner I got away from Gunville Place the better. Claudia and I had already begun taking up our childhood roles. Where was our sophistication that she felt obliged to be surly and I to soothe?

The day became one long informal party. The way that Grandmother organized the occasion impressed me. She was another who missed the War, or rather the activity and interest of serving a cause and being on jolly terms with people whose paths could never in the ordinary way of things have crossed hers. The bombing of London revived her taste for drama. Air-raid wardens and firefighters congregated in her basement to drink gallons of tea and chomp their way through hard buns. The flaw in her pleasure was anxiety for Grandfather. He refused to give up his clubs and she fretted dreadfully when he was not within her sight or hearing.

She had arranged for the far-flung guests (whose

natural instincts so horrified Claudia) to travel from remote outposts in Norfolk and Suffolk by train and taxi to London hotels. From there a small procession of motor-coaches carried them onwards to Dorset. Arguments she settled summarily. Her massive physical presence and uncompromising manner silenced all opposition.

She had always worried about Claudia. An unhappy match had at one time seemed only too probable. Grandmother married for love, and she showed a fine disregard for rank and fortune quite uncommon in the rich. Bill's tenacious devotion satisfied her. She divined that Claudia's chaotic oddity of temperament had found the solid rock on which it could rest.

'You are happy about Claudia, aren't you, Grand-mother?' I asked.

She regarded me in her usual dour manner and remarked that the Savernakes had produced many a hell-cat, monuments to greed and sensuality. 'I thank God that Claudia has inherited enough of my nature to counterbalance that undesirable blood-line.'

'I shan't develop into a hell-cat I hope.'

The remark was a sort of joke but she did not always understand jokes very well. Perhaps I sounded anxious. 'You're a Mottesfont, Amity. No need to worry about you. The women rarely diverged from the accepted path. Many died spinsters. Those who married compensated by breeding quantities of children and rearing them with a commendable lack of fuss.'

This glum and unexciting analysis explained the unusual number of cousins in various degrees. The Mottesfont women were still breeding away, and the choice offered to me by practically everyone was to follow their example or remain a spinster. Depressing.

The rehearsal (what could be simpler than a country wedding when you come to think about it?) went well.

I had always liked Gunne Magna church. From around the time of the Crusades an effigy in alabaster of an Earl of Osmington had slept beside his wife and seven children, staring blindly up at the cobwebby hammer-beams. Damage to the Earl's nose had opened one stone eye and given him a friendly squint.

'An honour to be asked to officiate,' Mr Moot said, one big happy beam. 'It seems no time at all since you were both little girls coming to the rectory for your lessons.'

'How is Mrs Moot? She isn't with you?'

Some of the joy went out of his smile. 'Very well, indeed. Today she's in Bristol, giving a lecture on Merlin and the role of sorcery in Arthurian legend, but she expects to be here tomorrow.'

'Up to her old tricks,' Claudia muttered in my ear.

The antiquity-loving Rachel Moot had once come a bit of a cropper in her pursuit of pagan Dorset. She didn't seem to be as cured as she ought to be. It was sad for Mr Moot, who probably would have preferred to spend his retirement making tours of the Holy Land or discussing liturgical details with other priests.

'Wasn't Arthur supposed to be the first Christian king under the guidance of Merlin, Mr Moot?'

'I dare say, Amy, I dare say. In these times it takes all one's faith to believe in God.'

I had no chance to pursue what I hoped was a comforting theme. A railway van pulled up at the churchyard gate and an embarrassed porter unloaded an enormous wicker hamper. Water dripped as he carried it up the path. In a spirit of forgiveness for Claudia's imaginary part in the loss of Singlet to Lettie Polkinhorn, Portia had sent flowers, madonna lilies and early chrysanthemums. ('Do use them to decorate the church.')

We might have known that she would run true to form and expect us to change plans to accommodate her last-minute gift. The flower-arrangers, headed by Gladys Bowells and two of her daughters, looked aghast. They had been working in the church for several hours. Vases overflowed with clove-carnations, rosebuds and feathery asparagus-fern. Tall stands of delphiniums stood on either side of the altar. Annie Bowells paused in the act of fastening trailing smilax to a window-sill and dumped her basket crossly on the top of the step-ladder.

'The damned things smell of funerals,' Claudia said. 'They're enough to frighten anyone into the grave. Why must the stupid woman interfere all the time? I'm getting married, not buried.'

'We'd better use un,' Gladys Bowells said with lack of enthusiasm. 'Her Grace'll be offended if us don't.'

'Get them out of here, put them on the compost-heap.'

'If you say so, Miss Claudia, but I 'ope we don't get blamed.'

Portia would be bound to follow the fate of every last leaf. I intervened. 'Don't worry, Gladys, take them up to the house and put them on a landing somewhere. I'll tell her that they arrived too late for the church.'

Gladys Bowells brightened and became coy. 'Just think, Miss Claudia, the next time you walk out of here it'll be as a married lady.'

'I am thinking,' she said morosely. 'If I'd known I had to go through all this I wouldn't have bothered.'

That evening the ballroom was closed to us. Valentine had thrown open Father's empty rooms and the French windows on to the terrace. The deafening jabber created the authentic and unmistakable sound of an English party. Feeling that I fed on honey and wine in my perfect love for Rudi, I viewed my kin with a gentle eye. Gaps had appeared in the family ranks. A Warwickshire uncle had died in the Coventry bombing and two cousins did not return from the beaches of Normandy. On Grandfather's side, the whole of a family of six, excluding the baby who miraculously survived, was wiped out by a V2 rocket in a leafy Kent suburb. Those with us showed more concern and fractionally less selfishness.

Claudia and I stood talking to Bill. At least, I talked. Claudia wore a glum, abstracted air and would not be drawn on the subject of the wedding and the honeymoon. Then without warning one of those weird silences occurred when an angel is supposed to be passing overhead. Two people appeared at the far end of the terrace. One of them was Pan, the other a tall, thin woman with a fly-away head of brown hair and horn-rimmed spectacles.

Claudia flung aside Bill's detaining hand and covered the small distance in a couple of strides. 'Pippa!'

The chattering groups glanced curiously then returned to their conversations. Pan turned away. The school friends came together in a laughing, weeping embrace. 'Bless my soul,' Pippa said, 'I'm drenching your shoulder.' She held Claudia awkwardly with her left arm and I noticed then that where the right should have been there was an empty sleeve.

I moved closer to Bill. The vile reality of torture hit me with sickening force, and my own smug flesh crawled with the dread of it. After a spate of questions and explanations, I heard the name of Dieter.

'You're certain he's dead?' said Claudia, speaking low.

'Five days ago. No appeal allowed.'

'I want to know everything. Come on.' Without so much as glancing back at us she ran down the steps towing Pippa behind her. After a few minutes Val's red sports car shot out of the stableyard and spluttered and banged its way down the drive. The bride had gone.

Bill became awfully quiet. 'It occurs to me,' he said suddenly, 'that I have never received a welcome like that.'

'You're not imagining—'

'Of course not, don't be an ass, Amy. She hasn't that much complication.' He lit a cigarette and drew on it so fiercely that little sparks flew. The life and humour went out of him.

'I expect she's taken Pippa to see the house. You could go over.'

Bill received the idea coldly. 'In view of the eagerness with which Claudia left us I really don't care to. I've tried extraordinarily hard, but I find I've had enough. All along I've been so damned sure she loved me. Over-confident. She gives nothing. Perhaps there's nothing to give – to me at any rate.'

It was futile to protest that she loved him, though I knew she did, or had done until Dieter Huppner turned up in Southampton. 'She's been bothered over something important that she needed to talk about. You wouldn't let her, you just shut her up.'

'A case of pure funk, Amy. I didn't want there to be any source of recrimination between us, the kind of thing inclined to crop up in anger. Was I wrong?' He frowned. 'Yes, I can see you think I was.'

Time passed very slowly. The car returned. Claudia wandered back to us alone with a defiant air. She and Bill looked steadily at each other. She smiled slightly. 'I haven't seen her for a long time.'

'It's not too late,' Bill said. 'All it needs is a simple announcement that the marriage won't take place.'

'Yes.'

'Well then?'

Claudia looked lost, as though the language of lovers were foreign to her, as maybe it always had been. The shrieks had become deafening. A Mottesfont infant dragging a blanket toddled onto the terrace and howled for his mother. 'Can we go somewhere out of the noise, please? I seem to feel rather tired.'

He nodded. They moved away. They did not touch each other. I followed them into the house. Bill opened a door and stood aside. 'In here please.'

The room chanced to be Sonia's former boudoir. The sofa that had been such a boon to her lovers was still there beneath a dust-sheet. Claudia, her shoulders hunched against reproaches, walked inside. The door shut firmly behind them. For a while I lingered, waiting, but I had no business there. I couldn't help them.

The old, bitter loneliness of the house began to swamp me. In this place love seemed a pretty hopeless emotion, bringing more misery than happiness and separating rather than uniting. I badly wanted to go home. Instead I went to my bed, cold without Rudi's warm presence.

For a while I slept, then awoke. I looked at the clock: ten past three. The darkness was not absolute. From my window I saw the harvest moon rolling down the slope of Bulbarrow Hill. I got up and crept along to Claudia's room. The light was on. I peeped in, but the bed had not been disturbed and the room was empty. Panic seized me. Flying downstairs on bare, silent feet I found that every trace of the evening's conviviality had already been cleared away.

Cursing the thickness of the panelling, I leaned an ear against the boudoir door and listened, hearing at first only my own heart-beats and noisy breath. From inside the room I detected the faintest stirring sound. Cautiously I turned the handle, opened the door a crack and looked in. By the dim light of a pink-shaded lamp I saw, on Sonia's big sofa, Claudia lying against Bill's shoulder. Her fair hair was spread out in a fan over the arm that held her. They both still wore their evening clothes and they were both fast asleep.

Stealthily I closed the door and retreated. Hope sprang up again. At least they were sleeping, not fighting. I noticed that I felt cold. Summer had ended and the nights were becoming frosty. I dragged back to bed and lay, half-drugged by the scent of the roses, counting the hours by the chime of the hall clock.

Some time after five a motor-car started up and rolled away. Bill returning to his hotel? Soft footsteps passed my door. Were we in for a fiasco or a wedding? I drifted on the fringe of sleep, half imagining, half dreaming of relatives cheated of a party, taking back their wedding gifts and departing in high dudgeon. For the last time I started awake to explain to them that none of this was my fault. Then I fell into a deep pit of comfortable oblivion.

Chapter Sixteen

After what seemed to be about ten minutes a hand shook my shoulder. 'Wake up, Miss Amy, and get your breakfast before it goes cold,' Annie Bowells said.

'A tray? Lovely,' I mumbled.

'Just for the family. We can't do it for they lot, too short-handed, and not one of un's thought to bring a ration book. You've got the last of the bacon.'

Cautiously I asked, 'How's the bride this morning?'

'Kittle-cattle.'

'She's awake then?'

'Went off like a sky-rocket. Wanting to bother her poor old Nan and Granddad, which I wouldn't let her, and the language! Then on the telephone. And up in the attics, if you please, looking for gramophone records.'

What interpretation did one put on these assorted activities? Wedding on or wedding off? 'I'll go along and see her when I've finished this.'

'Get your bath first. Here's the key. I locked up in case the guests got in before you. D'you want maiding?'

'No thanks, Annie.'

A queue had formed by the time I emerged from the bathroom. 'You take your time!' snapped a strange matron with a whiskery chin, presumably a connection in some degree, 'we all have a wedding to go to you know.'

On such a day I declined to apologize. 'I'm the bridesmaid.'

221

'Oh are you? We could all say that.'

'Hardly.'

I beat a hasty retreat before I managed to embroil myself in one of the endless wrangles so essential to our family life. The house echoed with the noise of children, from the three babies howling away in the old nurseries to a toddler demanding over and over again, 'Why not, Mummy? Why can't I, Mummy?' The sound of a sharp slap ended the irritating litany. 'Didn't hurt,' the child said tearfully.

The source of an unnerving and persistent howling proved more difficult to determine. We harboured no totally unhinged relatives as far as I knew, though in some instances they stretched the bounds of normality. The sound had rhythm of a sort. I stalked it down the corridor and came to Claudia's door.

'Do stand still a minute, Miss Claudia,' Annie implored.

'"This carol they began that hour, with a hey-hey-hey and a ho-ho-ho, and a hey-ya noninonino."' etc. Good heavens, the bride was swinging Shakespeare, and serve him right.

I dressed in my creamy-goldy frock and tucked a clean hankie in the top of a stocking. My hair sprang up nicely at the ends. My shoes had two-inch heels and made me look taller. The effect was not bad at all. I took a sniff at my not quite top quality scent (Chanel Number Seven – whoever had heard of it?) the best that post-war Paris could provide. I voted against it. With luck I could pinch a few drops of Claudia's.

Feeling braced for whatever news, good or bad, awaited me, I knocked at her door and went in. 'Where on earth have you been, face-ache?' asked the divinely tall, divinely fair vision in white silk. She tottered to and fro in front of a cheval-glass tilted at an odd angle. 'It won't stay put. Is this poxy veil on straight?'

'Don't say poxy and don't call me face-ache, it's

horrid. I know I look quite nice for once and I won't be put off.'

'A dear little pet name for a dear little sister. Smashing frock.'

The fatigue of my night-watches made me snarly. 'Quite the little sunbeam, aren't we?'

'Sarky beast, shut up will you?' She gave a lovely tremulous smile. All the agonizing had gone for something. Our rude and cursing burden shook with nerves and scowled and sparkled like an April morning. The wedding was definitely on.

In the church porch people came and went. The London contingent appeared by the first train and the Coritanum Rolls Royce drew up at the gate, decanting the Duchess, her son and a nursemaid. Portia's looks shocked me, and I instantly forgave all the tiresome 'phone-calls. Her extreme thinness emphasized her height. In a long grey-green dress and a distressing swathed chiffon toque, she seemed as brittle and breakable as a crack willow branch.

Grandmother (also wearing a toque, but with rather more style) said, 'How are you, Portia, my dear? Let Nanny take the boy. The church is too full for children.'

Portia clutched him defensively to her side until he began to wriggle, but she let him go. Arguing with our grandmother was a pointless exercise. Walking up the path she gradually collected her stately Duchess manner, and we exchanged nods and smiles as strangers do. Davy took charge of her then and led her to her seat. Almost immediately she popped out again. 'What happened to the flowers? Weren't they delivered?'

Those flowers still irritated me. When last seen, they were stuffed into a quartet of enormous Japanese vases outside the doors of the ballroom. Looking into her weary eyes a snappish remark died before it reached my tongue. 'They arrived rather late for the church, Portia, and they're too beautiful just to be seen for an hour. So kind of you to send them. We're reserving them for the reception.'

'The hothouses always do well at Hindlecote,' she said with a touch of her usual complacence.

When Pandel Metkin and Jimmy Raikes arrived David turned his back, pretending not to notice them. They kissed my hand, oh lovely continental courtesy. I controlled an urge to touch Pan's silver-grey curls, wondering about the contents of the letter to Davy that I had not been shown. They slipped unobtrusively into a rear pew.

Bill, with no appearance of urgency, stopped and chatted. 'At the last intelligence shortly after five this morning the bride had decided to turn up. How is she now?'

'On tremendous form, never fear. It is going to be all right, Frog dear, isn't it? You'll be happy?'

'We'll be married, which isn't necessarily the same thing. I would never have guessed about that damned Nazi. A rotten start to any girl's love-life. I'll have my work cut out persuading her that I'm neither censorious nor a cad. My tendency towards faithfulness and the quiet life may, of course, bore her.'

'The War more or less sated our appetites for brainless amusement, don't you think? Excitement wears Claudia out, though she's too pig-headed to admit it. She needs normality. We all do after having to be so supernaturally brave and cheerful for so long.'

'Children, d'you think? I broached the subject.'

'Oh dear, oh dear. You didn't propose them as a cure-all did you?'

'Wrong tactics, I suppose. I mentioned several. She expressed a strong aversion even to one. But she rather liked the idea, I think. She didn't rush away or slap me, in fact she kissed me with stimulating fervour and hardly blinked when I mentioned Weymouth.'

I thought it more probable that she hadn't been listening properly, but I didn't say so. 'Tons of luck, Frog. Go on, your best man's getting fretful.'

'Lord, I'm nervous. Can't wait for the speeches and champagne.'

Everybody was in church and seated when Pippa arrived wearing a blue dress with long loose sleeves. '*Bonjour*, Amy. I am excited beyond reason at suddenly being a matron of honour, and I am a mess. Never will I master lipstick one-handed.'

Diffidently I said, 'You make us proud, you know. Claudia told me about the medals.'

'*Merde alors!* If only they could give me back my man and my arm they could keep their medals! What do we do now?'

'We slowly follow Claudia up the aisle and try not to step on her train.'

David handed her a bouquet which she balanced on her left arm. Old Mrs Bowells had made it in a great hurry that morning and it looked rather as though it might fall to bits at any moment. I arranged a bandeau of flowers on her brown hair.

The summoning bell clanging out above our heads stopped. Time passed. I took a good look around the church. The numbers were about even. So were the potential embarrassments. On the bride's side we had Uncle Henry, and also Grandfather's Cousin Beatrice who had taken to drink in a big way after the death of her husband. She hadn't liked him much. But he died falling downstairs in a Liverpool brothel and, as he was a well-known circuit judge, the considerable scandal upset her. She was reputed to have said on hearing the ill tidings, 'His activities at home would certainly not have killed him, but then I have always distrusted Liverpool.'

225

For the groom, I selected his mother, a dear but a confirmed giggler, and an aunt who was deaf and sensitive about it. Her interest in figures such as the precise weight of the earth and the number of packets of pins sold each year killed any hope of conversation stone dead.

David slid past me. 'She's here.'

We braced ourselves as Mrs Moot at the organ slammed firmly into the Bridal Chorus from Lohengrin. (Claudia had wanted 'In The Mood'!) Father leaned on his sticks, supported by Valentine. Over her shoulder Claudia flashed a grin at me, laid her hand gently on his right arm and the slow procession up the aisle began. We were off at last.

Grandmother held a handkerchief to her eyes. I felt a bit weepy myself as the bride repeated in a quiet, clear voice, 'I, Claudia Louise Imogen, take thee William Alexander to my wedded husband.' A smooth passage so far. Nobody thought of a just cause or impediment, no shots rang out, Claudia showed no signs of incipient madness. The ring was safely on her finger and, oh the relief of it, she had passed into the care of Bill. Light years ago Rudi promised me that I need not worry about Claudia and in the end, after much wearying, he had been right.

While Bill and Claudia knelt at the altar, I heard behind me the voice of Uncle Henry raised in complaint. 'If the Almighty had my rheumatism he wouldn't expect me to keep bobbing up and down all the time. Place smells like a knocking-shop, Phylly, looks a bit like one, too, with all those damned tulip things. I'll be sneezing my head off before nightfall, I shouldn't wonder.'

'Carnations, not tulips. Do be quiet in the prayers, Henry, and stop advertising your familiarity with houses of ill-fame,' Aunt Phyllida hissed. 'It's almost over.'

226

'Good. I need a drink. Can't think why we had to come. Who's that nobby little bridesmaid in the goldy stuff?'

'Amy, of course, now behave.'

'God's teeth, she's changed. Used to be plain as an ironmonger's dog.'

'For the love of heaven, Henry, shut up or I'll leave you!'

'Don't do that, Phylly. I shouldn't care for it one bit.'

'Hush, Henry!'

'Sorry, Phylly.'

Pippa looked baffled. In the front pew on my right, I saw Mrs Deering's shoulders begin to shake. She spluttered and covered it with a cough. The deaf aunt stared at the stained glass window, her lips moving as though she were counting the little panes ready to tell us all how many. We had met once. She supplied me with figures for the rose window in Chartres Cathedral and the number of safety razors manufactured in Britain in 1939. I forgot them quite quickly.

Mr Moot read at tremendous length about duty and love and St Peter and St Paul, but I was willing Mrs Deering not to explode out loud and got no benefit. Claudia's borrowed, or rather loaned, aigrette of diamonds trembled slightly. Little flecks of light bobbed on Mr Moot's cassock. Then she and Bill stood up and Mrs Moot played the opening bars of 'O Perfect Love'. Grandmother sobbed, Mrs Deering dived under the pew and made muffled noises. My eyes got damp again. I find it a seriously affecting hymn.

But almost at once we moved towards the vestry for the signing of the register. Claudia lowered her lashes modestly and muttered in my ear, 'Bloody Henry!' She seemed to want to say more, but the bells pealed out above our heads drowning all hope of further conversation.

Everyone behaved impeccably for the photographs,

except for Uncle Henry who tried to tell the deaf aunt that at his age he didn't want some mountebank with a camera pointing a lens at him. Her vague, sweet smile annoyed him.

'Phylly, that woman's barmy, grinning over nothing.'

'She's deaf, Henry.'

'Then why doesn't she say so?'

'Do stand still and don't bellow. You'll offend her.'

'If she's deaf she's not going to hear me, is she?'

'Be quiet this instant, Henry.'

He subsided, grumbling. 'Shan't say another word so don't ask me.'

The Bowells family in general, and Sammy Bowells in particular, have been our constant godsend. Under his direction the caterers produced an amazingly sumptuous wedding breakfast. It's rather humiliating to have become so greedy about food. The exigencies of war made rationing acceptable and going without a virtue, but to win and get less than ever seemed a poor reward.

Sammy could not be trammelled with nonsense about economy or rationing. The Black Market had been drained to famine level of chickens, venison, trout, salmon and assorted crustaceans. Fruit and nuts loaded the wedding cake, cooked and iced by Gladys. Somewhere away from the eyes of Ministry inspectors, a pig had made the supreme sacrifice and donated a ham to be proud of.

'Er never saw the farmyard nor dustbin food,' Sammy said when complimented. 'Lived up in the oak wood er did, stuffing acorns and apples and a mash I'd eat myself if called on.'

After the feast I expected the reception to fall flat. Not a bit of it. Father must have spent years providing for the day, and the supply of champagne seemed inexhaustible. Claudia and Bill showed every sign of staying with us long enough to enjoy themselves.

In 1927 I had thought the aunts and the uncles ancient, tottering on the brink of the grave. Now they truly were old and we, the children, had moved up to take their places. The silly, frivolous world we knew then would never return. There had been too much loss, too much sadness, and I felt uneasily that our innocent expectation of better days to come might be disappointed.

'Champagne,' said Rudi, handing me a glass, 'brings out the best in everyone. Come and relax.'

'It's not like red wine is it? You won't let me get ill and whiny and jealous again will you?'

'I quite like you being jealous, but I didn't expect you to drink your way through the best part of a bottle of fine Corton because of it.'

'It was the other way round, wine first, jealousy later, but never mind. Pippa seems to have got Pan and David together. Davy's bristling a bit, no he's laughing now. Good. Is Val going to announce us?'

'He is. Be patient.' He led me to a chair in the centre of the room. 'We shall sit quietly within earshot and enjoy the passing show.'

'Rudi, do you remember how glittering and glamorous this room used to look? It's a poor gaunt relic now without the looking-glasses everywhere; and the velvet furniture's in store and full of moth.'

'I rather wish I'd never seen it like this, with black-out curtains still at the windows and the floor scratched to pieces. Your brother's a brave man, taking on a huge house before he even inherits.'

I nodded absently, glancing across at my father sitting with Gwennie beside him and in animated conversation with the bridegroom. Just as well, I felt, that the room looked different and that the glasses were gone. On a sultry day in 1937 they had reflected passionate and disgraceful movement, the final nail in the coffin of our family life.

I said, 'We're sitting at just about the spot where poor Sonia came to grief. If I'd known that Father already had Gwennie I don't suppose I'd have been nearly so shocked. What a mistake it is to get caught in the act of adultery.'

'Getting caught is always a great embarrassment, and difficult to carry off with flair.' Rudi spoke with feeling. 'I'm awfully glad you seduced me and made me reform.'

'I took a vow of perpetual virginity on that day. I only broke it for your sake, though I must say the sacrifice has been thoroughly worthwhile and ennobling.'

'Damn, Claudia's waving at us. Let's ignore her.'

'Some hope. We haven't inspected the wedding presents yet.'

They had been arranged on a long table under the windows to the terrace. In front of each rested a card giving the name of the donor. The largest card related to the largest object, a silver samovar, 'Gift of the Duke and Duchess of Coritanum and the Marquess of Stevenage.'

Portia stood protectively close to the table, talking to our grandmother and Claudia. For the reception and dancing she had changed into coffee-coloured lace which, as it was darned here and there and didn't much suit her, I assumed to be old and priceless. (Whoever boasted of buying lace new from Selfridge's bargain-basement?) Around her hair was bound a chain bearing a single drop-pearl that swung untidily on her forehead. It looked exactly what it was, a necklace. She might, I felt, have got decent jewels out of the bank for Claudia's day.

I tried not to resent her. In a room full of people she remained a solitary figure, and her careworn air touched me. The frock hung loosely on her. When the sleeves fell back I noticed large discoloured patches on her arms. Vaguely I mourned the failure of our attempts to know her better.

As Rudi and I joined them, Portia's son, the three-year-old Marquess, slid from her arms and hurled himself passionately at Claudia's legs. 'Kiss-kiss, Auntie,' he pleaded wetly, gazing up into her distant face with adoration.

'If you dribble on this expensive dress I shall break every bone in your body,' Claudia said with cold and indifferent calm.

The boy, on the pudgy side like his father, doubled up, clutching his knees and laughing. His immediate worship upset Portia, who picked him up in spite of his struggles and howls. 'Never mind, my darling Beau, never mind. Claudia, you really should have engaged a detective as I suggested to guard against theft. After all, we have given a valuable heirloom.'

Claudia, thoughtfully malevolent, studied the massive samovar. She said, 'So you have, Portia. One would deeply envy the strength of any guest who tried to make off with it. Does it *do* anything, or are we intended just to admire?'

'It's Russian; you make tea in it.'

'Me?' The bride's voice, clear and penetrating, rose a couple of octaves. Heads turned. 'Oh my poor bladder! Have you been trying to get rid of it for long?'

'You were a beastly vulgar child, Claudia, but surely you've learnt how to behave by now. A married woman can do useful work in the village – infuse new life into the Women's Institute, hold rummage sales and garden-parties to raise funds for charity and the church. Duties and responsibilities don't cease just because you're the wife of . . .'

Portia noticed Claudia's thunderous expression and fell silent. It was too late. 'Of whom? Of a common man without title?'

'A man of limited means is what I intended to say.'

'That,' Claudia said, 'is none of your damned business, Portia. Ever since you herded revolting Botty into a corner and became a duchess you think you've a right to run all our lives. You're a dreadfully bossy, interfering sort of female.'

Portia's face wrinkled miserably. 'I'm not like that at all, I'm not. That's a rotten thing to say. And please don't call the Duke Botty. The eldest son is always named Botolph, it's a family tradition.'

At that point Valentine stood on a chair and called for silence. 'Charge your glasses everyone, please. I have something pleasant and important to say. It gives me enormous happiness to announce the engagement of my youngest sister, Amity, to Rudi Longmire, already a friend to many of you. Let's drink to their long life and happiness.'

They did, though with a touch of my old paranoia I suspected that most of them had long ago forgotten my existence. (Amity? Which one's that? Oh, the plain one.) Aunt Phyllida, with Henry puffing at her heels, came to congratulate us. 'So pleased for you both, Amy, my dear. Rudi, your festival has never been forgotten. Henry was laid up with alcohol poisoning for a month.'

'A damned lie, Phylly, it was colic, something I ate. You've filled out, Amy. Used to be a damned ugly brat.'

Rudi bristled. 'She was an enchanting child. We were so busy picking off the great gaudy sunflowers that we failed to notice a budding orchid.' (Gosh!)

'There, such a charming sentiment. Take no notice of him either of you. Henry's never admired anything that wasn't busty, blonde and brainless, thank heaven. So easy to out-manoeuvre the little trollops. Dancing later, I hear. If you care to trundle me around, Rudi, I'll be grateful. Henry's long past it. And he used to be so frisky, poor old thing.'

They did not mention the tragedy that had aged them. Both their sons had died before the age of twenty in the wreckage of Spitfires shot down over the fields of Kent. The loss had taken the heart out of poor Henry. Not a pat or a pinch left in him. A skittish old hangover from the Naughty 'Nineties and always out-of-date, he no longer frisked, and his voice held a querulous note.

Grandmother's face lit up with ferocious pleasure. 'Surely you were in America, Mr Longmire? How very nice to see you again after so long.'

'Hallo, Mrs Mottesfont. You look truly regal in your tiara. The best Lady Capulet I have had the pleasure of directing.' She glowed at the compliment. Glancing at Claudia, beautiful in her bridal gown, and at fair-haired, stately Portia she asked on a rising note, 'Are you quite sure that it's Amy you wish to marry?'

'Terribly sure. She's my undeserved blessing. We hope you'll grace our wedding.'

'Certainly. The child has kept you a very deep secret. I trust you'll never hurt her as I imagine we all must have done. She's a Mottesfont, and tenderer than the others.'

'I would cut my throat first and that of any soul on earth who threatened her.'

She gave an appreciative grin. 'A typical theatrical overstatement but I'm inclined to believe you. How do you occupy your time at present?'

'I've leased a house in Bloomsbury where I intend to start a theatrical agency, so I shall be often in London. Would it amuse you to hear the gossip?'

Dignity struggled with curiosity and lost. 'Life's boring since the War ended. Socialists, pah, a grey lot. I am usually at home between two and four. Do call.'

After a single shocked exclamation Portia became

233

conventional and apathetic. 'How is one to understand the modern world? I suppose I must congratulate you both.'

'Well done, that wasn't so painful was it?' Claudia jeered. 'Amy, how do you fancy a samovar as a wedding present? You make tea in it for good works.'

'No thank you. Do go to Woolworths; they have lovely fat brown teapots, export rejects. Just the thing.'

Grandmother frowned at us and tapped Portia gently on the arm. 'There's no money, is there, my dear? I suppose yours is long gone, and your jewellery?'

She did not answer at once. Little Botty blew bubbles of spit and put his head on one side like a parrot to attract Claudia's attention. 'He knocks me about,' she said abruptly, 'when he comes home. Nothing's left but Mother's diamonds.'

I stood in absolute dismay, not daring to meet anyone's eyes.

'Shit,' Claudia muttered savagely, 'oh shit! Now what do we do?'

I think that neither of us had ever felt so awful in our lives, faced with our stupid, mindless, uncaring cruelty, our failure even to try to understand. Sudden apology would simply compound our offences. Portia had receded spiritlessly into a shadow world, rocking her son gently, suffering our mockery.

No remonstrance about bad language from Grandmother. Her face and voice were utterly kind. 'Spendthrift and brutal like his father; I feared as much. And you've done nothing about it?'

'He'll take Beau away from me.'

'Have you never read the terms of your marriage settlement? Gervase knew the old Duke. He tied it up very tightly.' Portia shook her head. 'Come with me, we must talk at once. Let Amy take Little Botty to his nurse, she's very safe with children. Claudia, we don't need you. Go and circulate, please. You'll excuse us, Mr Longmire?'

'Not Little Botty,' Portia said weakly, putting the boy into my arms. 'We always call him Beau.'

Claudia muttered horribly, cursing herself for being a spiteful bitch and asking God why Portia hadn't said something earlier instead of saving it for her wedding day. And how was she supposed to know something was up and what could she do about it now when it was too late? She always hated to feel in the wrong.

Rudi put a glass of champagne into her hand. 'Get that down quickly. Keeping up appearances is bound to lead to misunderstanding. There will be time for amends, but not today.'

'At least I didn't get around to suggesting that the damned samovar would be just the thing for Singlet and Lettie Polkinhorn. Which reminds me, I adore the heavenly emeralds. I wanted to wear them today but Grandmother insisted that they go on show.'

'Are you sure that you wouldn't have preferred a large fish-kettle with perforated serving-dish? Portia thought it an essential to any bride, but Amy vetoed it.'

'Sometimes, Rudi, you go on as though you're tired of life,' Claudia said. 'Where's Bill? I want him.'

'Talking to Father,' I said.

Just then the band began to play 'The Gold And Silver Waltz' and Bill hurried over to be greeted with rapture.

'Good heavens, missing me so soon? My dance I believe. We are duty-bound to lead off the junket before the rest can get going. Providential that it's a waltz. I can do those.'

Various people said with total lack of originality that they made a lovely couple, which they did. As other couples joined them Rudi drew me onto the floor. 'You're thinking that Portia and Botolph made a lovely couple once, and just look at them now.'

'I do wish you wouldn't read my mind so accurately. How am I ever to keep secrets?'

'Oh, you can tell me anything, everyone knows that. As lovely couples go Claudia and Bill aren't bad, but nothing compared with the stunningly lovely couple that we shall make.'

'Be quiet, Rudi,' I said, 'and dance.'

'Sorry, Phylly – I mean, Amy. Ouch, that's my foot.'

Chapter Seventeen

Champagne and dancing make an insidious combination. Even the most critical observer could not complain that we did not mix. Rudi danced with Grandmother, Gwennie and Aunt Phyllida, even with Cousin Beatrice, who readily put down her glass. 'Only soda water with the merest dash of scotch; very dull but I've had to join the temperance brigade,' she explained. 'They put me away, you know.'

'Surely not?'

'In Clerkenwell, with nurses, all man-haters. Off-duty they wore collars and ties and pork-pie hats. Rather suggestive, but excellent friends. Most restful not having to pretend to be a sorrowing widow. It quite set me up for the War which, unlike marriage, was seldom boring. Shall we be doing the okey-dokey later, do you think? Such a jolly athletic dance.'

'Indeed it is,' Rudi said, 'though I rather think it's been renamed the hokey-cokey, and perhaps is unsuitable for weddings.'

'The hokey-pokey, I must make a note of that. The younger members of my Band of Hope incline to be critical of errors. Abstinence does not always improve the nature.'

Uncle Henry declined to leave his chair, saying that he wasn't going to make a sketch of himself getting stepped on by a bunch of old women and tripped up by screeching brats; anyhow he hated damned weddings. But Grandfather Mottesfont and various elderly cousins took me sedately around the floor.

David and Pippa danced almost every dance, very close together. At the wedding breakfast Pippa had said to me, 'So David is the little half-brother, son of the Soapy Sonia? I had not heard until recently of the scandal and the divorce.'

'It happened a couple of years before war broke out.'

'We have here a mystery, I think. Amy, I know Pandel Metkin rather well and it is an enormous pleasure to see him again. He was a great friend of my French grandmother. At the age of sixteen I fell madly in love with him and felt a sadness that he was not for women.'

'You knew about that so young?'

'*Mais oui*, such things are much discussed in Paris. No young French girl is permitted to face the Huppners of this world in ignorance. And now I see Pandel born again.'

She waited expectantly. I said, 'David is his son. He knows, my father knows, most of the family don't.'

'But the two together in the same room, they will see it for a certainty.'

'Not them. They never notice us or each other, not properly.'

I told her briefly of the night in midsummer when Davy was conceived on a hillside under the moon.

'Such romance! This Giant I must see, but my coveted unicorn lost to Sonia! True she was perhaps more beautiful, but I see that I gave up too easily. I'm chagrined to find that it was a possibility after all.'

Pan had been following events too. He asked me to dance and in spite of my advancing years and almost settled state a romantic thrill shivered down my spine. Love did not enter into it. I was simply englamoured with him still, the prince of fairy tales. My head just about reached his chin. He smelt of something discreet, expensive and delicious, and as we danced I became aware of the strong movement of his thigh muscles. I think he exercised. Certainly he seemed the teeniest bit vain of his body, splendid as it was.

I looked up and found his dark eyes watching my face. He said, 'The last time I held you in my arms you cried and told me your secret heart. Do you remember?'

'Of course I do – under the old cedar tree. You mopped me up and asked who was with me in my imaginary house. I never dreamed then that it would turn out to be Rudi. You asked us to tea, just Claudia and me with no grown-ups. We were thrilled to the marrow!'

'And now you are not given – beastly rabbits was it that so upset you? – in place of affection?'

I laughed. 'Come soon and see my white house. It brims with love, and not a rabbit in sight. Pan, how is it between you and David?'

'With the help of Pippa we have achieved a state of civilized neutrality. It is, perhaps, a foundation to build on.'

'She had a crush on you when she was sixteen.'

'Ah, and now she is intent on seducing my son, who is enjoying every moment of it.'

'Heavens, how quick! Could it be this ballroom that incites passion? You began wanting Sonia in here, the night she gave a supper-dance. She looked gorgeous.'

'But unhappy, and you, Amy, had your eyes on us.'

'And ears. Tremendously fascinating to me because I always felt on the outside fringes of life and never quite in it.'

'But now you are thoroughly awake and your own woman,' he said. 'You have done well with yourself and with my son.'

Claudia joined me later. 'Lucky dog, I haven't managed a dance with Pan or Jimmy yet and my toes are throbbing from being stepped on by the elderly. Shall we get champagne and hide in a corner for a while?'

I hadn't quite believed what Pan said of Pippa, but we came upon her occupying the corner we chose and murmuring with David. She smiled up at us through her spectacles. 'Claudia *chère amie*, I have to leave. We shall meet soon. David will drive me to my hotel.'

'Pippa wants to see the Cerne Abbas Giant,' he said. 'Now seems a good time, don't you think?'

'We had better go quickly. A cousin – Beatrice would it be? – is pursuing us with a priest in tow. Your new vicar, Amy. He will not spoil with keeping.'

So all Bertie Gooch's efforts to sway the Bishop had failed. And Davy? I bit my tongue to avoid saying stupid irritating things like drive carefully, don't catch cold, will you be late?

'I've a feeling,' I said to Claudia, 'that the Giant is up to his old tricks. History may be about to repeat itself.'

'And why not? Pippa's been a widow for nearly two years and the French – well, they're not so inhibited as the English, and at least she's too sensible to go and get pregnant like Sonia. She lusted after Pan and here's David, the living image and available. Do you mind?'

'Why ever should I? I hope they have a perfectly lovely time. To be truthful, when Davy got so censorious with his mother I feared that he might turn out a bit of a prig. Some discreet sinning is the best thing in the world for him.'

It was past ten o'clock when Claudia and Bill changed into their going-away things. They bore the jokes bravely; may all your troubles be little ones, don't do anything I wouldn't do, as if you could, ha ha ha, and be careful not to wear yourselves out, there's plenty more where that came from. Quite a departure from the usual lofty disdain of vulgarity.

As I kissed her goodbye Claudia said, 'Legitimate sex, there's a novelty. No more undignified scufflings and wiping away of lipstick smears. I feel tremendously virtuous.'

'Enjoy it, then, and have a nice honeymoon.'

'I wonder what it's like doing sex in a boat. We could try. Bill's persuaded me to take up sailing again, so we're hiring a dinghy.'

'They're awfully small. I shouldn't think it's possible without falling overboard.'

'I'll send a postcard and let you know.'

'You'd better not, the postman reads them and passes on the news. Portia's diamonds, they are safe aren't they?'

'Val has them stowed away and let's face it, Amy, no self-respecting burglar would give this house a second look. It shrieks poverty. If you speak to her can you sort of hint that I'm sorry?'

'Portia? She'll have risen above us, but I'll try.'

'Wordless sympathy might get across; you're quite good at that.'

She threw her arms around me and hugged me so vigorously that I squeaked. 'Come along, woman,' Bill said, 'unless you intend to bring the whole family along.'

Dora Aphrodite had supplied me with a dozen boxes of rose leaves and confetti from under the counter, contraband frivolities until we had managed to Win The Peace. Hurriedly I passed them around. We pursued the bride and groom to their hired car. Cousin Beatrice, whose soda water had, I fear, gained in strength during the reception, hurled one of her shoes and hit the driver on the ear.

Then they had gone and a sort of flatness came over us. But the party went bravely on. Rudi and I danced to 'Small Hotel' and 'Room Five-hundred-and-four' and Ivor Novello songs, 'My Dearest Dear' and 'My Life Belongs To You', wrapped securely in each other's arms. I did not envy the glamorous women who had shone here like bright stars and faded. My time for romance in the ballroom had come round. I wallowed in it.

David returned quite late, looking sleekly content. He put an arm through mine and said, 'I've never thanked you for being a great sister to me. May I come back to Underhallow when Father's better?'

'Of course, my dear.'

'When my year here is up I shall go back to America and get my degree. Then I'm not too sure what I'll do. Metkin has given me a chance to rebuild the London end of the business, and I'm seriously tempted.'

Cousin Beatrice appeared behind us, a little elevated but by no means under the influence. She had recovered her shoe. 'Amy, you must meet Father Matthew Collison, soon to be Vicar of Underhallow.'

'Not another damned father,' David said. 'I've more than enough already.'

Mr Collison blinked. The young girl with him tucked up the corners of her mouth in a secret smile. 'And this is Frances, his daughter,' said Cousin Beatrice.

While Mr Collison talked boringly of ritual and whether Underhallow liked or disliked incense, Frances slid away. She would have been rather beautiful if she had not looked so sullen.

'What's the matter?' David asked her without much interest.

'I'm not his daughter really, I'm a bastard.'

'What a coincidence, so am I.'

'Are you honestly? How many fathers have you got then?'

'Four at the last count, including my American foster-father.'

'My real one's dead. Don't you think that being a bastard is terrifically degrading?'

'Not a bit,' David said, 'why should I? It wasn't our fault. Are you old enough to drink champagne?'

'I'm almost seventeen, but they're all practically teetotal and won't let me try.'

'We bastards are for trying everything.'

He led her away towards the bar. 'I'm a remote cousin,' Mr Collison was saying. 'My mother's mother was a Mottesfont. Such a pity about poor young Gooch. I do hope the parish won't resent me.'

Portia did not come back to the ballroom. Little Botty fell fast asleep in the arms of his nurse and later Grandmother swept them up. Mother and son were to stay with Father until Coritanum had been dealt with.

I yawned and shivered with tiredness. 'Don't go back to the Running Stag tonight, Rudi darling. I hate sleeping alone.'

'Eyebrows will be raised and I have no pyjamas.'

'They're all too tipsy to notice and you can do without or borrow from Val. We'll go home tomorrow early.'

In my single bed it was a bit of a squash, but very warm and cosy. The roses were drooping and dead in their bowl, but I felt almost reconciled to that ugly room. We didn't leave early after all. We overslept and were wakened by Val's one surviving housemaid who hadn't a clue who we were. 'Are you getting up?' she said. 'I'm to do the beds.'

Housemaids were not as they used to be before the War. Nothing was. The whole ramshackle structure of class and privilege had been bombed to rubble. I didn't mind a bit.

Creeping out unobserved proved impossible. In the hall Grandmother pushed her way back and forth among an awful crush, herding the departing guests on to their motor-coaches. I managed to trap her long enough to kiss and thank her.

We found Valentine strolling on the terrace. He walked with us down towards the stable-yard where I had left the car. 'That went rather well, I think. Did you two enjoy it?'

243

'Absolutely,' Rudi said. 'I fall in and out of love with the Savernakes, except for Amy. I love her all the time.'

'Young David's a pleasant chap. I'd like to offer him some place in the running of the estate, except that it would be a share of nothing.'

'Did Father say anything about him?' I asked as delicately as possible.

'Oh that. It didn't take a genius to notice, and I rather let Metkin think that I knew. How can it matter? David's been our brother for more than eighteen years and I'd be miserable if he suddenly disowned us.' He paused and looked back at the house. 'While I was at it I had a long talk with Metkin about this place. He suggests planning for ten years hence and gradually converting the house into a country hotel – separate entrances to each wing and the centre block reserved for family. Tennis courts, swimming pool, the lot. As he sees it, people will get sick and tired of austerity and want to play.'

'Rather a long time to wait with no money to speak of isn't it?'

'He offered to invest in me and naturally I refused. Hand to mouth for a while, but I have the land in reserve, hundreds of acres across Dorset, and standing forest too. Controls won't go on for ever. Wood can be cut and sold, and as tenants move out of the farms I shan't re-lease but sell when prices are right.'

'Val dear, the very best of luck and thank you for a lovely party. Do come and see us if you can find a few days.'

'Goodbye, my dearest girl. Nasty business about Portia. No wonder she scratched at us. Keep an eye on her if you can and let me know how she is.'

'Sorry, Val,' Rudi said, 'but from now on I'm appropriating Amy. Portia can be safely left to your Grandmother.'

My brother grinned. He bent down, picked up a

silver paper horseshoe from among the gravel and pressed it into my palm. 'For luck. The best I can do at present, but I promise to redeem it for the real thing when I'm a wealthy hotelier.'

As we turned out of the gates I said, 'Rudi, do you think I ought to try a bit harder with Portia, invite her to stay or something?'

A look of mock despair darkened his face. 'Will this torment never end?'

'All right then, if you'd rather I didn't.'

'Amy, I would so much rather you didn't that I shall stop this car and beg you on bended knees.'

'There's no need to go to lengths, silly. I don't want to a bit, so I shan't.'

'Heaven bless you, lady. Can we have eggs and toast soldiers for tea?'

'If the hens have laid and you don't mind the soldiers looking grey and chalky.'

'They'll be fine and bronzed. Gladys Bowells gave me a home-baked loaf to bring back.'

'You've been flirting again, you wretch,' I said.

It began to rain as we reached home. September drew to an end and summer was definitely over. I pitied Claudia in Weymouth, though I need not have done. The following week I received the promised postcard.

It read: *'Perfectly possible though dampish and only suitable for flat calm. Having a fairly lovely time. Blest are the ties that bind. How's Rudi? Love from Claudia Deering. (Doesn't that sound strange?)'*

'Is it a religious cryptogram?' Rudi asked. 'Or has she left something out?'

'She's sparing the postman's blushes. I shan't explain.'

'Ah, I rather think that if I worry at it I shall **understand.**'

*   *   *

In December snow fell. It thawed, but the weather remained raw and cheerless. After Christmas Rudi and I began to look forward to a spring wedding, then in January came the longest, most bitter winter of living memory. To make matters far worse, the pathetically meagre stocks of coal could not be moved from the pitheads. Paraffin for heaters ran out. Once the wood we bought in summer had gone we got no more. The trees froze to iron and electricity flickered on in sullen fashion, remained with us briefly and cut off without warning. Trains could not run, huge snow-drifts blocked the roads, the country lay frozen and near to starvation. We were locked in with crisis upon crisis. Rudi's hope of an early wedding was dashed.

My house became a shining palace, the garden like the fields of paradise. We lay late in bed, the only moderately warm place, and watched the unending blizzards driven by an east wind. It was killing weather, but beautiful.

I had wanted a May wedding and that in the end was what I got, in Underhallow, with my two sisters as matrons of honour and Little Botty as a page. Claudia rang a month before the date and mentioned in passing that she was expecting a baby. 'It won't matter, will it? Annie can let my dress out a bit.'

I ought to have asked questions. Bill's car arrived and disgorged at my doorstep a whale in clinging pale-blue jersey. 'For heaven's sake, how pregnant are you?' I asked.

'I don't know, about eight months I think.'

'Honeymoon,' Bill said proudly. 'Weymouth air.'

'Does it show a lot? I'll hold my bouquet over it.'

An entire rose-bush would barely have covered the bulge. The delivery of twin daughters five weeks later came as no surprise to me, though Claudia expressed

246

annoyance. 'Great greedy monsters, nothing but feeding machines and Bill didn't warn me there are twins in his family. D'you think I could give one away? No? I suppose not.'

My father, with a metal hip joint and pins in his bones, gave me away, walking with a single stick and no help. Valentine, safely engaged to Cristabel, looked wonderful, bronzed by Bahamian sun and glowing with content. As well as our present, a beautiful piece of Bohemian glass, he gave me a narrow silver chain bracelet bearing a little silver horseshoe. 'It's still a baby,' he told me, 'but it will grow up.'

Cyril Fox caused us a degree of consternation by proposing himself as Rudi's best man. He had enrolled with the agency and never lacked work. By then he must have been rich, though an outsider would never have guessed it in a thousand years. Fortunately Rudi had already asked David. Matthew Collison, the new Vicar, married us. We felt obliged to ask Cyril to the wedding, hoping for the best sartorially, and since Davy and Frances were friends we asked her too. Sonia did not respond to our invitation. I did not expect her to come, so I was surprised and touched to see her sitting with Robbie at the back of the church. They left before the photographs and did not appear at the reception.

Those photographs have unusual features that need explanation when shown to people who do not know my family. Cyril managed quite a nice dark suit, but his shoes pinched and halfway through the ceremony he changed into his plimsolls. They came out splendidly, complete with holes. Claudia looms exceedingly large, a captive barrage-balloon with nosegay. Stricken anew with love on seeing her, Little Botty threw a tantrum because she declined to carry him. His nanny, a starched and armoured female, tried to mop him up. 'I hate you!' he yelled, and kicked her hard with his shiny buckled shoes.

'Somehow I don't warm to that boy,' Claudia said. 'My hand itches to give him a sound spanking.'

Portia, wavering around to protect her lamb, sniffed angrily. Little Botty evaded all efforts to place him properly and made the front row in his frilled blouse and velvet knickers. Double snail-tracks run from his nose and a huge baby's comforter is wedged in his mouth. Definitely a Coritanum. And definitely a lovely, lovely day.

As yet it is too soon to know whether everyone will manage to be happy; or any of us, come to that. Portia discovered that a divorce would bankrupt the wretched Botolph. The parure of diamonds brought matters to a head. Needing cash, and intending to pawn them, he went confidently to the bank and demanded that they should be passed over. Disappointment overcame restraint.

Poor proud Duchess, she had suffered him and kept quiet for years but this time was different. Instead of simply hitting her about a bit in the privacy of their bedrooms, Botolph gave her a savage and semi-public beating that alarmed the servants and half-killed her.

The knowledge of her power changed Portia, not entirely for the better, since she shows a marked resemblance to that holy terror the old Duchess, Botty's mother. 'It's remarkably pleasant to have the whip hand,' she told me. 'Botolph is almost tolerable when he's frightened. We join for public occasions but live separately in different wings of the castle, as far apart as we can reasonably get. It works splendidly. He is a man without virtues or morals, but I couldn't possibly lose Hindlecote.'

Dominance and a slightly querulous manner suit her. I enjoy some of her remarks: 'Adultery has done little for him in the way of skill or finesse in making love, and executed badly it's a ridiculous exercise. I can't say I much care for it and I'm relieved that he reserves it for his mistresses.' She has still not forgiven Lettie Polkinhorn, blaming her entirely for seducing Singlet away. The two of them have a flat in Great Portland Street and occasionally I run into them when visiting Grandmother. 'Do you suppose they actually – you know – *do* anything?' Portia asked, proving that she is only human. 'Surely they're both past it?'

'Probably,' I said, pretty sure that they weren't.

The Duke employs a couple now, butler and house-keeper. The former housekeeper, a churchgoer and of strict moral standards, looks after Portia in her wing and allows no interference.

Abigail Golightly called several times at Hindlecote and was repulsed. (Her Grace is Definitely Not At Home.) As a recommendation she sent to Portia, in advance of her most recent sortie, a signed copy of her book set in Underhallow. Its title turned out to be *Reign Of The Vampire Witch*. On the cover a priest backs away in some surprise from a woman dripping blood from splendid fangs. She bears no resemblance to Josie Knapp whatsoever.

Portia insisted that I should have it, holding it by two fingers at arm's length. 'Perhaps you or Claudia can read such filth, I certainly cannot.' (Her attitude to us has not changed all that much.) 'Proud rearing manhoods indeed! The woman has a mind like a sewer.'

Naturally I read it and saw what Dora Aphrodite meant about thrusting and throbbing. I wonder some-times whether Abigail really is married. She writes as one thoroughly inexperienced and sex-starved, and I have this theory that in fact she is a virgin, unloved and undesired. The book circulated rapidly around the village, but we did not recognize ourselves or each other.

*　　*　　*

David spent eighteen months in America at Harvard. He returned recently to England and went up to Oxford for a further year. Frances Collison calls to see me and talk about him now and again. Poor child, I think she may be in love with him and finding mere friendship unsatisfactory. But I have given up trying to keep track of his girlfriends. Part monk, part playboy, in Oxford he works, and in his London flat he entertains. He never mentions Josie, but I imagine he sees her when it suits them both.

She left Cambridge loaded down with honours. We have heard her on intellectual wireless panels discussing this and that, and read about her in magazines. Remarriage does not seem part of her ambitions. Why should it when, judging by newspaper photographs, she is surrounded by a host of the most glamorous men?

The slow drift of Underhallow life goes on without her and without Ivan. Keys of the new scout hut are already circulating. Dora Aphrodite and I do those useful and charitable acts that Portia so applauds, though I draw the line at cricket teas.

When the theatrical agency got into its stride I became popular. A stream of up-and-coming actors, actresses, variety acts, musicians and playwrights began to track down from London in varying states of misery and hope, to weep on my shoulder or flirt with Rudi. The village loves them, they love the village. Rudi and I struggle to be alone but we rarely are. Fortunately we had the sense to keep the London flat very quiet, and we skulk there and don't answer the doorbell or the telephone.

This morning a posh doctor suggested that I'm pregnant. Given the obstacles to a wanton and exuberant sex-life it seems something of a miracle. Rudi is awfully proud of himself. 'Another mouth to feed. I wonder if there's an opening for infants. I'd better put it down on the books.'

'A typical agent,' I said, 'and please don't refer to the poor unborn as "it". We're bound to have a he or she, there isn't any other kind. I rather hope it's not two at once like Claudia's.'

'The more the merrier. I expect to be kept in luxury in my old age. No, don't throw things at me, Amy. I love you so hugely and I promise to take no commission from him or her. Amy, not the crockery, it's impossible to replace and I'm joking.'

'I'm not going to throw it, I'm getting tea ready. Are you certain you're pleased?'

'You sound rather glum.'

I glanced at the Cyril Fox mural and imagined it smeared with jammy paw-prints. 'We'll never be alone together again, not even here, and suppose I don't like it – I mean him or her? Claudia doesn't much like hers.'

'Have you forgotten how to translate your sister? She adores her twins, though no force on earth is going to persuade her to admit it.'

'She refers to them as those beastly objects.'

'In a tone loaded down with pride.' Rudi took my hand. 'Amy, you're nervous aren't you?'

'A bit. I do want to get this right, but the doctor made it sound awfully easy to do the wrong thing. He asked if I had any idea of what looking after a baby entailed. I haven't yet, and I absolutely refuse to have a nanny bossing me about.'

'Between us we should be able to rear a child perfectly, you'll see. Lots of people without our unique talents manage very well.'

The world looked brighter when he kissed me and told me what a clever girl I was. I managed to drop a plate. We picked up the bits between us and in a moment we were arguing about names and where he, she or it ought to be born. I am for Underhallow and no hospitals. Rudi is for twenty gynaecologists and a London clinic. I felt happiness flow over me. Then a dreary thought came into my head. If I'm not careful I'm going to turn out to be a true Mottesfont woman after all.

THE END

A Mislaid Magic
Joyce Windsor

'I LOVED IT. I THOUGHT IT FRESH AND SHARP AND FUNNY,
WITH A MOST WONDERFULLY ECCENTRIC CHARM'
Joanna Trollope

All the beguiling charm of Dodie Smith's *I Capture the Castle*
combined with the witty view of Britain's upper classes portrayed in
Nancy Mitford's *Love in a Cold Climate*. A totally compelling first
novel which is funny, sad, and utterly delightful.

Lady Amity Savernake, neglected, rather plain, and youngest
daughter of the Earl of Osmington, was seven years old when her
stepmother (disparagingly referred to within the family as Soapy
Sonia) took her to London, bought her a fitted vicuna coat with a
velvet collar, and introduced her (at the Ritz) to Rudi Longmire, the
genie who was to change their lives.

It was Rudi's idea that there should be a midsummer Festival of Arts
at Gunville Place. The ugly Dorset pile, seat of the Savernakes, would
be transformed into a pastoral paradise; singers, actors, musicians
and exotic visitors – as well as the family – would bring enchantment
into their world. As Rudi, Master of Revels and Lord of Misrule,
drew each and every one of them into his exotic plans, so excitement
spilled out into the countryside. A dead may tree threw out leaves
and blossomed. The local white witch absentmindedly gave her pig a
love potion, and two village maidens were accosted in the woods by
a genuine Dorset Ooser.

And within the family it seemed the enchantment would solve their
various discontents. Soapy Sonia, Grandmother Mottesfont, even
Claudia, Amy's corrosive and rebellious sister, bloomed in the
midsummer revels. And young Amy watched and listened and for a
brief childhood span was given the magic of complete happiness – a
happiness she never forgot – not even in the disruptive aftermath of
that heady summer, or in the years that followed.

'IT HAS ALL THE INGREDIENTS OF A FAIRY TALE . . .
WHIMSICAL . . . SHARPLY FUNNY IN PARTS'
The Times

0 552 99591 6

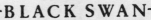

BLACK SWAN

The Golden Year
Elizabeth Falconer

One enchanted summer in Provence and its aftermath.

Summers, to Anna, had always meant the Presbytery, the
mellow old stone house in Provence where her mother, the
formidable Domenica, lived. Now that Anna's marriage to
Jeffrey was all but over, she thought that she had herself well
organized, dividing her time between her riverside home in
London, her two teenage children and her career as a gilder
and restorer of antiques. And then there were her summers in
France – a chance to eat and drink magnificently, to sit in the
sun and to recharge the batteries. She hardly realized how
narrow and lonely her life had really become.

But one summer her brother Giò, an antiques dealer in Paris,
brought down a new friend to the Presbytery. Patrick, a
handsome television director, suddenly opened up Anna's
life in a new and wonderful way, offering her a wholly
unexpected chance of happiness. But she did not
immediately see that others might not share her joy, and that
her beloved brother Giò could have quite different ideas
about Patrick and the future.

'A delightful evocation of the sights, sounds and flavours of
life in Provence'
Family Circle

0 552 99622 X

BLACK SWAN

Touch And Go
Elizabeth Berridge

'MISS BERRIDGE HAS AN EYE FOR THE BEAUTY OF HUMBLE
AND FAMILIAR THINGS . . . SHE HAS A QUIET, WICKED SENSE
OF HUMOUR'
Honor Tracy, *New Statesman*

When Emma Rowlands returned to Wales, to the village where she
had spent her childhood, she brought with her no more than some
favourite pieces of china, books, flowers, and her small pregnant cat.
Behind her she left a broken marriage and an eighteen-year-old
daughter who had fled to India to escape the marital fights.

As Emma, approaching thirty-nine, stood in the solid red brick house
on top of a Welsh hill, she felt a tiny sense of happiness displace her
apprehension. Years before, as a small child, the somewhat maverick
village doctor had asked her what reward she would like for being
brave, and she had asked for the shell house. Now, at a time of
uncertainty and despondency in her life, she discovered he had left
her not the toy house she had asked for, but his own home.

As – hesitantly – she began to renew old friendships and re-examine
her relationships with not only her daughter, but also her mother, a
widow who assuaged her loneliness by continual travel, so gradually
she began to interpret the meaning behind the gift of the house, and
with understanding came the chance to rebuild her own future.

'ONE OF THE BEST, BUT NOT ALWAYS ADEQUATELY
APPRECIATED, OF BRITISH NOVELISTS'
Martin Seymour-Smith, *Oxford Mail*

'ELIZABETH BERRIDGE HAS THE SHARPEST OF EYES. BUT
SOMETHING RATHER MORE IMPORTANT AS WELL . . . WHAT
HER PEOPLE DO AND FEEL AND REPRESENT MATTERS, SEEMS
MEMORABLE'
Isabel Quigley, *Financial Times*

0 552 99648 3

BLACK SWAN

A SELECTED LIST OF FINE WRITING
AVAILABLE FROM BLACK SWAN

99565 7	PLEASANT VICES	Judy Astley	£5.99
99629 7	SEVEN FOR A SECRET	Judy Astley	£5.99
99618 1	BEHIND THE SCENES AT THE MUSEUM	Kate Atkinson	£6.99
99648 3	TOUCH AND GO	Elizabeth Berridge	£5.99
99537 1	GUPPIES FOR TEA	Marika Cobbold	£6.99
99593 2	A RIVAL CREATION	Marika Cobbold	£5.99
99622 X	THE GOLDEN YEAR	Elizabeth Falconer	£5.99
99610 6	THE SINGING HOUSE	Janette Griffiths	£5.99
99681 5	A MAP OF THE WORLD	Jane Hamilton	£6.99
99503 7	WAITING TO EXHALE	Terry McMillan	£5.99
99561 4	TELL MRS POOLE I'M SORRY	Kathleen Rowntree	£5.99
99606 8	OUTSIDE, LOOKING IN	Kathleen Rowntree	£5.99
99672 6	A WING AND A PRAYER	Mary Selby	£6.99
99607 6	THE DARKENING LEAF	Caroline Stickland	£5.99
99620 3	RUNNING AWAY	Titia Sutherland	£6.99
99650 5	A FRIEND OF THE FAMILY	Titia Sutherland	£5.99
99056 6	BROTHER OF THE MORE FAMOUS JACK	Barbara Trapido	£6.99
99549 5	A SPANISH LOVER	Joanna Trollope	£6.99
99643 2	THE BEST OF FRIENDS	Joanna Trollope	£6.99
99636 X	KNOWLEDGE OF ANGELS	Jill Paton Walsh	£5.99
99673 4	DINA'S BOOK	Herbjørg Wassmo	£6.99
99495 2	A DUBIOUS LEGACY	Mary Wesley	£6.99
99592 4	AN IMAGINATIVE EXPERIENCE	Mary Wesley	£5.99
99639 4	THE TENNIS PARTY	Madeleine Wickham	£5.99
99641 6	A DESIRABLE RESIDENCE	Madeleine Wickham	£6.99
99591 6	A MISLAID MAGIC	Joyce Windsor	£4.99